A

I saw after the ~~first~~ ~~hand~~ ...vould have to work fa... ...t bad with a pack of cards, but these fellows was dyed-in-the-wool. With the sky for a limit, I made eight hundred in two rounds—and then I lost five of that at the next turn, and got six back in another minute. But here I knew that they were playing me for something real, and as the cards came to me for my deal, I made up my mind to make my clean-up on the spot. Those crooks were too fast for my company.

I was mighty liberal. I gave out three queens to the New Yorker, and two pairs to the Cotton King. And in the draw I let the Alabama man fill and handed him from New York a little sneaking pair of deuces. With two full houses up, I thought that a bit of betting might be in order, and it was. I got my whole wad of cash up. When it came to the showdown, I laid a straight flush on the table and collected.

When they saw that flush, they knew that they hadn't picked a sucker, and they looked a mite sick. They looked still sicker when I pushed back my chair and stood up.

They looked at each other, and the little white-faced runt from Manhattan laid the barrel of a mean-looking automatic on the edge of the table.

"Sit down, Oregon," he said. "Sit down and we'll talk it over. We don't play with pikers, y'understand?" He had some reason on his side, and that automatic was a good deal in his favor....

MAX BRAND®

JOKERS EXTRA WILD

LEISURE BOOKS NEW YORK CITY

JOKERS EXTRA WILD

TABLE OF CONTENTS

Speedy—Deputy

Frederick Faust's saga of the youthful hero Speedy began with "Tramp Magic," a six-part serial in *Western Story Magazine* that appeared under the Max Brand® byline beginning in the issue dated November 21, 1931 and ending with the December 26, 1931 issue. As other of Faust's continuing characters, Speedy is a loner, little more than a youngster, and able to outwit and outmaneuver even the deadliest of men without the use of a gun. He proved to be popular with readers, and stories of his adventures, appearing in *Western Story Magazine*, eventually numbered nine in addition to the serial. The serial has been reprinted by Leisure Books under the title *Speedy*. "Speedy—Deputy," published in *Western Story Magazine* (2/13/32), was the first of the short stories.

Straight Roulette

Mike was annoyed. In the first place, One-Eyed Mike did not believe in such follies as straight roulette wheels; he never had fixed this one, and he hated to watch it in operation, controlled by blind chance only. In the second place, he was troubled when he saw a patron winning honest gold in his employer's gambling house. Above all else, it drove a knife through his heart when a fellow who was obviously nothing but a lazy loafer started raking in hundreds of dollars.

Loafer was too mild a word, really, to be used upon the stranger. He was simply a tramp in rags, a youngster not much over twenty, with a darkly handsome face and a flashing smile.

Now, laughing at his own good fortune, cheerfully advising his neighbors at the roulette wheel to follow his betting chances, the lad spread his elbows at the board, so to speak, and so instantly increased the loathing that filled the manly breast of Mike Doloroso.

The name of the stranger irritated Mike more than all else.

Shoving some money toward him with the long

wooden rake, he had asked: "Here . . . this is for you . . . what's your name?"

"Thanks. Speedy is my name," the stranger had answered.

"Thank me for nothing," One-Eyed Mike said gruffly. "Where did you pick up that moniker and why?"

"I really don't know the reason. I only know the name," said Speedy.

"You're a polite cuss, anyway," said Mike Doloroso. "You been your mother's pride, I reckon. And joy, eh?"

His sarcasm brought wide grins from other players, but Speedy was not offended. It was plain that, like most other tramps, he had no trace of manly pride in him. The disgust of Mike increased. He presently saw two hundred dollars go down on a combination of four. A thousand and eight hundred dollars had to be taken from the bank and shoved across the hand-polished board in the direction of Speedy. Mike Doloroso felt his face turn hot—his neck swelled—there were sensations of strangling in his throat.

Finally he turned the wheel over to an assistant and went to see his employer, Sid Levine. When he had waded through the crowd of prospectors, laborers in the mines, teamsters, idlers, all the riff-raff that collects in a mining camp like froth below a cataract, he banged on the door that said in large letters PRIVATE.

A voice from within, the voice of his master, Sid Levine, answered: "Keep out of here, I tell you!"

"I ain't gonna keep out," said One-Eyed Mike. For his chief pride was his familiarity with the great man, Levine. He was one of the half dozen who, in the world, ventured to call him Sid.

"You keep out, Mike!" called Levine. "I'm busy."

"Who you busy with?" asked Mike.

"I'm busy with the sheriff," said Levine. "Go away."

"Yeah . . . the sheriff is what I wanna see," declared Mike.

He turned the handle of the door. It was locked. But presently a step crossed the room inside, and the lock turned. Mike Doloroso walked in.

It was the sheriff, Buck Masters, who had opened the door. Levine, fat as a carved Buddha, a Buddha of pale-green jade with a great jaw and a greater hook of a nose, sat immovable, as usual, behind the table, a cigar fuming in his hand. He looked like up-all-night, ache-in-the-head, and gout-in-the-foot, accompanied by disturbances of the mind.

The sheriff was another type. He was a great, swarthy man. He had been a singer in his youth; he still sang, generally after midnight. He had gone from singing into the prize ring, and he had made more money at the latter game until years and a bad reputation had ruled him out of the business. After that he had taken his blunt jaw and his gleaming eyes to other parts of the world, and finally he had drifted to the West and wound up, in the middle of the gold rush, in Sunday Slough. There he met Levine. When Sunday Slough grew up so far that it needed an official representative of the law, Levine, who owned Sunday Slough, caused Buck Masters to be elected sheriff, because he was the kind of sheriff that Sid Levine wanted.

He was the sort of sheriff that One-Eyed Mike wanted, also. Now, measuring the man of the law from an equal height, Mike said to him out of the twisted corner of his mouth: "Move over and let me in."

"What call boy went and paged you?" asked the sheriff.

Mike shifted slightly the patch of leather that covered his missing eye.

"I went and called myself," he said. "Get out of the way, Buck, will you?"

"Gonna have this big stiff in?" the sheriff asked Levine without turning his head.

"Aw, leave him come in, then," said Levine. "He's always butting in. He ain't got any sense about where he's wanted."

The sheriff stepped to the side and closed the door behind Mike. There was no false pride about the sheriff when he was among his intimates. Then he returned to the table and sat down again. Mike was leaning a hand on the table top, looking at the wad of papers that Sid Levine clutched and moistened with his fat, sweating hand.

"Look-it," said Mike. "Whacha talkin' about, you two? What kind of a crooked game you cooking up?"

"Listen at him," said Levine without enjoyment. "That's the way this bird talks. He thinks it's funny. You ain't funny, Mike. Back up, will you? Show us a clean pair of heels, will you?"

"It'd be the only clean thing in the room, then," said Mike, pleased with his retort. "What I wanna know is, whacha got on the table?"

"Hands," said Sid Levine. "Now you go on and tell us what's biting you. I was talkin' private with the sheriff. But you gotta go and butt in. Now talk yourself to death."

This sneering abuse pleased Mike. He knew what cold dignity could be in his employer, and it tickled his fancy to have the great boss speak in such terms to him.

Mike said: "There's a bird out there that something's gotta be done about."

"Drunk?" asked Levine. "Why don't you bat him on the jaw and throw him out, then?"

One-Eyed Mike looked down affectionately at his

burly right hand, which was now supporting his weight against the table.

"No, he ain't drunk," he said, "but he's wrecking the roulette bank." He turned to the sheriff. "Say, whacha know about a guy like this Levine that has to go and put in a roulette wheel without no brake on it? Whacha know about that, eh?"

"Yeah, that's pretty cute, ain't it?" said the sheriff. "But I'll tell you what, he's law-abiding. That's what Levine is. He's afraid of the law, is what he is."

He laughed. All three of them laughed at the good jest.

"Yeah, I'm afraid of the law, all right," said Sid Levine. "I'm afraid of the sheriff, too, because he's got the law behind him. I uphold the law because I uphold you, you big stiff. That's what I do." He grinned, an act that caused his nose to lengthen and his pointed chin to rise.

"Go on," said Buck Masters. "What about the bird that's breaking up the roulette bank?"

"Aw, what I mean," said One-Eyed Mike, "he ain't nothing but a bum that's crazy with luck. He calls himself Speedy."

"I went and heard that name somewhere," said the sheriff thoughtfully.

"Yeah, you maybe think you heard it because it sounds familiar," said Mike. "But you never heard it about him. He's just a kid . . . kind of a smiling fool. Just a bum . . . just a tramp. That's all. He's having a crazy run of luck, what I mean."

"What kind of a run?" asked Levine, flicking the ashes from his fat cigar.

Day and night, through all his waking hours, this idol of the mining camp kept such incense burning in his hand.

"What I mean is," said Mike, "he bumped the bank

7

for eighteen hundred the last spin of the wheel. You gotta go and put in a wheel without no brake. That was bright. I told you it was bright to do that!"

Levine flicked his cigar again, although there was no ash on the glowing tip of it.

"Eighteen hundred, eh?" he repeated.

"Yeah. Eighteen hundred I said, and eighteen hundred I mean," answered Mike.

"Well, we gotta do something about it," said Levine.

"That's why I come and talked myself to death," said Doloroso.

"All right. You kind of showed some sense," declared Levine.

He turned his massive head toward the sheriff. Buck Masters acknowledged the glance by yawning.

"We was talking about something important," he said. "You gotta go and drag in a low bum like this Speedy," commented the man of the law.

"Whacha been talking about?" asked Mike.

The sheriff looked up quickly at Levine.

"Aw," said Levine, "he's inside. Mike is inside. He's a friend of mine."

The sheriff turned his glance upon Mike again. "We was talking about Derrick," he said.

"Which?"

"Cliff Derrick," said the sheriff, and waited.

A wave of excitement spread across the damaged face of Mike. "Derrick!" he gasped. "What's he gone and done now?"

"He's gone and bedded himself down on this here range," said Buck Masters.

8

Fixing a Tramp

The single eye of Mike looked up and far away. It was clear that he was seeing things in the past.

"Derrick," he murmured again.

"Yeah, Cliff Derrick," said Levine. "That ain't so easy to say, neither."

"No, it ain't easy to say," murmured Mike. "It ain't so easy to take, neither."

"Neither is dynamite, or lightning, or arsenic," commented Buck Masters.

He looked down at his right hand, spread it, folded it into a fist, admired the row of knuckles, and yawned. He always yawned when he grew interested. He felt that it was unmanly to betray excitement.

"Well," said Mike, "Derrick is dynamite, all right."

"He's arsenic, too," said Levine. "He's slick, is what he is."

"Yeah, he's slick," said the sheriff. "He's poisonous slick, is what he is."

"What's he mean, coming out here?" asked Mike.

"Air, maybe," suggested Levine gently. "Wanted a change of air. I guess that's what he wanted. He wouldn't be bothered none wanting the free and easy that's floating around this here camp."

"Look-it here," said Mike. "He ain't gone and come into town, has he?"

"Aw, he ain't that much of a fool," said the sheriff. "Say, Levine, is he a friend of yours? You ain't told me that." The sheriff hesitated.

Levine pulled carefully at his cigar, which was almost out, a thing so strange it almost took his mind from the subject under discussion. At last, abstractedly, he answered: "We never done no business together."

"Then he ain't been trimmed," said Mike.

He and the sheriff laughed loudly. Levine smiled broadly with gratified vanity.

"What I mean," he said, "we got some mutual friends. That's all. I dunno nothing about Derrick. I read the papers. I dunno nothing about Derrick personal."

"The papers is enough," said the sheriff. "Even the papers can't go and lie all the time."

"Yeah," said Levine, "I guess he's pretty tough."

"Like a boiled owl, is all he is," said One-Eyed Mike. "Say, where's a drink around here?"

"You always gotta drink," remarked Levine. "It makes me sick, the way you always gotta drink. Aw, go on over there and help yourself, then. You know where it is. You take Mike," he added to the sheriff, "he's always gotta be sliding something past his front teeth. That's a fault of yours, Mike. Someday I'm gonna fire you. I ain't gonna have a lot of booze hounds around my place."

"Make it two," said the sheriff as Mike opened a filing cabinet and pulled out a bottle. "Yeah," he went on, "there's some people that ain't ever satisfied unless they're half tight. You gotta be a man to drink like a man oughta. You gonna have a shot?"

"I'll have a taste," said Levine. "Not them glasses, you dumbbell. Them are for the ladies. You take a skirt, they can't hold no liquor. It's a funny thing. You take a skirt, a coupla shots sink 'em. They dunno nothing about holding nothing. They ain't got any head, that's the trouble with 'em. Well, here's how, boys."

Mike lowered his glass and smacked his lips.

"Whacha always gotta have a chaser for, Sid?" he asked. "There ain't any use having a drink if you can't let it smoke a while."

"He's gonna teach me how to drink, too," commented Levine coldly. "That's all he's gonna do. He knows how to drink, is what he knows. What I mean about Derrick, is he the kind that stands in or is he the kind that stands out?"

"He'll stand in," said Mike wisely, "but he's a hog."

"He wants it all, does he?" asked Levine with a sad eye.

"You gotta throw a bluff with Derrick," said Mike. "That's all you gotta throw . . . but you gotta throw it big. Know what I mean? He ain't a pup. You can't pull nothing over Derrick. He's wise, is what he is."

"Yeah, he's no pup," agreed the sheriff.

"Well, whacha say?" asked Levine.

"He's the kind," said Buck Masters, "you sock him on the chin, and then you help him to stand up again. That's the way to get started with him."

"You sock him on the chin, you go and bust your hand, that's all," said One-Eyed Mike. "Who's gonna go and sock him on the chin, what I mean?"

"Oh, I dunno," said Levine, "anything can be managed, one way or another."

"Don't you go and make any mistake," said Mike, frowning with the intensity of his belief. "You better declare Derrick in. You better give him a cut. It'll save you money any time before you're done with the game. But

11

there's a roulette wheel in there without no brake on it. What're we gonna do about that?"

"The wheel's all right. The wheel'll take care of itself," said the great Levine. "About the guy that's running in luck, we better do something about him. What about you, Buck? What about you doing something?"

"Well, what would I do?" asked Masters.

"Use your brain on it," said Levine. "That's exactly what you would do."

"I'm the law," Masters grinned. "I gotta have a charge ag'in' him before I can go up and slam him in the hoosegow."

"I'll give you a charge," said Levine. "He's a bum. Go and sock him in jail for vagrancy."

"And him with five or six grand in his pockets that he's just taken out of the roulette?" The sheriff shrugged his shoulders as he asked the question.

"Well, whacha want?" asked One-Eyed Mike. "Ain't that the kind of fish that you wanna catch? Two minutes after he's been pinched he won't have any five or six grand, I guess."

The face of the sheriff grew still, and his eye burned. "Roll him?" he suggested.

"Why not? Half for you and half for the house," said One-Eyed Mike.

"Half for the house?" echoed the sheriff, frowning.

"Well, you hunt on our land, so you gotta pay a commission. It ain't every place in the world that the gamekeepers hold the game by a halter while the hunter comes up and gets the kill."

"You ain't such a dumbbell, Mike," murmured Levine. "You got a kind of brain in your head, at that. Fifty-fifty, Buck."

Masters shrugged his powerful shoulders. "I don't

mind," he averred. "Fifty-fifty is all right. But it's kind of raw . . . rolling a gent for vagrancy when he's got five, six thousand bucks in his jeans. Never mind. I'll slam him in the hoosegow, but I hate to bother the judge with that kind of a deal. I know the judge is fixed, but he don't want to be bothered except for something big. The way he says, the straighter he runs and the better judge he makes, the more use he'll be when it comes to a pinch that means a fortune or the rope. Daly, he don't wanna be bothered by no vagrancy dope."

"Aw, whacha talkin' about the hoosegow for, anyway?" asked One-Eyed Mike. "What I mean, slam this bird, trim him, and give him a run out of town. Make it so hot for him, he won't stop running for a coupla weeks. That's all I mean to do."

"Well, all right," said the sheriff. "I'll go and do it now. So long, Sid. See you later, Mike."

"Say," said Mike, "I'll be on hand when you shake him down . . . just to see what falls. Besides, two do a better job than one. You sock him on that side, and I plaster him on this side."

"Maybe you're right," agreed the sheriff. "I never say no. I don't seem to have no mind of my own no more."

"You're just growing up, brother," declared Sid Levine. "Go on and roll that baby, and come back and tell me about it, will you?"

"We'll come back with something more than talk," said One-Eyed Mike. And he led the way out of the room.

The sheriff, half a step behind him, said: "Travel heeled, you guess, this bird you're talking about? This Speedy?"

"Him? He never seen a gun except in a window. He

ain't nothing. Nothing but lucky. He's the kind that the women like. Soft and sweet, is all I mean."

"All right," said Buck Masters. "I'll just give him a squeeze and let the dollars fall where they may."

"Sure," said One-Eyed Mike, laughing. "Hew to a line, is the idea."

He returned to the roulette wheel at the very unpleasant moment when Speedy was drawing in a five hundred dollar win.

One-Eyed Mike began to perspire. It seemed to him something approaching a mortal sin when he saw good money was going to waste as rapidly as this.

Besides, others in the crowd had begun to follow the choices of Speedy and were placing their money on the same numbers or the same color, or odd or even. A regular run on the game was starting.

In the middle of this excitement came the sheriff. He moved with the long and easy stride of a very powerful man, and, as he walked, he waved a jovial hand to right or to left, singling out some one of his acquaintances. For he was well known, and well liked, also.

At last he came through the crowd to the place where Speedy was standing, and instantly he laid a hand on the shoulder of the boy. That is to say, he started to lay his hand on the shoulder of that young man. But he failed to do so. Speedy, at that very moment, glided a little to the side, laid a bet on the odd, turned, and faced the sheriff with a polite smile.

"I want you, brother," said Buck Masters.

"Want me?" asked Speedy, his brows lifting.

"I'm Sheriff Masters. You come along and don't make no fuss, is all."

"But why do you want me, Sheriff?" asked the boy. "What have I done? It isn't because I've been winning money at roulette, is it? It isn't because Mister Levine has sent for you, is it?"

He said those words in a slightly louder voice, and they drew instant attention from the crowd.

A Good Story

A mining crowd is never gentle and never dull-witted. This group of men was instantly irritated.

"Look, Masters," said one of them, "what kind of a raw deal is this? Can't Levine lose a few grand without bringing in the police?"

The sheriff arched his black brows and roared: "What kind of a gag are you pulling on me? What kind of bunk is this? Back up, will you, and leave the way clear. Kid, face around and get out of here before I throw you out!"

"Oh, I'm going out, all right," said the boy. "It was simply that I wondered what I'd done."

"Why, you're a bum, you're a tramp, for one thing," said the sheriff. "And . . . well, you know what your record is, you worm!"

As he broke into this tirade, Speedy seemed to shrink away through the crowd in fear and trembling, and the sheriff followed after him.

The crowd did not follow. After all, arrests were common in Sunday Slough.

As Mike again turned the roulette wheel over to his

16

assistant and hurried in pursuit, the sheriff reached again for the shoulder of the boy, and again missed his grip. He thought that was odd—as though the young-ster had eyes in the back of his head and knew when to side-step without turning to look!

They came out the rear door of the dive. Suddenly it was quiet. The voices inside of Levine's Grand Palace were shut behind a stout wall, and the noise of labor up and down Sunday Slough—the clinking of double and single jacks on drill heads, the calling of orders, and the rumbling of wagons over the roads, deep with white dust—came thickly through the mountain air.

Mike came out behind the sheriff and Speedy. His face shone with sweat; his eyes shone with hungry ex-pectation. He saw the sheriff poking a big, capacious Colt revolver in the direction of Speedy's stomach.

"Stick up your hands, brother," said the sheriff.

Speedy lifted his slender brown hands, hardly larger than the hands of a child. "What do you want?" he asked. "The money I've won?"

"Fan him," said the sheriff.

Mike fanned him. He got a stuffed wallet, a bundle of money out of an inside coat pocket, and some more money from a trousers pocket. There was a small sewing kit, an undersized pocket knife, a pair of hand-kerchiefs extraordinarily clean, and nothing else.

The sheriff almost laughed aloud. "Tramp royal is about all you could say of him," he said. "He travels light, all right. Got a hoss?"

"Yes, I have a horse."

"But maybe you'd as soon walk as ride when you leave Sunday Slough?"

Speedy did not answer, because it was fairly obvious that no answer was required. He looked with gentle, helpless eyes from one face to the other.

17

"Well, give him a start," said the sheriff.

"I'll start him, all right," said Mike.

He had stepped around so that he was just opposite the man of the law, and now he gathered his strength and launched a pile-driving blow at the back of the boy's head.

Unfortunately, at that moment, the youth stooped a little and stepped to the side, so that the great, balled fist of One-Eyed Mike whizzed past the head of Speedy, missing it by a mere fraction of an inch, and shot at the sheriff.

It was a beautiful punch, long and straight, and with almost as much follow-through as a golf stroke. It very nearly reached the face of the sheriff. In fact, he had to throw up a sudden guard, and his left forearm was bruised by the violence of the blow.

"Why, you big ham!" said the sheriff. Then he himself, putting up the revolver, stepped in to flatten Speedy with the practiced might and skill of the prize ring.

Once an artist always an artist! It was a short and snappy left hook that he tried on the boy, who stood blinking and bewildered, with his hands at his sides, hanging loosely. It was plain that there was so little manhood in Speedy that he did not even know the first elements in the art of self-defense. Not even enough to lift his arms.

He was so paralyzed by fear that he was even unable to turn and run. The sheriff, on second thought, might have refrained from striking such a helpless target, but he was not using second thoughts just now. He was too irritated by the ache in his left arm, where Mike's fist had grazed him. Therefore he struck with the precision, with the lightning speed of a cat's paw.

It seemed as though the wind of the blow preceding

it knocked the boy back upon his heels, and the good left fist of the sheriff jarred home on thinnest air alone. He grunted as his own shoulder and stretching side absorbed the shock. But he balanced himself and stepped in with a long, overhand right smash.

The boy staggered again, and literally fell to the ground in helpless fright. But it so happened, just as he dropped, that One-Eyed Mike came charging in with furious violence. Over the kneeling form of Speedy, he tripped and pitched with violent impetus into his friend and comrade, Buck Masters.

They were heavy men; they rolled in headlong confusion upon the ground, while over them hovered the slender form of Speedy. He told them that he was sorry for their fall. He did not see how it could have happened. He wanted to assist them to their feet. But when the sheriff regained hands and knees and then feet, he found that a pair of big revolvers dangled from the hands of the boy. He held them as though he had never seen such weapons before.

"Look out!" gasped the sheriff. "That's hair-trigger, that one of mine."

"I hope that nothing happens," said Speedy. In his other hand he held a considerable wad of paper money and his own wallet. "I took this," he said. "I thought you had had it long enough to know what it was all about, Sheriff? Am I wrong?"

"Sleight of hand, eh?" said the sheriff. "Circus stuff, jujitsu, and all that, eh? That's all right, kid. You made a good play. But don't you think that I'm done with you!"

One-Eyed Mike had been stunned by the violence of the fall. Now he got to his feet, reeling. His brain was ringing with mighty bells; the leather patch had shifted, and the horrible, dark cavern of the missing eye was visible.

"Leave me at him, Buck," he pleaded.

"Why, I ain't holdin' you back none," said the sheriff. "Go on and catch him if you can, but don't let him drop a gun on your toe while you're chasing him around. That's all. Sail right in and catch him, brother!"

"You ain't funny," said One-Eyed Mike. "Hold on! Gonna let him go sneakin' off?"

"I won't sneak far," said Speedy cheerfully. "When you really want me, just send for me."

"Give back that gun," said the sheriff. "You leave that gun behind!"

"I forgot which is yours and which belongs to Mike," said Speedy. "But I'll do my best to find out which belong to which!"

He moved away as he spoke, and the sheriff leaned a hand against a tree trunk and stared gloomily after the lad.

"He's a slick one, all right," he said.

Mike rubbed a hand across a troubled brow. "He's so slick," he commented, "that he's gonna get all roughed up before he leaves this here town. You hear me talk?"

"I hear you talk," said Buck Masters in some disgust. "I seen you fight, too. You can knock a hole in the air, all right, you can!"

"That's the way of it, is it?" demanded One-Eyed Mike. "Who was the big dunderhead that comes and slams into me just when I had the kid measured for a home run? Who was it that up and got in the way when I was just about to plaster him? You used your hands like a coupla loads of hay. And that's a fact."

"Did I?" asked the sheriff softly. "But where you were shining most, Mike, was in the ground work. Yeah, that's where you done handsome. The way you dived, that was the best thing about you. He went and hypnotized you, and you thought that you was takin' a swim. Ain't that right?"

"You're all thumbs when it comes to kidding," said One-Eyed Mike. "But I'm gonna point out something to you. Except when I fanned him, we ain't either of us laid a hand on him."

"No," said the sheriff, "we ain't, as a matter of fact. I wanna see that kid again."

"I'm gonna see him again," said the gambler, "if I gotta walk miles and swim rivers all the rest of my life to get at him. And the guns, too. Walkin' off with our guns!"

Young Speedy, in the meantime, had sauntered into the main street of Sunday Slough until he came to one of the most flourishing shops in the street. It was a place where one could buy anything from dynamite to drills. Every whim and fancy, whether for the hunter of bird and beast or the hunter of man, could be satisfied there. Shotguns in one long rack and rifles in another begged to be handled and used. A whole wall of the place was decorated with blue cardboard boxes filled with ammunition.

Speedy, once inside the door of this shop, paused a moment to admire the display. Then he found an idle clerk and laid the two revolvers on the counter.

"I picked up this pair of guns," he said. "Who owns 'em?"

The clerk frowned at them. Then he jerked up his head with a start.

"Why," he said, "that's the criss-crossing that the sheriff cuts into the handles of his guns to roughen up the grip. And this here with the sight filed off, wouldn't that belong to One-Eyed Mike?"

"I don't know," said Speedy. "I suppose the right men will come to claim those guns."

With that he walked out of the shop and went on down the street, regardless of the clerk, who followed him as far as the entrance, and then stared after him agape. It seemed that the clerk had many things that he wanted to say, but all stopped on the verge of his lips. Then he saw the editor, reporter, business manager, and sales agent of the Sunday Slough *News*.

"Hey, Bill!" he cried. "Come here and get a story!"

Speedy's Threat

Bill came to get the story. There was plenty of news in Sunday Slough, running from cheerful gunfights to new gold strikes up and down the cañon. But the appetite of Bill for new items was an amazing thing.

"What's the idea, Pete?" he said. "Got a new kind of a gat in stock?"

"Say," said Pete, "tell me the moniker of a kid all kind of dressed up in rags and patches, with one kind of a coat and another kind of trousers, and mostly everything oversize, with a sad kind of a soft look about his eyes, which, once you'd seen him, you'd remember."

"Yeah, I seen him in the Grand Palace," said the reporter. "I seen him making a run on the roulette wheel. Five, six grand was what he picked up. Along comes the sheriff and gives him a run. Slugs him in the hoosegow for vagrancy, they say."

"Ain't that kind of thick?" said the clerk. "Slugging a gent in the hoosegow for vagrancy when he's got all that kale in his poke?"

"Yeah, kind of thick. But they're deep, some of the people around this here town."

"They're deep, all right," said Pete. "But they didn't slam the kid in the hoosegow, after all."

"No?"

"No, they didn't. Look-it here. Did anybody go along with the sheriff when he run the kid in?"

"Yeah. There was one went."

"Was it Mike Doloroso?"

The reporter stared. "Who told you that?" he asked.

"Leave that be," said the clerk. "The name of this kid . . . who does he call himself?"

"Speedy."

"That's a funny name."

"Yeah, it's a funny name, all right."

"Look-it," said Pete. "Maybe there's something to him besides his eyes."

"There's luck to him. I saw him have that run at roulette."

"Maybe there's something more than luck. Come here!" He took Bill to the counter and showed him the pair of revolvers. "There's the sheriff's cannon. And that one belongs to Mike Doloroso, or I'm a one-eyed sucker," declared the clerk.

"What are you doing with them guns?" asked Bill.

"Speedy left 'em here."

"Hold on! Speedy left 'em here?"

"Yeah, he says that he found 'em in the street. Is that likely? No, it ain't likely. He brought 'em in and says I'm to hold 'em till they're claimed. Now, look-it here. The sheriff and Mike go out to run Speedy into jail. They don't run him into jail, though. Instead, he walks off with their guns. If you're a bright guy, you might find a story buried in that somewhere."

"By Jove, this is one of the best!" cried the reporter. "But if I print anything, Mike and the sheriff and the whole inside gang will cut my throat."

"They won't," declared the clerk. "Look-it what I do. I put them two guns in the window, and I put a big show card under 'em, and on the card I say that Speedy left these two guns with me, and anybody that claims them can have 'em. That's gonna bring every gent in Sunday Slough to look at the guns. And everybody's gonna know, before night, who really owns those guns. And everybody is gonna be asking questions how Speedy got 'em. All you do is to write a little item in the paper, and maybe it's worth a box on the front page!"

Bill writhed with pleasure. "It's worth a three-column head," he vowed. "It's a beaut'. It's new and it's tender and it's true, is what it is. But they'll murder Speedy, is all they'll do. The thugs, I mean."

"Yeah, and maybe they tried to murder him before, and, instead, he just takes their guns away from 'em. Who is this here Speedy, anyway?"

"I dunno," said Bill, "but I'm gonna find out!"

In twenty minutes he found Speedy in the Best Chance Saloon, far down the street. The sounds of sweet singing and the twanging of a guitar drew Bill Turner into the place, and there he found that a good-size crowd had already gathered. They leaned their backs against the bar and faced toward a lad who sat cocked back in a chair in a corner of the room, with his battered hat on the floor before him and a guitar across his knees.

It was Speedy, singing songs of old Ireland, and the crowd listened, hushed and respectful. It does not take many drops of Irish blood to color all the rest in a man's body. Every one of those listeners, although the names might have ranged from Russian to German and Portuguese, gave reverent heed as though to the songs of a fatherland.

25

Showers of big silver and dollar bills fell into the hat at the end of each song. But Doc Wiley took firm hold of the ceremony at this point. He was a prospector whose flaming red hair was gradually being dulled to gray, but his shoulders were as ample and his voice as huge a roar as ever in his famous youth. For a famous man he had been, up and down the range, following his fortune wherever he could find it, and throwing it away again as fast as found.

Now he said: "I got three hundred dollars, kid, and I'm gonna hear three songs. Tune up, you wildcat, and lemme hear you yip good and loud!"

He named his songs. They were sad and wailing affairs, every one of them, and they proclaimed the miseries of the green island and the cruelty of the oppressors, but someday, far away, happiness would return again. So Speedy sang them to great applause, and after every one of them he threw in a whirling, jolly, dancing tune for an encore, until the whole roomful of men was roaring and stamping with the chorus and beating time with foot and hand.

Then Doc Wiley, the prospector, very drunk, but very solemn, crossed the room and put his three hundred dollars in the hat.

He said: "Kid, if I'd ever been in old Ireland, these here songs would put me right back there again. And I tell you what I'm gonna do. When I make another pile, I'm gonna pull out and go to Ireland and buy me a dog and a potato patch, and be as Irish as any of 'em all!"

He turned around and made a slow, stately way toward the door. Just as he reached it, Speedy, on noiseless feet, overtook him, and the three hundred dollars glided from his hand, unnoticed, into the pocket of the big man. Then Doc Wiley went out into the street.

The Best Chance Saloon broke into deep-throated murmurs. It is easier to take three hundred dollars, after all, then to return it, and Speedy would have been heavily plied with liquor had not Bill Turner, of the *News*, got the lad into an obscure back room.

Turner explained: "Speedy, I'm a newspaperman. Sit down and tell me about yourself."

The soft eyes considered Turner gently. "I'm poor newspaper copy," said Speedy. "You ask me questions, and I'll answer 'em."

"Tell me, where you from?" asked Turner.

"Over there," said Speedy, with a gesture that included half the points of the compass.

Turner grinned. "I see," he said. "What's your line?"

"Everything but work."

"No work, eh?"

"No."

"Never?"

"Never a stroke."

"Gentleman of leisure, Speedy?"

"You can call it that if you want to."

"What brought you out here, anyway?"

"Travel," said Speedy.

Bill Turner laughed. "That's the way most people get around . . . by traveling. Been on the stage?"

"I prefer blind baggage to a stage," said Speedy.

"You've had a good deal of education," said the reporter.

"That was when I was young and didn't know any better," said the tramp.

"How old are you?"

"Old enough to vote."

"Usually travel around and pick up your money singing?"

"I don't care how I get money," said the boy, "so long as there are no sweat stains on it."

"About the sheriff and One-Eyed Mike. . . ."

"What about 'em?"

"What did you do to them?"

"Nothing," said Speedy.

"Hold on! Down there in the shop window there's a pair of guns. You took 'em from the sheriff and One-Eyed Mike. The town's gonna be buzzing about it, Speedy. You might as well tell me the straight story."

"No story is straight after it's been told once," said Speedy. "There's nothing for me to tell you, partner."

"You did nothing to 'em, eh?"

"I didn't touch them."

"Just persuaded 'em to give up their guns?"

Speedy shrugged his shoulders. "I just found the guns," he answered.

"You don't have to touch a man if you get the drop on them," suggested the reporter.

"The drop? Oh, I never carry a gun," said Speedy.

Bill Turner rose slowly to his feet, as though lifted by an unseen hand. "You . . . never . . . wear a gun?" he echoed.

"No, never."

"Well, I'll be dog-goned!" said Turner. "Is that all you're going to tell me?"

"I can't think of anything else to say."

Turner looked steadily upon his companion. "Speedy," he said, "you won't talk, but I'm gonna talk to you. I'm gonna tell you something."

"Yes?" said Speedy.

"After that story of the two guns gets around, they're gonna make you walk the plank. You better leave Sunday Slough."

"I can't," said Speedy. "I'm too interested in cleaning it up."

"Cleaning it up?"

"Yes," said Speedy, "I want to help the sheriff do his job!"

The Scoop

Turner had plenty of news to print day by day, but, as has been said before, he rarely had such a feature as he carried that evening. It was read by every man in town. The edition was sold out before dusk. He printed a new edition, an extra, and charged twenty-five cents a copy. He sold out that edition, too, and ground his teeth because he had not made a printing twice as large.

However, it was a good day, a grand day, for Bill. He was not in the newspaper game to make money merely. He was an artist, and his soul as a creator was satisfied with his performance. He had built out of Speedy a new feature, and one that would be remembered. He wrote a good head in the first place.

BETTER SUNDAY FOR THE SLOUGH
OR
A BETTER SUNDAY FOR SUNDAY.
SPEEDY ARRIVES TO CLEAN UP THE TOWN!

Under that beginning he wrote that Speedy, wandering guitar player and singer, dancing genius, parlor magician, sleight-of-hand artist, had come to Sunday Slough, found money easy in the Grand Palace, and had then been arrested on a charge of vagabondism by the sheriff, assisted by formidable Mike Doloroso.

But something had happened. What was it?

On the way to the jail the sheriff and Mike had lost their prisoner and both their guns! Could they explain!

Perhaps the guns would offer an explanation. And they were both on view in the window of the gunsmith!

Yes, it was a story that made Sunday Slough gasp, and then laugh loudly, although somewhat up its sleeve, for no matter what might have happened to the sheriff in the course of this misadventure, he was known to be a formidable man.

His humor was not of the best the next morning as he sat in his office blinking whisky fumes out of his brain and trying to get the taste of his first cigar of the day. But his brain ached. A cloud was still drifting before his eyes, and through that cloud appeared, with increasing brightness, the image of Speedy, the tramp entertainer.

Mike Doloroso came down the street at this moment and paused to scowl at the sign beside the sheriff's door. It read:

WANTED, A DEPUTY SHERIFF,
A MAN WHO KNOWS THIS RANGE, HIS HORSE, AND HIS GUN.

The pay was high, but even forty dollars a week no longer tempted men in Sunday Slough. They had seen too many others apply for the job, get it, and then disappear from the tale of the living at the end of a few days. Sometimes the people of Sunday Slough referred to those fellows as "Buck Masters's seven-day men." That was about the average of their incumbency. After seven days they faded from the picture, and the pay they drew was just about enough to pay for their funeral. Therefore, it was generally said that a deputy sheriff in the Slough was working for his grave.

One-Eyed Mike eyed the sign with disfavor, also with thought. He had come with evil will to call upon the sheriff, now he remembered that, although the deputies came and went with the weeks, Buck Masters had remained in Sunday Slough for twenty times that long, and still he was alive. Neither did he assign the hardest jobs to his assistants. In fact, there was nothing that Buck liked so well as a brawl, and his favorite diversion was meeting an out-of-town badman and beating him at his own game of general, all-around badness. It was true that Buck was open to influence, but that did not mean that he was hand in glove with every yegg who visited the Slough.

So, having considered these things, One-Eyed Mike came into the office with more respect than he had intended to show. He merely said: "We turned up an ace yesterday, Buck."

The sheriff puffed at his cigar and, instead of looking at Mike, seemed to be regarding only the bad taste in his mouth.

"I been by the window and seen them guns," said Mike. "Whacha think about that, Buck? Whacha think of the nerve of that bum?"

"Whacha think of it yourself?" asked the sheriff, coughing out a cloud of smoke afresh.

"I think heads we win, tails he loses," said One-Eyed Mike. "Got a drink around here?"

"Not this early in the morning," said the sheriff. "I ain't gonna tempt the young, like you and me. You seen the guns, did you?"

"Everybody else has seen 'em, too. There's a crowd

all the time in front of the window. That cross-hatching, it stands out pretty strong on the handles of that gun."

"What about the filed-off sight?" asked the sheriff sharply.

"Yeah. You can see that, too. How are we gonna roll this bum, what I mean?"

The sheriff turned his head slowly away and looked at the colored calendar that hung beside his window, showing a bonnie lass with golden hair over her shoulder and a mouthful of teeth and a prop smile. Through the window he looked out over the ragged, staggered roofs of Sunday Slough, with the bright smoke of the sun already rising from them, and beyond the roofs he saw the cliffs of the upper valley, gleaming gold or blue. He loved that valley, and he loved that town. His twenty weeks in it had been profitable; more than that, they had been happy weeks. He felt that his finger was upon the main pulse of life at last, and that he mattered vitally to many people.

At last he said: "The dirty bum is by way of makin' a fool out of me!"

"Me, too," said One-Eyed Mike. "It was a funny thing, what happened yesterday. I dunno that I understand it."

"Sure, it was funny," said the sheriff. "It's so funny that just remembering of it gives me the gripes. The cool gripes!"

"I dunno what happened," said Mike.

"You never heard of a fool that was crazy with luck, I guess?" suggested the sheriff.

"Yeah, I've heard of that, too. He was crazy with luck, all right."

"Then shut up and let me think," said the sheriff.

Nevertheless, Mike went on: "What I mean to say is that this bird, with five or six grand in his jeans, he goes and gives a show in the Best Chance and pulls down some small change and does a song and dance. What I mean, he's lousy with coin, and he goes and works his head off for forty, fifty more. Doc Wiley is tight and slips the kid three greenbacks, and every one of them says a hundred dollars, soft and tender and true. And the kid passes them back into old Doc's pocket as he goes out the door. What I mean, the brat is still in town, and he's staged a gun show in a big window, and I dunno what he's all about."

"He dunno what he's all about, either," said the sheriff. "He's just kind of dizzy with himself, and he's pulling a grandstand just now. Pretty soon the floor'll jump up and sock him in the chin so hard he won't ever wake up."

"Yeah, he's gotta be rolled, I guess," said One-Eyed Mike.

"Rolled? He's gotta be rolled and plastered, picked up and dropped. Even if he's a hard-boiled egg, I'm gonna crack him wide open. Only, I was just thinking how."

"So was I. So was Sid," declared Mike.

"Didn't Sid have no ideas?" asked the sheriff wistfully.

"He didn't have no good ones," said Mike. "Sid is green as fresh lobster when he thinks about that kid getting off with five or six grand. But he says what's the difference? If you take and pinch the kid a second time, everybody in town will know that it's just a grouch. And what can you pinch him for? Vagabondage? Not with him so flush and the whole town knowing it. Resisting arrest? You couldn't bring him up for that, because you and me would have to tell what happened, and we couldn't do that."

"So that leaves what?" asked the sheriff.

"A rap over the bean is all, I guess," said Mike.

"Yeah," suggested the sheriff. "Or a fake gunfight in

any saloon where he's working, and the only bullet that hits anything but air is the one that splits the wishbone of this kid. This Speedy, this what's-his-name, has anybody else found out what he is?"

"He ain't nothing but a greasy bum," said One-Eyed Mike. "Nobody don't know anything at all about him. And we got people here from all over the world. He won't talk about himself."

"That's nacheral enough with a lot of gents," said the sheriff, who sometimes drew a curtain over sections of his own life. "I bet he's done time."

"Most of Sunday Slough has," said Mike. "What of it?"

"Nothing of it," said Buck Masters. "That ain't anything against a man. Anybody's likely to run up against a piece of time, I guess."

"I guess, too," said Mike. "But we ain't no nearer to rolling this here bum."

"We're gonna roll him," said the sheriff. "But I dunno. Something kind of holds me back."

"Like what holds you back?" said Mike.

"Him not packing no gun, I mean."

"What makes you think that he don't pack no gun? Him saying so?"

"Yeah, him saying so. It kind of stuck in my craw. Suppose that I go out and salt him down with a handful of lead, and then they turn him over and find that he don't pack no gun. It wouldn't look so good. We didn't find no gun when we fanned him."

"He's sleight-of-hand, is what it is," said the other. "You can't tell about a guy like that. They can do funny things."

"They can't put a Colt Forty-Five into a hollow tooth," objected the sheriff.

"I dunno . . . they can do funny things. You wouldn't believe your eyes," said Mike. "And don't you worry

35

about that baby. If you sock him between the eyes, nobody is gonna go and say that you've robbed the cradle none."

"Put on the brakes and skid to a stop," said the sheriff. "Here comes that ham-and-eggs deputy marshal, Tom Gray, the honest man. Honest Tom. What's he coming butting in for around here?"

"Federal officer?" asked One-Eyed Mike, his eyes enlarging.

"Yeah, shut up," said the sheriff. And just then the deputy marshal came in.

Two Visitors

The deputy marshal looked far from an important or a fighting man. He was short, stoop-shouldered, and very gray. He wore a close-cropped mustache, as gray as the hair of his head, and his upper lip twitched nervously. Only his eyes were steady—very tired, patient, and sad eyes.

He wore an alpaca coat, his trousers were pulled down over his boots, and there were no spurs on their high heels. He had a low, turned-down, stiff white collar, rather soiled where it touched his sunburned neck. He looked like a third-rate businessman in a small town, one about to enter a crisis in his affairs. He talked in a husky voice.

"Hello, Masters," he said. "You haven't forgotten me?"

Masters summoned a smile and a handshake. "How's every little thing?" he asked. "This is Mike Doloroso."

The marshal turned about and looked quietly, earnestly, at One-Eyed Mike.

"I know Mike," he said, "but Mike doesn't know me." That was his only greeting to the gambler, then he turned back to the sheriff. "I've come hunting for help," he said.

"Have you?" asked Masters, surprised. "What can I do for you, Gray?"

"Cliff Derrick has jumped into this part of the world," said the marshal.

"Has he?" asked the sheriff innocently.

"Yes, he has. Know him?"

"I dunno that I know him. I've heard about him. But this is away off your beat, Gray."

"Yes. It's off my regular beat. But I go where the men I want have gone. I want Derrick. I want all of him, and I want him forever."

"Life, eh?"

"Yes. Even if he had nine lives, I'd want all of 'em."

"Yeah, Derrick's been a busy boy," commented Mike, who kept on the outskirts of the conversation.

"He's what I'd call a handy man to have around the house," said the marshal. "Anything from running chinks to smuggling dope across the river. He's not particular. He goes where his luck leads him, and he covers up his trail with the handiest thing that comes his way . . . something red, usually."

"Derrick's a killer, they say," remarked the sheriff. "That's all there is to it. He's a killer. He ain't a bad man. There ain't no fun in Derrick. He just up and kills you. That's all there is to it!"

"That's all there's been to it so far," said the marshal. "I hope to add something to the story, though, a sort of conclusion. And I thought you and your boys might help me, Masters. We haven't always been friendly. But I forget the past. I take men the way I find 'em. I hope you can do the same."

"Sure, I can," murmured Masters with a certain air of relief.

"Derrick is no particular help to anyone," said the marshal. "Although you're policing a big county, Masters, I dare say that you'll be crowded for room now that Derrick has moved in."

"I reckon that I might be," said the sheriff. "Where d'you reckon this Derrick to be hanging out now?"

"Somewhere around the Castle Ford."

"He would be." Masters nodded. "That's a regular hole in the wall."

"That's what it is," said the marshal. "Do you stand in with me?"

"Of course, I do. I'll give Castle Ford a stir and see what comes to the top. I'll let you know."

"That's all I want," said the marshal. "Glad I've seen you. So long. So long, Mike. Be a good boy."

He went out into the fiery sunshine of the street with his short, quick, impatiently stumbling step. Like many a horseman, he was uncertain on his feet.

When he was gone, the pair inside stared at one another, and Mike spoke first, cautiously.

"Well, whacha think?" he asked.

The sheriff removed his cigar and snarled his lips around the issuing cloud of smoke. "That snake give me the run once," he said. "Like I would throw in with him now! I could eat him sliced for cold salad, is what I could do."

Mike grinned. He actually sighed with relief. "Like you would throw in with him instead of a man like Derrick," he said. "There's thousands in a fellow like Derrick. Thousands is just small change for him!"

"Sure. I know that. It ain't the money, though," said the sheriff. "But this Tom Gray, he gave me the run once. I don't forget a thing like that. Now he comes around and finds me in the saddle, and he wants to ride on the same horse. He can go to blazes. I don't

39

work with his kind. I work with my own kind."

"Sure you do," said Mike. "This gives you an easy break with Derrick, too. You can tip off Gray's hand to him. Levine will give me a day off. I could carry a note from you up to him."

"You couldn't carry no note for me," answered the sheriff, sneering a little at this absurdity. "I don't write messages to birds like Derrick. But you can go and tell him what I think. It's only about six miles to Castle Ford. You can be back pretty soon. Try to find out how many men are with him, and what they're like. He don't play a lone hand ever. And if. . . ." He stopped. "Now, dog-gone my eyes," said the sheriff, "because I don't believe what they're tryin' to tell me!"

He stared as he spoke. Through the door of his office, out of the burning sunshine into the thick, cool shadow streaked with powerful tobacco smoke, came none other than Speedy! He stood just inside the doorway, and, taking off his ragged hat, he smiled upon the two, and then mopped his forehead with an extraordinarily clean handkerchief.

"Here we all are again," he said.

One-Eyed Mike arose and stepped back toward the wall, a strategic post of importance. The sheriff leaned forward in his chair and drew open—a silent inch farther—a certain important drawer of his desk.

"Yeah," Masters said, "it looks like we're all together again for a while. Just come in to pay me a little call, brother?"

"I came in to laugh with you about that newspaper article," said Speedy. "What an impression that gives . . . as though somehow I had managed to manhandle you both!"

He was as good as his word and broke into the most

cheerful laughter as he said this. He took a chair and tilted it back against the wall. One-Eyed Mike moved closer, stepping sidewise, like a spider, and looking at the sheriff rather than at his intended victim, as though the direction of his eyes would be a mask to his physical movements.

"Yeah, that was the impression that the story gave, all right," said the sheriff, his teeth set so hard that the jaw muscles bulged.

"That was the impression," said Speedy. "I knew that you'd be laughing about it, and so I dropped in to join you. There was something else on my mind, too."

"Oh, was there? And what was it?" asked the sheriff softly. "Something about the gun show down the street, maybe? Or the cleaning up of Sunday Slough?"

"You know," said Speedy, "I don't like steady work very well, but I thought that forty a week sounded like pretty good pay."

Both of them stared at the lad with amazement, with bewilderment. At last One-Eyed Mike said hoarsely: "Do you hear him? He means nothin' but the deputy sheriff job!"

"He don't mean that," said the sheriff.

"You know how it is," said the boy. "I understand that the deputy sheriff would have to do a good deal of riding. I'm not a first-rate rider, but I like the open air pretty well. Never feel quite healthy unless I'm well tanned. You know how it is."

The sheriff moistened his tight lips as far as the bristles of his unshaven beard.

"You wanna go and be deputy sheriff, do you?"

"Why not?" said the boy.

"Well, why not? Know what they call a deputy sheriff here?"

"A seven-day man?" asked the boy. "Yes, I've heard that. But they must have been rash people. A little tact will get one around all sorts of difficulties."

The sheriff pointed his forefinger as though it were a gun. "What's your phony game?" he demanded. "What aces have you got to deal off the bottom of the pack? What's all this about cleaning up Sunday Slough?"

"Well," said Speedy seriously and gently, "you know how it is. Every man ought to have some civic interest in his life. Everyone ought to take a vital share in the life of a community. I was reading about it just the other day. And it seems to me that I might take a hand with Sunday Slough. You agree?"

The sheriff blinked. It took him some time to digest the meaning of these words. A few of them were new to his ears. At last he leaned back in his chair. "What would you do to Sunday Slough?" he asked.

"I'd make it quiet at night," said the boy. "I could hardly sleep last night, if you'll believe me."

"Well, I'll be . . . ," began the sheriff. He broke off to remark: "Yeah, I'll believe you. Son, if you wanna be a deputy to work under me, it means signing a paper and swearing an oath to do your duty and execute the law."

"I know that," said the boy.

"I have a paper here. You slap your name down on this line . . . that's right . . . John Smith is what you call yourself, is it? Well, that's all right, too. Now, here's a Bible to swear on. Where's that book? Here it is. You lay your hand on this and repeat after me."

So, hand raised, Speedy repeated the oath of service.

When he had ended, the sheriff swallowed hard and said: "Now you're my man. The law's man, I mean to say."

"That's correct," said Speedy.

The sheriff cleared his throat. He looked down to the desk to keep the burning delight from showing in his eyes.

"You can start on the job right now," he said. "Up at Castle Ford there's a man I want brought into town. His name is Cliff Derrick. I'll write out the description for you!"

A Few Tricks

The written description of the famous Cliff Derrick did not amount to a great deal, but the running comment with which the sheriff eked out his written phrases was interesting. He wrote down: Height about five feet eleven, weight a hundred and sixty-five, complexion fair to medium, features average, habits quiet, no scars or distinguishing marks. Age, anywhere between twenty-eight and forty.

Then he said aloud: "You see that he's kind of an average. He looks tall to a short man and average to a tall man. To you he'd look about the right height, Speedy. What I mean, he wouldn't seem either tall or short. Now you take his complexion, there's a lot of difference of opinion, and I've seen some that said he was sandy and some said golden-haired, some brown and some black-haired."

"Yeah," said Mike, "I met up with a gent from Carson once that said he knew Cliff Derrick personal, and knew him well, and he said that Cliff was a dark gent that had black hair and black eyes. I didn't think that he could mean what he said. I didn't think he was more than bluffing about knowing a great man. But he wasn't bluffing. He meant what he said."

"Perhaps he dyes his hair or wears a wig," suggested Speedy with an amiable smile.

"How would he go about dyeing his eyes?" asked the sheriff rather sternly. Then he added: "No, he's just kind of average all over. He's the kind of a looking man you wouldn't expect nothing special from him. You'd just write him down average. You wouldn't expect him to be quick, or smart, or brave, or nothing. He's the kind of a gent that'd lose himself in a crowd as quick as he entered it. He dresses the same. In town he's like any ordinary townsman. In a swell city he fades right into the swells on one side, or among the toughs on the other. And out here on the range he just looks like a kind of rusty cowpuncher, is all. Understand?"

"He must be a clever fellow," said Speedy, nodding.

"Clever? He's Cliff Derrick!" said One-Eyed Mike. "Don't forget that. You write that down in your books, will you?"

"Yes, I'll write that name down in my mind," agreed the boy.

The sheriff stood up, brusquely ending the interview. He said: "You get paid off at the end of each week. But you get traveling expenses and the price of a hoss . . . cost of hoss to be charged ag'in' you unless it's used up logical and right in the execution of business."

"For instance," said One-Eyed Mike in kind explanation, "suppose that Derrick was to choose to dump your hoss before he dumped you, that would be regular execution of your duty, eh?"

"Yes, I'll have to get a horse," said Speedy. "How much should I pay for one?"

"About a hundred dollars ought to get you a high-grade mustang . . . really high. Hosses are dirt cheap around here. You can get a ride for twenty dollars. But I'm talkin' about a hoss that might be able to follow Derrick's dust for a coupla miles."

"Where shall I look for a horse?"

"Down at Seeman's place. He's always got a flock of hosses on tap. You go down and try him. So long, Speedy. Here's luck to you."

"Thanks," said Speedy. "I hope the talk dies down and the newspaper chokes before I get back from the trail."

"By the time you get back," said the sheriff, "there won't be any more talk. Don't you worry about that. When you come back here with Derrick in your pocket, there won't be any more talk at all."

They watched the youth through the doorway, and One-Eyed Mike was rubbing his red knuckles still redder against the side of his trousers.

"I dunno how it is," he said, "but every time I see the mug of that kid I want to take and sock him on the jaw."

"It's a kind of a nacheral instinct," agreed the sheriff. "The butt of a gun would suit me as well as a fist, though. I'd like to mix his face all up . . . I'd like to scramble his features for him, what I mean."

"Leave Derrick to do a better job than we'd do," suggested Mike Doloroso. "The beautiful part about Derrick is that he don't care what tool he uses. He's choked men with his bare hands and he's knifed 'em in the back. He's shot 'em down in a fair fight, and also from behind a rock or a bush. He's killed men at midnight and at noon. He's poisoned their food, he's blown up their houses, and he's dropped bombs on 'em from a high place. I wish that he would use all of them methods on that kid . . . all of them together . . . blowing up, and blastin' down, and knife and gun, a strangling, and a club to finish things off with. That's what I wish."

"I hope your wish works out," said the sheriff. "Now, you climb the frame of the best hoss you got and slide up the trail to Castle Ford. You find Cliff Derrick, and you tell him that there's a deputy of mine that's got out of hand and that is sure to gun for him. Give him a description of the fool, and leave the rest to Derrick. He'll scramble up Speedy so that even his mother wouldn't know the remains. Still, I got a feeling that I'd like to have a hand in on the hashing of Speedy. No, you mush, and don't quit galloping till you see Derrick face to face. When you get near the Ford, you start whistling two notes, one high and one low. They say that's the call for Derrick or one of his trusties. Beat it, Mike."

Speedy had gone not to the corral of Seeman, the horse dealer, but to the hotel where the federal marshal was staying. Thomas Gray never refused to see a man; he saw Speedy now, and the boy said to him: "Marshal Gray, I've heard a lot about you, and I've come to ask some advice from you, because I've been appointed deputy sheriff here, and I want to know what I should do to follow in your footsteps."

The marshal heard this odd speech without enthusiasm. He said: "Are you another one of Buck Masters's seven-day men? Well, son, tell me, were you born in the saddle? Can you shoot, too?"

"I can hit the side of a barn when it's not too far away," admitted Speedy.

"Are you being funny?" said the marshal.

"No, I'm saying the truth, and nothing but the truth. I can stay on the back of a horse so long as it doesn't run too hard. When it comes to bucking, the first jump slams me to the ground."

The marshal mastered his sense of scorn. "Let me see your guns," he commanded.

"I don't carry any guns," said the boy.

"What?"

"Guns go off and hurt a lot of people by accident," suggested Speedy by way of explanation.

"Yeah, they hurt a lot of people," said the marshal. "You're planning to go out on the trail and catch men when you can't ride a real horse and can't shoot with a gun? You mean a revolver. Of course, you're at home with a rifle?"

Speedy had come near. He talked after the fashion of those people who seem incapable of expressing themselves in words unless they have buttonholed a victim. The marshal shrank twice from this close approach, until the wall was at his back. Then, in great disgust, he was forced to remain in his place.

"No, I'm not at home with a rifle, either," said Speedy. "I don't believe in bloodshed, Marshal Gray," he added with a frank smile. "I couldn't use either a knife or a gun on any man."

"Boy," said Gray, tormented almost beyond endurance and actually raising a hand to brush away the protesting gestures of Speedy, "you dunno what you're talking about. Either you're a born fool or a fool by cultivation. I tell you what. Some of the men that have to be chased on these mountain trails would turn around and swallow you. About one in three of them would as soon die as be caught by the law. And every man jack of them can ride anything that walks, and shoot the eye out of a turkey's head at a hundred yards."

"You don't think that I'm worth giving advice to?" Speedy asked sadly.

"Son," said Thomas Gray, "I hate to be rude. But I

also hate to waste my time. I'm a busy man. This is right in the middle of a busy day. I've got to say good bye."

"That's all right," said Speedy, and left the room at once. He even paused in the doorway to nod and bow and regret that he had come at the wrong moment. The marshal watched all these pretty manners with increased contempt until Speedy suddenly bowed to the floor, exclaiming: "Hello, what's this? Somebody leaving gold watches instead of calling cards at your door, Marshal?"

He came back, carrying the massive old watch in his hand, the great chain with huge links dangling far down. He said: "Who could have done this, Marshal?"

Gray found something very familiar about the look of that watch and chain, and now he fumbled at his breast pocket. His fine old watch was gone, and so was the heavy chain and the bar that kept it attached to the buttonhole in the lapel of his coat.

He exclaimed: "What in blazes!" Then he reached out and took the watch. It had belonged to his father before him; he loved it as the apple of his eye.

"And this pencil was lying there beside the watch, silver case and all," went on Speedy. "To say nothing of this lapis lazuli stone and the scarf pin that it's set in."

Marshal Gray took back his property, item by item.

There was even a handkerchief that must have been drawn out of the side pocket of his coat, although he knew that he kept a leather wallet of tobacco in the same pocket. Finally, when he had stared his fill upon the naïve face of Speedy, he uttered a great sigh, went to the door, slammed it, and came back to his guest.

"Sit down!" he commanded.

Speedy sat down gently, gingerly, on the edge of his

chair, like a man presuming upon the time of some great personage.

"Now," said the marshal, "who are you, anyway?"

"Just a fellow with a friendly feeling and idle hands," said Speedy. "That's all. One must have occupation for the fingers, or the mind practically dies of boredom. Am I wrong?"

"You could keep a whole crowd entertained," said the marshal. "You oughta do this thing on the stage."

"I left the stage to find excitement," said Speedy. "I want you to show me how to get it around this town. D'you know?"

The Hunt Begins

The marshal was a man with a sense of humor, although as a rule his smiles dawned but slowly. On this occasion, however, he grinned very widely, and afterward he said: "Now, Speedy, since that's the name that you choose to be called by, tell me just what your game is? What is this stuff of yours about going after badmen? What do you want, Speedy?"

With his ingratiating smile, the tramp said: "The fact is that I'm working as a sworn deputy sheriff. It wasn't a hard job to get, either. And I want to hold that job until I've cleaned up Sunday Slough."

The marshal grew sober and nodded. "What sort of cleaning up?" he asked. "Or is this just a little lark for you?"

"I'll tell you the story in short," said Speedy. "I've never worked with my hands. I never intend to. And the same feeling is what puts a lot of fellows on the bum."

"The very same," said the marshal, while his teeth clicked on the last word and his eyes glinted.

Speedy did not seem to notice these signs of disgust.

He merely said: "Some of the boys who go overland like the life. They never tire of it. I'm one of that kind. But some of them don't take to it at all. It goes well till the first frosts, as you might say, and then they wish that they'd been ants instead of grasshoppers. I knew a big Swede of a lad by the name of Pier Morgan who was on the bum for two years because he wanted to be President of the United States and didn't wish to start in by selling newspapers. Maybe you've met that kind yourself?"

"Yeah. I've met 'em," said Thomas Gray with another *click* of his strong, short-ground teeth.

"But after he'd been a tramp for two years," said the boy, "he decided that there was nothing in travel except a pain in the head. He decided that he'd go to work. I told him that he ought to go back East, where there's more law than order, so to speak. But he wanted the West because he was Western. He picked on the new mining camp, Sunday Slough. He told me that the West was the land of opportunities and new-made lives. I agreed with him, all right. But I told him that Sunday Slough was also a place where he would have plenty of opportunity to get a knife in the back or a bullet through the head. He listened, but he wasn't impressed. He was one of those fellows who trust the strength in their hands. He never hit a man when he was down, and he never used a club or a gun or a knife, not even on a shack. Personally, I'd make an exception against the brakies. Wouldn't you?"

The marshal could not avoid another smile, but he put it out like a snuffed candle.

"Go on," he said. "What happened to Pier Morgan?"

"He came out here and struck it rich," said the boy. "For three months he worked like a sailor and rolled up a big pile. Then the crooks got hold of him. A thug jumped his claim. He asked the law to help him. The law dumped him in jail. Then he tried to fight his way out, and the law brained him and put a couple of bullets through him. It threw him out on the junk heap, and there I happened to come along and find him. So I packed him to a safe place."

"What place?" asked the marshal.

"A place out of town," said the boy calmly. "And spent the time in between seeing how a tough lad could beat a smashed head and a high fever when he only had about a quart of his blood left in him. It was a good show, and the last I saw of it he seemed likely to get well. When I saw that, I thought that I'd come into Sunday Slough and see some of the wheels that run it. I mean I wanted to see Judge Bertram Daly, and Sheriff Buck Masters, and Sid Levine, who owns them both. I haven't seen the judge yet, but I've heard a good deal about him." He paused.

"You mean," said the marshal, "that you think these men double-crossed your friend?"

"I mean," said Speedy, "that Sid Levine owns that mine today through one of his hired men, that the sheriff rolled poor Morgan for his wad, and that Judge Daly put him in jail to keep. I mean that Buck Masters beat up Morgan when he tried to get away, and shot him up just for fun afterward, and threw him out on that junk heap, as I was saying."

"What do you mean by the junk heap?" asked the marshal.

"I mean the hospital. You know they have a hospital. It isn't a place to cure a man. It's a place to show him the quickest way to the grave."

"Speedy," said the man of the law, "I'm afraid that you're one of these fellows who thinks that every sheriff and judge in the land is a crook."

"You're wrong," said Speedy. "I've had a good deal to do with sheriffs and judges here and there in my day, and I've found them pretty hard but pretty fair on the whole. I don't cry with joy when I think about 'em. On the other hand, I've found them straight, as I said before. And that's ninety percent with me. My own hands follow their own way to a living, but I admire the fellows who go it straight."

"You're a queer fellow, Speedy," said the marshal, knitting his brows. "I don't think that I'll ever find another of your type."

"I'm not a type. I'm a new kind of business," said the boy.

"Let it go at that. But what is your idea in being made a deputy sheriff?"

"I'm going to get a hold on this town. I'm going to get such a hold on public opinion that the sheriff and the judge and even Sid Levine can't throw me out. So I angled for the deputy sheriff job, and the first thing I'm to do in that capacity is to go after Cliff Derrick."

The marshal shook his head. "I see how it is," he said. "You're still young enough to daydream. Derrick is a wildcat. A wildcat with brains better than his claws, even. He's a graduate student, my lad."

Speedy merely said: "I'm going after Derrick. I don't want your help to get him. I want your help to hold him."

"Say that again," suggested Thomas Gray.

"These thugs who run Sunday Slough," said the boy, "will never keep a fellow like Derrick in their jail. He has too much money to oil their hands. They couldn't keep their grip on him. But you could. Would you do it?"

The marshal said: "There's nothing that I want more in the world than to lay hold on Cliff Derrick. He's poison in the world's system. Particularly in the part of the world that I know."

"Good," said Speedy.

"My lad," said Gray, "I'll tell you what I'll do. I'll ride with you."

"That's a compliment," said Speedy, "that I appreciate a lot. But the fact is that I have to play my game alone or not at all. I can't explain. But I have to ride my own way. I just want to know if you're with me . . . if you'll take two steps in my direction in case of a pinch, and if you can take over Derrick on a federal charge when I bring him in. Later on, if I should corner the Levine gang, would you back me up to the limit? I supply the men and the evidence. You simply stand at my shoulder to show people that I'm on the right side. Can you do that?"

"It's the strangest suggestion that I ever have heard," said the other. "But I think offhand that I'll agree to it. I'm to be your ace up the sleeve. Is that it? Well, Speedy, if you act the way you talk, you can play me for all I'm worth."

Speedy smiled gently on him. "That makes everything twice as easy for me," he said.

"Except," said the marshal, "that I still don't see why you should risk your life by trying to capture Cliff Derrick, when the men you really want to get at are the ones here in Sunday Slough."

"Now," said Speedy, "I'm nobody. I've barely introduced myself to Slough. It doesn't take me seriously. But suppose that I could manage to land Derrick . . . Slough would know me, then. And all the Levines in the world couldn't discharge me unless I wanted to lose my job."

At this the marshal nodded. But he was still frowning. "I've heard of many strange things," he said, "but I've never heard of saving a town for law and order in spite of itself. There are ten crooks here for every honest man. But try your luck. I hope that everything goes smoothly for you. But if you were a son of mine, by thunder, I'd throw you into an asylum for the insane!"

"Oh, I know how it is," said Speedy. "Nothing is any good until it works! Good bye, Marshal Gray, and thanks a lot."

He left the marshal and went toward the horse yards of Seeman, the big dealer.

He found that worthy in person and in a softened humor because he had just succeeded in selling a dozen Mexican mules for double their real value and three times what he needed for the making of a legitimate profit.

"Well, whacha want, son?" asked Seeman.

"What's the wisest thing on four feet?" asked the boy. "Something that can't step in a gopher hole, or step on a rock that's likely to roll over, or get dizzy with height, or lose a trail in the dark."

"What about speed, good disposition, and such things?" asked the dealer, yawning. "Want them things?"

"I don't care about 'em," said the boy. "I don't want a beast that bucks. But it can have a mouth like iron, and a pace like a snail. I don't care, so long as it doesn't mind a guitar jangling on its back and a rider that doesn't keep a tight rein."

"You've given me the word picture of a mountain mule," said Seeman, grinning. "An old mountain mule. There's one over there. Forty dollars' worth of him. He's eighteen years old. He'll never work in a team. But he'll carry a rider or a light pack. Is that long-drawn-out piece of nothing what you're looking for?"

"He's mine," said the boy, and counted the money into the hand of the dealer.

A twenty-dollar excuse for a saddle completed the picture. Speedy loaded onto his new purchase himself, his guitar, some jerked venison, and some parched corn. Indians could travel on such rations, and so could he.

When all of these preparations had been completed, he moved out of Sunday Slough mounted upon the back of the gray mule, a back as stiff and twice as high as a hurdle.

But he was quite content, and, as he reached the open trail, beyond the town, he unlimbered his guitar and sang to himself and the great mountains as cheerfully as a lark.

The Old Gray Mule

For a mile they stumbled up the trail toward Castle Ford in this fashion, the gray mule going slower and slower, but, at last, the rider abandoned the mule altogether, seeming to prefer to walk in the woods or the shrubbery at his side.

The gray veteran of many a whip-stroke strove vainly to understand this. He knew men in all their moods, he felt, but never in a gentle one. If he had given thanks to the god of mules, it would have been for the thickness of his skin that received and turned the edge of the most powerful blacksnake cuts and softened the impact of mighty bludgeons. The tempers and the sticks of men had been broken over him many and many a time, but still he continued upon his enduring way through the world. He seemed to have the curious ability of the tried cynic, enjoying life through the extremity of disgust that he felt for it. For all extremes are somewhat pleasant to the extremists.

But never before in his experience had he encountered such a master as this. Even when the man was on his back, it had not mattered whether he went fast or

58

slow, until at last his progress had simply been from one bunch of grass on the trailside to another.

Now the man abandoned him entirely to his own devices.

The gray mule felt lonely. For he knew how to employ wile against wile, and endure brutality until he had a chance at the year's end to repay it all with a single stroke of the hoof. If Indians counted scalps and coups in their glory of battle, the gray mule could have reckoned in his list of prizes scores of broken ribs and cracked skulls, to say nothing of the bruises from glancing strokes of the hoof. On one occasion, above all others glorious, he had kicked a fat and cruel master straight through the side of the barn. For that coup he had waited and planned for weeks and months.

However, there was nothing to be done about this master, at least, for the present. The gray mule was not one to make up his mind suddenly. Neither did he think that the world was made in a day, but he chose to bide his time and await, always, a fuller judgment. For some time, as he forged slowly up the trail, fairly eating his way along, he took it for granted that man, the ugly brute, would suddenly rush out of the trees and belabor him.

In his younger days he had fled from pain inflicted by the hand of man, but with increasing years he had learned that flight is folly. A noosed rope waits at the end of the flight, and a sure return to the old master who will repay with a day's bludgeoning. He had learned that the only way to live is to endure the master until the moment comes for a signal revolt. A new master did not usually mean less pain, but usually it was pain of a different kind.

Some thumped him on his hard ribs with their fists. Some kicked with their heavy boots. Some jerked and sawed on his mouth with the reins. Some cut him with whips. Some beat him with clubs. Some—and these were worst of all—thrust at him with jagged prods. His hips and quarters were ragged with the scars of this treatment. So his one delight was to repay pain with pain, and to hope, in the end, that the page would be turned, although the new one might be fully as bad.

Now, however, he was introduced to a master of a different kind. If he wandered from the trail far to either side, or if he attempted to turn back on the way, he was quickly herded back in the desired direction. But on the whole, there was no point in turning back. The trail was dim with the grass that grew upon it; the trail was a shallow hollow in the grass that grew higher on either side of the way. What a luxury it was to eat one's way through the working day.

So the gray mule contentedly marched ahead. Now and then he paused for a mouthful. Now and then he even defied almost certain fate, as it seemed to him, and stood deliberately still, chewing the last bite and looking about him with his red-stained, cat-quick eyes.

No, it seemed literally that the blow would never fall. Once he actually trotted a furlong down a steep slope. But no voice sang out after him. In fact, nothing that he did mattered very much, it appeared, to this young master who drifted through the tall brush and the woods to the right of the trail.

The gray mule began to grow mildly excited. It was impossible that real hope could ever again warm that scarred heart of his, but he was filled with wonder; he wanted to know when the catastrophe would occur. Presently he thought that he had the answer.

He had gone on into the golden end of the day, when the sun was almost ready to sink behind the western mountains. Their eastern sides were black;

their flanks and the heads were rimmed with glistening fire. Now, when the woods were growing as dark as thickly rolling smoke, out of a copse came a rider, moving cautiously on a horse of fine fettle that threw up its head and danced over the ground.

The mule passed and would have sneered except that his upper lip was crammed too full of grass. He despised horses even more than he hated men. For horses were the willing servants; they were engines all of fire and enthusiasm. They were stupid beasts, ready to lay down their lives for a kind word. They were fools who would not rebel against whip or spur.

He tossed his head, which was rather lightened than weighed down by this consideration.

The rider came close and peered at him, and rode still closer and lifted the flap of a saddle pocket. He pulled out a strip of dried venison, examined it with his eyes, sniffed at it, and then threw it away with an oath of contempt. It was apparent that he himself lived upon much better fare.

He was a big man on a big horse. He had a rough black mustache that thrust out on either side of his face, almost as far as the edge of the brim of his sombrero.

Now he cursed again and shrugged his shoulders.

"This oughta be the mule," he said. "That son-of-a-bitch, that Mart Ransome, he's cut in ahead of me and snaked the kid out of his saddle. I'm gonna give Mart Ransome a good bust on the jaw for that trick!"

He sat his horse again for another moment, pondering, hand upon hip. Should he take in the mule? Well, there was no use in taking the mule. His orders were for the man, not the saddle he rode in.

So presently, with a shrug of his shoulders, he rode on up the trail at an easy dog-trot, the supple fetlock joints of the horse so bending that the rider did not stir in the saddle. In this manner he reached a point not many yards ahead of the patient mule, where the brush grew up close on the right-hand side of the trail.

Here a shadow arose softly and suddenly upon his right hand. He did not really see it. He sensed it, as a man of hair-trigger nerves will receive indications from the very corner of his eye. In one instant he leaned forward, spurred his horse, and snatched out a revolver.

He was turning his head about, naturally, in the very same instant, when he saw a lithe youngster springing at him, already shooting through the air as if jumping from a spring. Then, like the flick of a whiplash, a lean, hard, sinewy arm jerked about his throat and hurled him backward over the croup of his saddle, with all the more force because his mount was springing away under the stroke of the spur.

He landed hard, but he was not knocked senseless by the fall. He was a rugged fellow who had had plenty of falls before this, and now he loosened his muscles and fell with an inertness that distributed the shock instead of concentrating it with bone-breaking force upon the point of the impact.

He landed and rolled as he landed. He strove to roll on top of the assailant, but hand and knee missed the mark. In his second effort he succeeded, for the stranger had concentrated an instant too long in getting hold of the gun hand of the rider close to the wrist.

Yet, just as the man of the black whiskers struggled on top of his foe a strange thing happened, for it seemed as though a band of hot iron contracted around his right wrist and then twisted. It was exquisite pain, for the tendons rubbed against both the surface muscles and the underlying bone. His fingers were numb. There was no question of volition or lack of it on his part. The senseless fingers were simply forced to abandon their hold, and the gun fell.

It was picked up at once, and the hard muzzle of it pressed against him.

He was brave, he was rough, he was experienced in many battles. But, like the little boy when the blood from his own nose stains his hand, he knew when he was licked.

He grunted: "That's enough."

"All right," said Speedy. "Take yourself off of me, then, will you? Wait a minute." Reaching his other hand inside the coat of the man on top, he pulled out a second gun.

The latter arose slowly. To the last instant he was hoping against hope that the confidence of victory would dim the hawk-like coldness of the eye that watched him. But that eye did not dim, and, like a wise man who cares something for his own scalp, he stood up and watched the youngster rise slowly and shake himself, getting rid of the dust of the trail just as a dog would have done.

"Well, here we are," said Speedy, "and I take it that you know me, but that I don't know you."

"Name of Doc Morris," said the other. "And I don't know you, brother. What made you jump at me like a ferret jumps at a rabbit?"

"What sent you down this trail as far as a gray mule and then back again?" asked Speedy.

"I had the bad luck to meet up with Bud Henderson," said the other, "and Bud, he said that there was a crook that had stole an old gray mule from him, and that he didn't mind about the mule, but that he'd give a hundred bucks to the gent that brought in the thief. Bud, he was laid up with a sore ankle he twisted a while back. I come along and found a mule that kind of looked like the one that Bud spoke about, but it's pretty plain that I must've been wrong. That's all, partner. Who are you?"

Speedy regarded him for a moment with those dangerously gentle eyes of his. Then he said: "Did my friend Derrick only offer a hundred dollars to you for bringing me into camp? Is that all he offered?"

"Derrick?" said the other. "Derrick's got nothing to do with it. Derrick ain't in this part of the country, is he?"

"Where is he, then?" said the boy.

"Why, he's down Tucson way. That's where he is."

"Is that where he is?" said Speedy. "But I think you'll lead me to him this side of Tucson just the same."

The Big Man Talks

The big man scowled. Then he said: "Look here, brother. You've handed me some strange language. As if I could tell you where Derrick is. As if I could lead you to him!" He put a great deal of astonished and half-scornful emphasis into the last remark.

Speedy lifted one of the guns that he was now carrying, balanced it in his hand, and advanced the muzzle until it was only a few inches from the breast of the other. Then he said: "Why should I hold off? If I hadn't seen you first, you would have made hash of me, eh? Or else you would have taken me back to Cliff Derrick. I'd like to stay here and bandy lies with you. But I haven't got the time. I've got to be quick and mean, and that's hard luck for you. I know it, and I'm sorry about it. But facts are facts. I'm telling you a fact now. If you can't talk, say your prayers. Make them short, because I don't know how long it'll be before another of your gang pops up on the trail."

He fingered the trigger of the gun as he spoke, and the big man suddenly groaned, and his knees sagged.

"Don't do that," he whispered, as though loud speak-

65

ing might touch off the explosion. "Don't do that, because those guns shoot by looking at 'em. They really do. Quit monkeying with 'em, will you?"

"Do I care if I put a slug through you?" asked Speedy.

The other replied: "Do you care if you hang for it afterward?"

"After I collect the reward on you," said Speedy, "I'll have to be hung for some other job."

"Reward?" gasped the big man. He seemed to wilt, like lettuce under hot water. "Reward?" he repeated.

"Why d'you think I'm here?" said Speedy scornfully.

"Why, you're trying to get at Derrick like a. . . ." He stopped himself. He realized now that he had already said too much.

"I'm here for Derrick," said Speedy, "and you're the fellow to lead me to him. Or else you're the man to drop right here on the trail. I'll collect on you after I've handled the rest of the job." He jerked the gun a trifle higher. "You poor fool," said Speedy, "d'you think that I value your life for a nickel? You're wanted, and you're wanted badly by those who will pay for your scalp. I'd as soon shoot you as shoot a coyote in a trap!"

The other raised a hand and pressed it against his face. Then he said: "I reckon you would. I didn't know that anybody in this part of the world knew me. I didn't know they knew the price on me. But bad news will jump a thousand miles of range like an open ditch. Only, you tell me who sent you after Sam Morrison, will you?"

Speedy could hardly refrain from smiling. He was rather glad that, as the sun began to set, the rosy glow was somewhat of a veil over his features. Certainly the pressure he had put upon the other had brought forth more than barren results.

"You don't expect me to talk, Sam," he said, "when you're the one who ought to answer questions? I told you before what I want. Now give me an answer. You're walking the tight wire, but you're not dropping off it yet."

"Ask me again what you want," said Sam Morrison. "You see how it is. I'm kind of dizzy. I dunno what struck me from the time you jumped out of the ground and exploded a ton of dynamite under my nose. What is it that you want to know?"

"The way to Derrick."

"I dunno," said Morrison.

"Sam," answered Speedy, "I'm trying to be patient, but every minute I know where you ought to be, and every minute I'm trying to keep myself from putting you there. Are you going to use sense or are you going to bury yourself here?" He added: "I don't much care. Perhaps I ought to bump you off for a beginning, and take on the trailing job myself later on. I couldn't trust you. You're a liar now, and you'll still be a liar five minutes from now."

The big man sagged again, saying: "Speedy . . . that's what they call you, isn't it? Speedy, you've got me cold. I don't want to turn the chief in, but what else is there for it? I hate to turn him in, but it's either him or me."

"What would he do if he were in the same pinch?" asked the boy curiously.

"Maybe he wouldn't double-cross nobody," admitted Morrison. "He's kind of funny that way. He sticks to his word, all right. They say that he'd sooner die. But I'd like to see him in a pinch like this. You'd get some chatter out of him then, I lay my coin. Speedy, I'm gonna come clean. I'll tell you where the score is. I'll take you inside of a hundred yards of Derrick's camp. After that you can find your way. Is that a bargain? I take you there, and then you turn me loose."

"You'll have to talk a little more, first," said the boy.

"Our friend Derrick, what are his plans about Sunday Slough?"

"Well, there's a lot of easy pickings over there in the Slough," said Morrison. "You know that, or I guess you wouldn't be there with your song and dance. Why shouldn't Derrick clean up on some of the easy dough, eh?"

"Why not?" murmured Speedy. "Who does he hook up with?"

"The bums that tipped him off that you were coming."

"The sheriff?"

"His pal, One-Eyed Mike."

"Oh, One-Eyed rode all the way out here, did he?"

"Nothing but One-Eyed. He don't like you much, brother."

"No, he doesn't like me much," agreed Speedy comfortably. "Did he go back to town?"

"Yes."

"Who else is there with Derrick?"

"Nobody but Joe Dale and Lefty Quinn and Ray Parker."

"Aha," murmured Speedy, to whom all the names were new.

Morrison misunderstood the exclamation. "Yeah, he don't take all the names in the telephone book with him. He don't carry no army along with him, but he goes pretty well heeled, all the same."

"He had you, too," said Speedy.

"I'm the only roustabout in that camp," said Morrison. "You know that. I've made my little play here and there. I ain't done so bad, but over there in the Derrick camp the positions don't go by seniority. They go by order of merit. That's the way that they go. Little Joe Dale . . . of course, he's the kingpin. He's only eighteen, but he's got him a man a year for the last five years. And as the saying goes, that don't count Negroes and greasers. He don't publish his own life and letters. Not little Joe! He ain't that way. You know Quinn and Parker, too, I guess. They figger pretty high in any society. That's all you'll find over there in the camp, besides Derrick himself."

"Thanks," said Speedy, "it looks as though we can do a little business together."

"Yeah," said Morrison. "I'll tell you the way it is. I never liked the business none too good. I always wanted to be on the other side of the fence. But I got in a pinch. You know how it is."

"Yeah, I know how it is," said Speedy with sympathy in his voice. "If you decided to open up, you could tell something, Morrison. Everybody knows that."

"If I come all the way clean," said Morrison loudly, "I could wreck a lot of camps. I dunno that I'd come all the way clean, though. It'd have to be worth my while. You know how it is. I'd have to get a stake big enough to make a new start in life. Somewhere in the South Seas, say. That's about where I'd have to go."

"Well," said Speedy, "there are all sorts of ways of arranging. About Derrick . . . it was Tom Gray that made him pull in his horns and try to find a new pasture, wasn't it?"

"No, it wasn't Gray," said Morrison. "He don't care about any one man."

"Doesn't he?" said Speedy dreamily.

"He don't give a damn for any one man," insisted the other. "But it was Tom Gray and a lot of others. They was all bringing a lot of pressure to bear. Running chinks is a good game. But it wasn't good enough finally to run all the risk."

"But Derrick kills them and lets them lie where they fall," said Speedy. "I should think that he would have cleaned out the bunch that had been following him."

"Kills them and lets them lie? Who's been telling you that, Speedy?"

"Wrong?"

"Dead wrong!"

"I've heard people say it, though."

"Sure, every four-flusher in the land is always giving everybody the low-down on Derrick. But it ain't true. The fact is that he don't like killings. He says that one killing is worse than stealing a million dollars. It leaves something in the air. It's the one thing that leaves a trail so rank that the sheriff can follow it. Even a sheriff!" He laughed, but not heartily, for he still was not feeling quite up to himself.

"So he didn't try to shoot himself out of the trouble?" said Speedy.

"No, that's what he didn't do. Some of the boys said that, with Tom Gray gone, the rest would scatter, but he wouldn't see it that way. He said that he wanted a change of air, anyway. Maybe he did, because he's always working pretty hard. That's the way he is. Got his nose to the grindstone all the time."

"I see," said Speedy, somewhat vaguely. Then he added: "Lead off, old son, and I'll follow. I want to get to that camp a little after sunset. Is there time, do you think?"

"Plenty of time, and the shooting light will still be pretty good," said Morrison. "You know, I can tell you a lot more later on, while we're riding in."

"You've said enough, Sam, already," said a quiet voice.

Speedy remembered afterward that big Morrison screamed as he heard the first sound of the voice, screamed before the report of the gun, before the bullet could possibly have reached him. Then he toppled slowly backward, his arms flung out, and seemed to be trying to touch the ground behind him with his hands, like an acrobat. Then he collapsed along the grass.

Outlaws' Shack

There were two guns in the hands of Speedy, but he made no attempt to use them. His reason was, first of all, that he knew the man who had spoken behind him was beyond doubt a master of such weapons; in the second place, he had never used a gun, and it was written in the strange list of his principles that he never should. It was not a matter of principle that constrained him now, of course. It was merely a slowing up of what would have been an instinctive action in another man.

The gunman in the rear did not speak. Sam Morrison lay on the ground with one arm twisted under his head, as though he were asleep. From that sleep, Speedy knew, the man would never awaken.

He said: "If you don't mind, I'll turn around and take it from in front."

"Why do you care about that?" said the quiet-spoken stranger from the rear. "You'll fill the same spot in hell whether you go there backward, or face first, or upside down."

"It's a question of tombstones," said Speedy.

"There's still a bit of light good enough for shooting," said the man to the rear. "Tell me the riddle about the tombstones."

"What are they going to do back there in Sunday Slough?" asked Speedy. "I mean, what will they do for a fool who was shot while he was running away? Why, they'll simply put a half-rotten shingle at the head of his mound of earth, and then, in pencil, they'll write on the name and the date. That's all. But suppose that I'm shot between the eyes, they'll wrap me in silk and drop an American flag on the coffin, and they'll put up a chunk of granite half the size of a house and write on it with chisels about another of Sunday Slough's seven-day men, gone in the good cause."

There was a breathless pause.

"You're a wit," said the man behind. "I came near laughing at that, Speedy."

"Besides, you ought to consider yourself," said Speedy. "If you get me from behind, you're just a thug. If you nail me from in front, it's another good scalp to dry over the smoke of your lodge fire. You ought to think of that, Derrick."

"You know my voice, do you?" said the other.

"I don't," said Speedy. "I know your ways, though."

"Turn around and tell me what you know about my ways," said the stranger.

Speedy turned, and he saw a form that did not at all conform with what he had heard about Derrick from the sheriff. Rather, this man was neither tall nor short, but distinguished by a sense of animal strength and adroitness, as perceptible as it is in the form of a deer that stands startled in covert, or a wildcat about to spring. He carried his gun not more than hip-high, but it was plain that even from that position it would not miss its mark.

"Nobody else would have been so sure," said Speedy as he looked at the outlaw. "When men have a double target, they make the second shot come tripping on the heels of the first one. But when you had Morrison out of the way, you preferred to wait for me."

"Why didn't you drop and start shooting from the ground?" asked the other, calmly curious.

"There would have been no good in that," said Speedy. "You would have split my backbone before I'd dropped halfway to the ground. I know how fast a fellow shoots when he fans a gun. Most of the gun fanners are pretty wild. But you hit the mark, and even if you missed dead center with the first slug, it would roll your man over and rattle him while you got in the second wallop. No, I'm pleased enough to be standing here for a few seconds, and to get the pepper in the eyes instead of behind the ears."

"You have your own viewpoint," said the outlaw. "We might even have a chat together, you and I, if you wish to. Mind you, at ten o'clock I have to be riding, and before I ride, you're going to be a dead man, Speedy. Is that clear? But if you want to sit about a while and chat, you're welcome."

"Of course, I'd rather come along," said Speedy. "You know how it is. We all have plenty of time to push the daisies, but not so long for talking with a Derrick or a Speedy. You want these guns, I suppose?"

"Just drop them on the ground," said Derrick, "and then turn about and walk straight ahead. Morrison had started you on the right track."

Speedy obeyed. Behind him, he heard his captor following closer and closer. It was the golden dusk just before twilight that filled the air and filtered among the trees. Overhead, he heard the last chattering and scolding of squirrels, the sleepy murmurings of birds, and, above all, the loud, raucous yell of a blue jay as it dipped across the treetops.

They went on through the trees for hardly more than half a mile, and then they came very suddenly on the ruins of a cabin. It had once stood in a clearing. The great primeval forest rose at a little distance, but between it and the house a few acres were covered with second-growth timber. Long, long ago, forty or fifty years, perhaps, some family or some one man had come here to the end of the world and started making a home. The wilderness had conquered, and it was still the master. The sight of the little house through the thickly growing trunks of the lodgepole pines was like the dimness of a ghost in midday.

Inside the house a light burned. A fire glowed inside it.

Before they quite reached the place: "Hello!" sang out a voice.

"It's all right," said Derrick.

"It's the chief," said the other, and stepped out into view. He was carrying a shotgun, a fellow who looked very much like a cowpuncher. He walked with a limp, and he had shoulders so broad and hips so narrow that the belt seemed to be pinching him in two like one of those monkeys an organ grinder keeps on a strap.

"Who's this?" he asked.

"This is Speedy," said Derrick.

"You got the man-catcher pretty pronto," said the other without excitement.

"This is Lefty Quinn," said Derrick by way of introduction.

All three of them went on toward the shack together, and outside of it, at the fire, they found two more men busily roasting meat on the ends of small sticks. The fumes of coffee were fragrant in the air.

75

"This is Joe Dale," said Derrick, pointing to the smaller of the pair, a quick, nervous boy. "And this is Ray Parker."

The latter was a handsome fellow in a dark, rather greasy fashion. He smiled and nodded as he heard the name of Speedy. But Dale said: "What's the idea of leading up a sheriff to mug us all, Derrick?"

"My idea is that he'll never report the good news," said the chief.

"But what . . . ?" began Dale in a complaining voice.

"Aw, don't be a fool," said Parker. "He means that Speedy is gonna . . . well, he's gonna put on wings before very long."

"Some time before ten o'clock," said Derrick, "but he wanted to see us before we parted. I thought that it would be a shame if he had to be disappointed. So I brought him along in. He's not like most of the others we've had on the trail here and there. I'm glad to feed him before he passes out." Then he added: "Look here, Lefty. Back there you'll find Morrison's horse, and Morrison, and a gray mule. Drag Morrison over to the first patch of rocks south of the trail, and drop him in a crevice. You might use a stick of dynamite to blow some stones over him and make him a grave."

"Did the kid, here, kill Morrison?" asked Lefty angrily.

"No, I did," answered their chief.

"It's a dirty job you've signed me up for," said Lefty, more gloomily than before.

"You can reward yourself," answered Derrick. "He still has something in his pockets."

"He owed me forty dollars," said Ray Parker. "Don't forget to set that aside for me out of what he has, Lefty."

"He can pay his own debts," muttered Lefty Quinn, and left the camp, swinging with a creak of saddle leather onto the back of one of several horses that stood in readiness for instant use.

As he disappeared, Parker said: "I don't like that. Morrison owed me forty dollars. I oughta get that money out of him."

"You should have got it living," said the chief. "The loot that's on him belongs to Lefty Quinn now. I said it did."

"What about his horse? That ain't 'on him'," suggested Parker.

"That's about a four-hundred-dollar horse, but you can have it to pay back the forty," answered the chief. "I'll tell Lefty when he brings it in."

"Lefty'll be wild," suggested Parker, grinning.

"No. There's a two-hundred-dollar watch on Morrison, and those emeralds in that ring of his are worth four or five thousand of anybody's money."

"Great Scott!" cried Parker. "You letting Lefty go west with all that loot, and for nothing but chucking a stiff among some rocks?"

"That's all. I have to pay my men high to keep them contented," said the chief. "You've had your turns here and there, Ray. You'll have more turns later on."

"Well," said Parker, "it's a dirty break, though. That's all I mean."

"It may look like a dirty break to you," said the chief, "but that's the way the cards were cut today."

Joe Dale had taken no part in the conversation. He remained squatting on his heels, taking charge of the turning of half a dozen of the spits, on the ends of which large chunks of meat were smoking and roasting, black and brown.

Into that rising smoke he exclaimed suddenly: "Whacha go and kill my partner for, Derrick?"

There was a ring of cold animosity in his voice. He did not look at Derrick, but he did not need to. That voice was the last growl of a dog before it jumps for the throat.

Derrick regarded the angry boy with a faint smile, as though he enjoyed this attitude of the lad. He said: "I never knew that he was a partner of yours."

"You know it now," said Dale in the most offensive way. "Whacha go and kill Sam for, Derrick?"

"Because he'd double-crossed all of us, and was bringing Speedy in to bag us," said the chief.

Dale jumped to his feet. "You lie!" he cried.

Itching for a Fight

It is almost the only word that cannot be used in the West. You may curse a man in ancestral terms and still remain within the terms of familiar conversation. You may, indeed, call him all sorts of a liar in the most colorful vocabulary. But never, if you are wise, use the verb. Never tell a man that he lies.

Now, Speedy, with a spark of growing hope, watched the pair. If they fought, he would wager his chances at better than even that he could get away during the tumult.

Perhaps Derrick realized it, also. At any rate, he controlled himself. The flash of a gun would have been justified at that moment, but instead he said: "You're letting that meat burn, Joe."

Dale barked: "I'm gonna have an answer!"

"You'll be answered when your hide is full," said Derrick.

Dale was as small as he had been described. But it was the smallness of a bull terrier. No mastiff could bully him with impunity. Now he shivered and shook like a dog with his beastly desire for battle. He had been called by Morrison the cream of the lot of Derrick's men. Speedy thought that he seemed more like a stick of dynamite than a man.

"I'm going to be answered," insisted Dale, but his voice had grown more quiet, and he sank down on his heels to tend the meat again, scowling.

Ray Parker, from the farther side of the fire, looked on complacently at this scene, as though he would enjoy the fight, even though it meant the end of the gang's work. He even shrugged his shoulders with disappointment when he saw Dale sit down again.

But the latter was not finished. He said presently: "What makes you think that Morrison double-crossed us?"

"By hearing him talk," said Derrick, as calm as ever.

Yet, in some strange manner, he had not in the least compromised his dignity. Without lifting his voice, without betraying the slightest emotion or resentment, he seemed as ready to put a bullet into Dale as the boy was to shoot his leader. Speedy almost forgot his own predicament in the interest of that scene.

"You heard him talk? To who?" demanded Dale, turning the spits, blind with anger.

"To Speedy," said Derrick.

"It don't sound likely," said Dale. "It's hard to believe."

"You've called me a liar once," said Derrick.

There was only a shade of emphasis on the last word, but that shade was deadly enough. It made Dale look up fiercely, as though ready to spring. But he checked himself long enough to ask: "What made him talk? What made him talk to Speedy? Was he going out for blood money? Is that what you mean? Tell me what you mean!"

"I mean," answered Derrick, "that he was caught by Speedy, snaked off his horse, and threatened. When he was threatened, he yelped like a dirty yellow hound and started to tell everything he knew."

"Dirty . . . yellow . . . ," began Dale, enraged more than ever. Then he altered his voice and muttered: "You say that this here . . . this kid, here . . . he snaked Morrison off his horse? Speedy may say so, but he never done it."

"Speedy did it. I saw him do it," said the leader. "What's more, he worked from the ground, and jumped Morrison and jerked him off his horse. Morrison landed on top, and had a gun in his hand. Speedy took the gun away from him and shoved the Colt against Morrison's hide. Then Morrison gave up and begged."

The boyish face of Dale twisted with passion. But he was silenced for a moment. Only his harsh breathing was audible. Then he said: "I guess it ain't all made up. I guess that it's straight. But it sounds damned strange to me! That's all."

The chief smiled gently at Dale. "Furthermore," he went on, "Speedy could do the same thing to you."

"He could do the same thing to me?" asked Dale. He jerked his head around. The cords of his thick neck stood out. His broad, blunt jaw thrust forward. "He could do the same thing to me?" he demanded again.

"He could tie you in knots," Derrick declared calmly, obviously enjoying this bit of torment.

"Me on a hoss and him on foot?" gasped the other. "There ain't a man in the world that could do it. Guns or no guns, there ain't a man in the world that could do it!"

Derrick smiled again. "So you say," he remarked.

It was plain that the insulting conversation that he had endured from Dale had got under his skin.

Dale stood up from the cooking meat again. "This is

the rottenest fool talk that I ever heard," he stated. He stalked up to Speedy and measured him with his eye. "This here kid," he said, "is maybe an inch or so taller than me, but I'm ten pounds heavier. I'll break him in two."

"You ought to," said Derrick, "what with your wrestling and your prize fighting. You've had enough training and experience to do it, but, still, you won't be able to manage it. Will he, Speedy?"

Speedy paused and considered the boy from head to foot. "No," he said. "He won't be able to manage it."

The rage of Joe Dale lifted him to his toes, and only slowly he came down to his heels again. "I'll take him now and trim him," he said. "I'll smash him flat is all I'll do to him. You won't need to use a gun on him when I'm finished!"

"You're talking to a dead man," answered Derrick. "He's dead by ten o'clock. D'you think that I'll risk him in your hands and give him a chance to slip away?"

"Chance to slip away?" cried Dale. He shuddered from head to foot, so great was his nervous eagerness for the battle. He moistened his lips, and his eyes burned. "Why," he cried, "I'd lay you a thousand. I'd lay it at a thousand to five hundred."

"I can't risk him, but I'll tell you what, Joe," said Derrick. "I'm almost ready to. You'd be worth your weight in gold to me ten times over if I could get the bad temper out of you . . . if I could make you understand that you're not the master of every man in the world. Nobody's too big for you to tackle with bare hands, or a knife, or a gun. But you can't tackle this one. I can't teach you your lesson with him. He might manage to slip away in the fracas, and I'll tell you this, my bright boy, of all the men who ever trailed me, I have an idea that this same lad with the soft eyes here, this Speedy, is the hardest of the lot to beat."

"Afraid to risk him with me? You're afraid to risk your coin," said Dale. "That's what you're afraid of. You know well enough that you're afraid for your money, and not afraid that he'll get away. Get away? Once I lay a hold on him, he'll stop thinking about getting away. Right here in the light of this fire, I'll make him get down on his knees and beg!"

"You sound big and you sound sure of yourself," said Derrick, "but a chance is a chance. And I don't want to lose this beauty."

"Two thousand dollars!" cried the other. "I'll make it two thousand dollars and my return hoss! I'll throw in my Betsy along with my pile of cash. I'll throw it all in against four or five hundred. If you're a short sport and a cheapskate, back out now!"

Derrick, for a time, reconsidered the suggestion. At length he said: "I understand how you feel, Joe. You haven't had a fight for almost three weeks, and you're hungry for blood. I understand so well exactly how you feel that I think that I'll give you a chance to get a good, thorough beating."

A sound of whining joy came from the throat of Joe Dale. He tore off his coat and flung it on the ground. He stood dancing on his tiptoes. "Pull him out here and make him stand up to me!" he said. "That's all I ask. Make him start to stand up and I'll do the rest for you. Right here, by the side of the fire, I'll make him yell for mercy. I'll make him beller like a hound under the whip. You hear me talk, you black-eyed, slant-eyed greaser, you?"

He thrust out a hand to indicate Speedy as he said this. The latter leaned a mere trifle forward and watched.

Derrick said: "We'll call that horse of yours worth a thousand. That makes your bet three thousand. I'm going to put up that much cash against you. Parker, you can hold the stakes."

He counted out a sheaf of bills, and Joe Dale, panting with eagerness, snatched out a wallet and hurled it toward Parker.

"You know where Betsy is standing hitched," he said. "Here's my wad. Now, get the kid out here."

Speedy had been sitting on a fallen log. Now he rose and stretched himself, bit by bit, as a cat does before it rises from the warm place at the fire. When it thinks of night trails and night hunting, the great outdoors with all its frost and dangers becomes more sweet to its mind than the lazy comfort of the seat by the hearth.

"You know, Derrick," he said, "that I've heard a lot of talk about how much you'll get from Dale, here, if I win for you. But what do I get for myself?"

Derrick smiled his cold, thoughtful smile. "You'll get," he answered, "an extra fifteen minutes. I'll delay my start till ten fifteen."

"Well, that's a bargain," said Speedy. "It won't take me more than two minutes to put down your wrestler, I suppose."

He came closer and looked from his full height into the eyes of the other. It was true that he was taller, and in spite of the much more solid and powerful build of the other, Speedy seemed to look down upon a lesser man.

He said: "Are you ready, Joe?"

"Ready, and crying to go," said the other.

"That's pretty good," said Speedy. "But you'd better get on your horse first. You'll need that much height added to the little that you've got."

Dale threw back his head and strove to laugh. The

sound strangled in his throat. "I'll need it, will I?" he said.

"Yes, you'll need it," replied Speedy. "Give the word, Derrick, whenever you want us to start."

"He'll need a horse to help him get away," said Derrick thoughtfully. "This lesson will do you a lot of good, Joe. It ought to help make a man of you."

Parker came back, leading a magnificent bay filly with a beautiful head and a wise and kindly eye. "I've put the money in this here saddlebag," he said. "Either way the fight goes, the mare goes with it!"

Into the Fire

The preparations were not yet complete, however. For Lefty Quinn now returned with his errand accomplished, leading the horse of Morrison and the old gray mule. He came with his singing voice as a herald flying before him. It was plain that he had found much of value on the body of the dead man.

Now the tale of the wager in the camp had to be explained to him. He had no hesitation in plumping on Joe Dale.

"I've got four or five hundred that ain't doing a thing, Ray," he said to Parker. "I'll bet it all on Joe."

Parker wistfully, as one who loves a sporting chance, looked at Speedy and shook his head. "He ain't got beam and muscle enough to please me," he said. "And I know what's in Joe's arms and back muscles. If he was stripped, the fight would be over before it started. Speedy would be scared to death."

"All right," said Lefty Quinn. "It looks like for once in my life I've gotta stand by and watch a fight without having bet on it or a hand in it. I don't like it, but I suppose that it's gotta be that way."

"You may have something to do before the wind-up," said Derrick. "You and Parker are going to help me referee this fight, and, if Speedy wins and seems likely to slip away, I want you to help me shoot into him. He's a tricky cat, but I think that our three guns ought to be enough to bring him back if he starts running. If he should get off, I'm going to be on Betsy, here. You don't mind me riding her, do you, Joe? She's the best horse in the world when it comes to dodging her way through timber."

"She's the best horse at everything else, too," said Joe Dale. "Supposing what ain't gonna happens, that the kid, here, busted loose from me, and got into the woods . . . why, she'll run him down like a bloodhound."

"That's why I want to be on her," said Derrick, mounting as he spoke.

"You're gonna bust your heart because you can't win her," said Joe Dale. "Nobody's ever been on that hoss without wishin' that he could pay some of his heart's blood to get her."

"That's what you felt, Joe, when you first sat on her," said Lefty Quinn. "That's why you stole her, eh?"

"Stole her? You lie!" shouted Joe Dale, now quite mad with rage. "I . . . I'll have a word to whisper in your ear, Quinn, you thug, when I get through with this set-up."

"All right," said Quinn, "but you'll never talk to me with your hands, you poor little man-eater. I've seen you work with 'em before. It'll be guns between us, baby!"

"I've talked till I'm blind in the face," said Joe Dale, "and now I'm gonna finish this little lunch and then. . . ."

He did not wait for the word of signal from his leader, but, making a long, light step forward, he suddenly drove his fist in the face of Speedy.

At least, so it seemed. Although the balled hand seemed to drive straight through the head of the more slender fighter, Speedy had dipped his head to one side.

As Joe Dale, with a grunt of wasted effort, whirled about, Speedy stumbled the wrong way—stumbled toward his formidable foeman, and reached out a long left arm as though for support. The hand struck the face of Joe Dale. It struck him on the roof of the nose and bobbed even his thick head back a little. Dale did not rush in.

It looked like an accident, but he was not sure. Instead, he danced a little, got his balance perfectly, and felt the blindness of his excess of rage leaking out, as it were, with the meager trickle of blood that was running down from his nose. He did not mind punishment. But it seemed to him that the slender fist of Speedy must be made of iron.

Now he came in dancing, in the style of a true pugilist. But he had changed his mind somewhat. He would not merely strive to batter his enemy with fists. That was, to be sure, the most satisfactory style. Then the work could be seen and admired by others. Instead of that, he would try a long lead, follow with a short-arm punch, and then, if neither of them stunned the youth, he would close and set his iron clutches upon Speedy.

So he came in lightly, gracefully, in spite of his bulk. He was like a toe dancer. He floated over the ground with a sure and light footing, and before him Speedy retreated, or seemed to retreat. It was hard to tell where his wavering and uncertain, fumbling steps would take him.

Only once, Derrick, from the back of the mare, cried

out: "If you get that close to the edge of the trees again, Speedy, you'll take a leaden pill through the brain!"

"Oh, all right," said Speedy. "I'll watch that."

How did he dare to turn his head as he spoke? How did he dare, when such a tiger was drifting in toward him?

Joe Dale, with a brutal gleam of joy in his eyes, tasted the satisfaction that would soon be his before he had actually reaped it, and gritted his teeth as he smashed for the head with his right.

He missed the target. Yes, strange to say, the turned head jerked down at just the awkward moment, and, as Joe lurched forward behind his punch, a fist circled up from nowhere and finished its looping, over-handed course by landing again exactly upon the end of his nose.

Again he felt as though someone had struck him with a solid section of lead pipe not even masked in a rubber bit of hose. His head jerked back. A shower of sparks flew upward across his eyes, as the stars fly when a ship rolls. He went backward, and, as he went, shaking his head like a dog out of water, he tried to clear his brain, but again and again and again that same section of leaden pipe whanged across his face.

He staggered. Numbness ran down out of his brain like a poisonous fluid, through his spine, and down into his limbs. His knees sagged. Dimly, out of the distance, he heard voices calling to him. But the voices were as nothing compared with two things that he saw in shadowy fashion.

The one was his chief, sitting on the back of his beloved Betsy and smiling his faint, derisive smile. The other was his antagonist standing in the middle of the fire-lit circle, with one hand carelessly resting upon his hip.

Speedy was not smiling. No, he seemed far too bored for that expression of contempt. And the fire of that great anguish, self-scorn, cleared the wits of Joe Dale as if by magic.

He heard Parker's voice saying: "Science, that's what it is. He knows how to hit."

"It's footwork," answered Lefty Quinn. "Got footwork like a dead leaf flutterin' in the wind. I never seen such a pair of feet dancin' . . . never in my life!"

Let them talk. Joe Dale could endure words, but he wondered if he could endure many more of those lead-pipe concussions of the brain. Suppose that a punch found a resting place upon the point of the chin?

He heard his chief saying: "Now, Speedy, tap him on the button and put him to sleep. I'll count the ten seconds. I'm going to make it an extra half hour for you, Speedy, instead of an extra fifteen minutes. I knew that you'd lick him, but I never dreamed that you could do it in thirty seconds!"

Thirty seconds! Was that all that had elapsed?

During that interval Joe Dale had crossed a whole continent of wretchedness and self-abasement. Yet he had faith in himself, if not in his schooled powers as a pugilist, at least in those hands of his, for when had their grip been broken by any antagonist, even by lumberjacks made of iron and twice his size? He looked out from his jaw, running in with a high guard close to his face, and saw Speedy standing with a negligent hand still upon his hip. What trick was coming, what sudden dodge?

Joe Dale hesitated as he ran, swerved like snipe in a gale, and then, confident, leaped forward with both arms stretched out to take a wrestling hold. Yes, there might be magic tricks of boxing, but, in wrestling, sheer, solid might of body and hand would be sure to count.

To his amazement, he found that the youth stood for the charge, and his thick-ribbed body struck that of Speedy and bore him back before the charge—far back toward the perilous verge of the fire, where Derrick, sitting the lovely mare beside it, called out to his champion to beware or he would be stepping soon on live coals.

But Joe Dale, laughing drunkenly deep in his throat, had secured a grip, a plain round-the-body hold. The game was his! Then he felt something like a whiplash and a club stroke combined across the upper part of his right arm. It bruised the muscles to the bone. That was not all. It bruised the nerves as well. That scientifically placed stroke paralyzed his whole arm and broke the grip in which he was so secure.

He looked up, bewildered and baffled, and saw the face of Speedy without a trace of the stain of battle rage upon it, a calm, thoughtful face. He saw the lean hand of Speedy raised, not as a fist, and not as a grasping claw, but rather as a cleaver, with the hard and seasoned rim of the palm as the edge of the cleaver. It is said that the Japanese, by long practice, so toughen this part of the hand and so perfect the science of delivering the blow that they can break a rounded bar of stone an inch thick. It was such a blow that fell now, high on the left side of Joe Dale's tensed neck, where the big cords begin to stand out just before the neck joins the head.

The head of Joe Dale flopped to one side as the head of a flower drops when struck by a child's stick. Then followed a singularly light shoulder hold, aided by a tripping foot, and Joe Dale fell on his back straight into the center of the fire.

He rose again like a rocket, screeching, right under the nose of the mare that reared high. As it reared, Speedy, or a great cat that bore his semblance, sprang upon the back of Betsy behind Cliff Derrick.

Bringing Him In

It was not that Derrick failed to see the flying danger. He had it well in mind and eye, but just at that moment Betsy, the amiable mare that never had been known to have good manners, was trying to cakewalk and even leaning a little backward in her effort to stand straight. He had to employ his hands to keep his place, and in the half second of the crisis, as she began to pitch down toward the ground again, Speedy landed behind the saddle and gave to the great Derrick almost exactly what he had given to Joe Dale.

But in this case the cleaver edge of his palm struck more carefully at the base of Derrick's head rather than behind his ear. He managed to draw a gun that simply fell out of his useless hand. Only vaguely his darkened eyes saw the shadowy trees flutter past swiftly, as a pack of cards flicked under a thumb, and his ears heard the dull booming of guns and the cracking of bullets that pursued them.

Bullets were not the thing. He knew that, even as he reeled in the saddle, half fainting. No, bullets were not the thing. What was needed was an instant riding in

93

pursuit, for shooting from any distance was all too precarious by such a light as this.

The pursuit began. As his brain cleared a little, he could hear shouting, and then the crashing horses through the brush.

The best man of all was out of it now—Joe Dale, who must be wallowing in the cool of the mud, trying to get that coolness against every part of his seared flesh at once.

But the others were good men. Where could one find better, except that young fire-eater, Joe himself? Yes, Parker was a man in ten thousand, and Lefty Quinn was one in a million. If for no other reason, they would ride their horses hard and well in that pursuit because each of them was mounted on a nag given by Derrick himself.

In fact, he heard the noise of that pursuit speed closer. They were gaining fast, as in fact they were bound to do, considering that the good mare carried a double burden. It gained, it burst full upon the ear of Derrick, as he regained full consciousness, and then it swept on by him.

Amazed and bewildered at first, after a moment he understood the simple thing that had happened. Speedy had merely taken the grave chance of pulling up the mare suddenly into the deeper shade of a thicket. His trick had borne fruit, for in the dimness of the trees the two riders had rushed past.

There was something else for Derrick to think of now. He found his hands tied behind his back, and his feet bound beneath the mare. A gag was passed between his teeth, and the cord that secured it lashed securely around his head.

A momentary hope came to him. It was the looming of a bright figure at the side, but now he recognized it as the old gray mule that had accompanied Speedy up the trail to the old Castle Ford. Now it had followed again, and, arriving at the place, it fell contentedly to grazing.

On its back Speedy mounted, hitched a rope to Betsy, the peerless mare, and went on at the dragging pace of a mule walk toward distant Sunday Slough.

His manner was not that of one who has done a strange and important thing. Rather, it was like that of a boy who had been sent to find a stray horse and had succeeded in the venture. He unslung a guitar that was encased at the side of the mule, and on this he began to strum softly and to sing in a voice softer still.

> *Julia,*
> *You are peculiar . . .*
> *Julia,*
> *You are queer.*
> *Truly,*
> *You are unruly,*
> *As a wild Western steer!*

The great outlaw had heard that song before. Never had he heard it so well sung as at present, and never had he enjoyed the singing less. He saw the implication. He saw, moreover, the picture he would make if he were brought in this fashion into Sunday Slough, tied hand and foot!

They did not take the main trail up the valley, but obscure cattle paths that meandered back and forth, getting on at the gait of a lazy worm rather than a mounted man.

Would intelligent fellows like Lefty Quinn and savage Ray Parker surmise such a thing as this? Would they not rather feel that they had been outdistanced by the uncanny strength and speed of the mare and left hopelessly behind, even though she was carrying double? Yes, in ten minutes they had probably given up the ride, or at least when they came close to the shining lights of the town.

Cliff Derrick groaned. He looked back over the course of events as they had befallen between him and the boy. It was true that he had been rather foolish. It was true that from the first moment he had recognized in the lad an enemy of peculiar powers. Yet it seemed that he had taken all reasonable precautions. He had sat his horse, armed to the teeth, ready to strike down the tramp with a bullet during that fight with Joe Dale.

Surely such an opportunity to give fiery Joe a lesson was not to be wasted. Keen as a whip, ready for any emergency, brave to a fault, all that Joe needed was a severe lesson in order to make him the most valuable man that had ever worked under the leader. It was only that Derrick had failed to foresee what the mare might do, faultless as she was, if a fiery rocket exploded under her very nose. That was the turning of the tide, and he wondered in bitterness of heart if the thing had been an accident, or if Speedy had deliberately planned it. Yes, he felt that it must have been a plan, because that would explain the manner in which Speedy had retreated with such apparent blindness to the very edge of the fire. The final flurry in which Joe had been cast into the embers of the fire was merely a part of that plan.

Cliff Derrick sat helplessly on the mare, bound hand and foot, gagged, incapable of sound or of motion.

Well, it would be a great day for Sunday Slough, a great day for young Speedy, the tramp. He would become famous overnight. At least, it was a consolation to know that the reputation of the boy would be so enlarged that no other gunman who had him under the nose of his revolver would ever take a chance with him again.

But, ah, the misery of it. To have so many years of brilliant and happy endeavor wiped out and buried in a landslide of ridicule. He could endure the rope that would hang him by the neck until he was dead; he could not endure the laughter with which the world would greet his capture in this fashion by a man who did not even carry a gun.

Still the thing seemed impossible!

The music continued. Other songs followed, but, as the bright moon rose and hung above the trees, silvering the tops of them, a coyote cried with a sharp yelp in the distance, and again the boy was singing:

> *Julia,*
> *You are peculiar . . .*
> *Julia,*
> *You are queer.*

They came, in this fashion, around the shoulder of a hill, and there a solitary horseman hove in view. He waved a hand.

"Hello, stranger," he said.

"Hello," said Speedy.

"Ain't you Speedy of the Best Chance?" asked the stranger.

"That's my name. I've been in the Best Chance," said Speedy.

"I'm glad to see you," said the other. "I was driftin' on back to camp. There ain't anything like a little yarning to kill time. My name's Cleveland, if you wanna know it. I was hearing today that there was a. . . . Hello, who's this here with you?"

He had discovered the condition in which Cliff Derrick was riding, and the face of the outlaw became hot with shame and with rage. Close up to him came Cleveland, gaping more and more, and then, with a shout: "It's Derrick! Dog-gone, it's Derrick! How did you . . . where . . . what . . . ? Great Scott, this'll drive Sunday Slough crazy! You went out and got Derrick, did you? That's what comes of having you for a deputy sheriff, is it? By thunder, the boys'll plate you with gold and set you with diamonds."

To this outbreak, Speedy replied nothing at all, except a few casual words. He did not appear in the least excited. He merely said something about "good luck" and happening to be "at the right place at the right time."

Derrick ground his teeth in a hopeless fury.

"Well," said Cleveland, "there's one thing that we can thank a seven-day man for. And Buck Masters, too. I was kind of losing all faith in that gent. I thought that he was a crook plain and simple."

He was still talking in this vein as they came around the shoulder of the hill and entered a narrow defile, the farther end of which was bright with the light of the town. When they were halfway down the shallow little ravine, there was a sudden rush of dark horsemen from the trees. They came upon them inescapably close.

Speedy stood his ground with his prisoner, but Cleveland did not wait. He had a glimpse of the lot as they spurred ahead, their faces illumined by the moon, and now he turned his horse about and galloped it with all its might for freedom.

There was no pleasure in the heart of Derrick as

these strangers swept about him. He could guess why they were come. He could imagine that a mob and a lynch scene would now quickly end his career. But was that not better than the prolonged wretchedness of a trial?

He heard the voice of a big man saying: "Hello, Speedy. Dog-gone my ribs if you ain't gone and done it. Pretty slick, my boy. This is gonna go and get you famous. Here's the man. Here's the old slickster! Derrick himself!"

"Glad to turn him over to you," said Speedy. "It's not too comfortable, having a red-hot piece of iron in your hands . . . a fellow like this, I mean. You watch him, will you? I'll jog on up to town and get them ready for him at the jail. Watch him, Sheriff, because he's a slippery one."

"Go ahead, Speedy," said the sheriff. "You're gonna get a lot of fame and credit for this."

"Thanks!" called Speedy, and hurried the mule down the trail.

The Deal

When the captor had left, there was a sudden change in the demeanor of the big sheriff. He said: "We got you pretty easy, Derrick. We thought that we might have to fight for you."

He removed the gag as he spoke, an act of grace that allowed Derrick to breathe deeply for the first time in whole minutes. As the outlaw pulled the sweet night air into his lungs, he heard the sheriff continue: "I didn't know that Speedy had tricks like this up his sleeve. He's a pretty smart boy. But we can't do business with him. He's too smooth for us. We might as well do a little introducing. This here is Sid Levine, that has Sunday Slough in his pocket. And this here is Mike Doloroso, that only has one eye, and that's maybe why his last name is Doloroso. And me, I'm Buck Masters, that happens to be sheriff of this county just now."

Derrick could sense that something was in the air. He could not tell exactly what, but he found himself at ease among these men.

"I'm glad to meet you, boys," he said. "I'd like to

shake hands all around, but you see how it is. My hands are not exactly at my disposal just now."

"We'll be fixin' that, too, in another minute," said Sid Levine. "What we wanna do is just talk a little minute with you, Derrick."

"I'm glad to talk," said Derrick, "as soon as I can get the ache of the gag out of my jaws."

"That's too bad," said Levine, "but that little rat, Speedy, he's gonna get his own share of poison some of these days. I may not be a wise guy, but I can guess that."

"Yeah, so can I," said Doloroso.

It was music to Derrick to hear these words. Sudden hope flowed in upon him.

"Business is what I wanna talk, Derrick," said Levine.

"All right," said Derrick.

"Tell him, am I the guy to talk business?" said Levine. "You tell him, Mike."

"He ain't the guy to talk nothing else," said Mike.

"You can trust Levine," said the sheriff. "He's never let anybody down. Nobody that was right."

"I'll hope to be right," said Derrick.

"You'll be all right," said Levine. He came closer. The moonlight shone upon his vast and greasy nose as he spoke. "I know some of the things that you've done for yourself, and you'll be all right. I can say that to begin with."

"That ought to make things easier, then," said Derrick. He knew that at least a part of the game was in his hands. He no longer thought about public shame and the hangman's rope, but about what vengeance he should pour out upon the head of Speedy when the day came for him to turn the tables on that youth.

Levine continued: "You see how it is, Derrick. I

wouldn't wanna see a fellow like you, that's got brains . . . I wouldn't wanna see him go to waste, would I?"

"Thanks," said Derrick.

"Not in jail, would I wanna see him wasted," Levine stated warmly.

"I hope not," said Derrick.

"Nor under ground, I wouldn't wanna see him, would I?" said Levine, pressing the happy point.

"Thanks," said Derrick again, but rather more shortly. He warmed up this word by adding: "Why shouldn't you and I do business together, Levine?"

The latter made a gesture, swinging both hands out and shoulder high. "What would I be talking for here," he said, "except I had an idea like that, I ask you?"

"Go ahead," said Derrick. "I'll talk turkey, too."

"What I mean," said Levine, "turkey is the only thing I ever like to talk. Meat, and meat closest to the bone. That's what I mean."

"Good," said Derrick. "I imagine that you have some ideas of how we could club together."

"Ideas?" laughed Mike Doloroso. "He ain't got nothing else but. Ideas is what he's made of."

"Shut up, Mike," said Levine. "Mike, he's always gotta be butting in. Don't let that make you sore, Mister Derrick. He means well, Mike does, only he ain't got any savvy. He don't know what it's all about. Look-it here . . . what I wanna say is I got Sunday Slough in my pocket. I take it out and polish it once a week, that's all. I got my initials carved into it. You know what I mean?"

"I know," said Derrick gravely. "There's a lot in Sunday Slough."

"Gravy. That's what there is," said Levine. "It's all full

of nothing but gravy, is what I mean to say. Am I wrong, Buck?"

"You're never wrong," said Buck Masters. "Is he ever wrong at all, Mike?"

"He can smell a dollar ten miles off and upwind," said Mike.

"Shut up, Mike," said Levine, more good-humoredly than ever. "He can't keep his face out of it, but don't you mind him, Derrick."

"All right. I won't mind him," said Derrick, with a broad wink.

"I say that I got Sunday Slough in my pocket," said Levine, "and here's the sheriff to make everything safe, and Mike Doloroso, that can break iron bars in his teeth, and that eats a pound of tacks every morning for breakfast just to put gravel in his craw to get ready for the raw meat.

"Now I say, ain't the three of us enough? Sure, and we oughta get all there is in Sunday Slough. But the trouble is that we been too polite. We own that town so deep down that it don't know that it's owned. And there had oughta be somebody that could step in from the outside and know the right places to step. We know the right places to step, but we're too far inside, if you know what I mean."

"I know," said Derrick. "You want an outside man, somebody you can trust, eh?"

"Derrick, there's a clean million in that town," said the other, answering indirectly. "There's a clean million, and only about three jobs to get the whole caboodle."

Derrick narrowed his eyes. "That's a lot of money," he said slowly. He repeated: "A million is a whole lot of money."

"I ain't no piker," said Levine. "Either I bust everything open wide, or else I let everything go. What should I wanna go and be a piker for? I got money. So have my friends. I see that they have money. Don't I, Buck?"

"You never gotta worry if Levine's your friend," said One-Eyed Mike.

"Shut up, Mike," said Levine.

"I had to say that," said Mike. "I couldn't let that pass. I had to tell the truth about that."

"Shut up, will you, you big Irish bum," said Levine tenderly. "Now you go on and tell me how the idea sort of strikes you, Mister Derrick. I wanna hear from your side of the case."

"I play on my own, usually," he said. "I have my own schemes, and I make no splits outside of my own men. But, except for you boys, I'd be the laughingstock of the world inside of another half hour. I'd be buried in another day, with not even a shingle to mark the spot. I say, you name the jobs and give me the frame, and I'll do the work for you and turn over the whole loot, without a penny for myself. I'd be glad to."

The eyes of Levine kindled with a deadly fire of joy. But this first thought he mastered. The next instant he was blinded by a rush of Christian kindliness.

"I wouldn't do that," he said. "No, sir, I wouldn't do it in a million years. All I want is my fair split, and I never wanted no more."

"That's all he ever wanted," said One-Eyed Mike.

"Shut up, Mike," said Levine, "and get those ropes off Mister Derrick. Why don't you do something to make yourself useful instead of always shooting off your face?"

Buck Masters interjected: "Levine, you fix a date to meet up with Derrick and frame the whole job. We gotta get back into town or there'll be trouble in there waiting for us. We gotta let the boys know how we had this Derrick in our hands . . . because we were seen with him . . . and then he out-slicked us and beat it away. I gotta raise a posse and start some trouble. We gotta go in on the gallop, because we was seen to take him over. One was Speedy, but the other . . . who was the other bird, Derrick?"

"A fellow named Cleveland. Picked him up on the road. That's all," said Derrick. "Outside of you fellows and Speedy, he's the only one who saw me in ropes."

"I'll fix Cleveland," said Levine. "I'll fix anything in the town, what I mean. Only Speedy . . . I wish that you'd batted him one over the head like you said you was going to do."

"I would've," said Buck. "But you know how quick he cleared out. And the way he handed over Derrick and didn't make no fuss, I didn't hardly have no excuse for slamming him. You seen how it was. But now we gotta get back into town and get fast. You frame it with Derrick."

"Tomorrow night, right here, and right at this time. I'll bring plans and all the details. You'll need some soup, though. Want me to bring it?" said Levine.

"I've got the soup and the makings," said Derrick. "Good bye, boys. We're going to do business together." He turned his horse, the lovely mare of Joe Dale, up the ravine and rode on very slowly.

The other three wheeled about and galloped at full speed toward Sunday Slough. Levine grunting and protesting—his fat bulk reeling in the saddle.

They came into Sunday Slough with a rush, and there they found that everything in the town that was "in Levine's pocket" was oddly changed. The saloons, the dance halls, the gaming establishments, even the Grand Palace, appeared deserted, and, instead, on the street about the entrances to these places, stood grim-faced men, silent and still, with guns in their hands and eyes that followed gloomily the galloping trio.

Noose Talk

The sheriff strove vainly to rouse any enthusiasm. He dashed up to a group and yelled: "Boys, get your horses! I want twenty picked men. We've had Cliff Derrick in our mitts, and the damn fox slipped away from us. Meet me at my office in five minutes. I'm gonna get him again if I have to pull up the mountains and juggle 'em around!"

But no one answered. The silent, staring faces regarded him and made no response.

At the office, Masters, Levine, and One-Eyed Mike stood panting around the sheriff's desk, with the light of the single lamp in their faces.

"What's up?" said Levine, green-gray with fear. "They don't seem like they used to be. What's happened?"

"Something's busted," said the sheriff, scowling. "This town don't look good to me no more. Go on, Levine. You own it. Now wake it up and make it dance like you used to!"

"I need a little time," said Levine, loosening his collar. "What could've happened? They didn't seem to rise none or get excited none when this yell was thrown at 'em. Why didn't they pile on their horses and come chasing?"

"I dunno," said the sheriff, "but if. . . ."

"Cheese it! Back up! Hold everything!" gasped One-Eyed Mike, as he made warning gestures behind him.

Through the doorway now, with a slow and relentless movement, poured many of the men who had been gathered in the street. Their grim eyes surveyed the three. A big man, whose face was covered with a red stubble, was the first and the foremost.

Sid Levine backed up before them until his fat, loose shoulders were pressed against the wall. He was accustomed to smiles and cheers. Explosions of wild rage he also understood. But this cold and steady and purposeful advance unnerved him.

Where were his men, his hired men, his bouncers and advocates of all sorts, who always percolated through every gathering in Sunday Slough, ready to swing the mob according to the dictates of the master? Not a single familiar face did he see. These were men lean and hard with labor. He had not dreamed that there were so many of them in the town. They looked ready for anything. And what did they want here?

The man of the red beard said: "You wanna know why we're here. I'm gonna tell you. My name's Cleveland. I met up with Speedy and Derrick on the trail outside of town. I seen you three come busting down on them. I guessed what was up right then. You'd make a deal with Derrick. You'd slam Speedy and roll him under the leaves, or put a bullet through him and say that Derrick done it. But Derrick didn't do it. You did it. Speedy's a dead man . . . and you're dead, too, all three of you!"

A stern murmur ran through the crowd.

"Mike, say something!" gasped Levine, putting out his fat, helpless hands.

Mike, although gray of face, said: "You boys are all wrong, crowding Levine like this. He never done a crooked turn in his life. He's the best friend that most of you ever had."

"He may be to some," said one blunt-jawed man of middle age, "but he looks to me like a crooked gambler and hound. Boys, I think we wouldn't be wasting rope if we stretched the necks of these three . . . unless we find out where the boy is . . . Speedy, I mean, who went out by himself and got Derrick. It's a thing I would have sworn that no man in the world could do!"

Cleveland burst out: "What did you do with Speedy?"

"Do with him?" said the sheriff. "We didn't do nothin'. We didn't touch him. Nacherally he turned his prisoner over to us and rode on in to get the jail ready. . . ."

Loud, derisive laughter closed over that protesting voice. With a sudden movement, like the sway of a wave, a hundred hands mastered the three. The strength ebbed out of Levine. His eyes rolled up like the eyes of a dead fish. His knees turned to pulp, and his loose body sank to the floor.

But now, from the street, a sudden uproar, a wild and riotous cheering broke out, rose and filled the air, rang and re-rang. It was a name that they cheered, and it was as life to the three captives. It was also a complete shock to the vigilantes. For that name, many times repeated, was "Speedy"!

The sound came closer. Pressing to the door of the office and to the windows, then back again into the street, they saw an old gray mule and Speedy himself on the back of it. Behind him followed a magnificent mare on which, gagged, feet and hands tied, was none other than the great Derrick!

"Sheriff," said Cleveland, "I've done you all wrong. There's Speedy, and he's still got his man. I didn't understand. We're all in the soup for this. Let's get out, boys!"

The next morning, Speedy sat with Marshal Tom Gray in a hotel room, writing on a scrap of paper and yawning as he wrote.

"But after that, how did you know that you'd get him again?" asked the marshal.

"I didn't know," said Speedy. "I simply played a pretty fair chance . . . not a very long one. I went up to the ravine and waited with a noose in a rope, and, pretty soon, up came Derrick, riding with his head down, like a fellow who has something to think about. I'm no expert with a rope, but it was no trick at all to drop the noose over him and bind his elbows to his ribs. No man can put up a fight in that shape."

"Well," said the marshal, "he's in jail, and watched by my men. I'll have his neck in another sort of a noose for another purpose before long. I think that you've broken the back of a very big gang, Speedy. But if you had waited a little longer before coming in, all three of the thugs would have been wiped out."

Speedy sighed. "If I'd guessed that," he said, "I would have waited, of course. As it is, I have to go and report to the sheriff and have a drink with him and let Levine slap me on the back. They don't know where I stand now. And before I'm through, I'll surely spring the trap under them good and proper."

"You may," said the marshal, "but I'd rather make down my bed in a rattlesnake cave than be in your skin in this town from now on. What are you writing?"

"A note. Got a boy who'll do what he's told?"

"In the next room," said the marshal. He called, and a lad of fifteen came to them.

"Partner," said Speedy, "take this note and go down to the stable and put the saddle on the mare that Derrick rode into town last night and lead that mare straight up the valley toward Castle Ford. Lead her, mind you, and don't ride, or you're likely to get a terrible fall. When a man comes out and claims her, give her to him, and come back. That's all." He reread the note, which ran:

Dear Joe:

The Japanese tricks are the very mischief to stand against until a man knows them. I hope you'll find Betsy safe and sound, and we'll meet again.

Yours,
Speedy

Satan's Gun Rider:
A Sleeper Story

"Satan's Gun Rider," the third entry in the Sleeper saga, appeared in the short-lived pulp publication, *Mavericks*, in the November, 1934 issue. It was one of five stories Frederick Faust wrote about his hero named Sleeper, a character with many similarities to another of his creations, Reata, whose stories had appeared a year earlier in Street & Smith's *Western Story Magazine*. Both are loners and adept at outsmarting their enemies—Sleeper with a knife and Reata with a lariat.

Pop Pays a Visit

Sleeper stood very still for a second on the deep creek-bank. In the meadow across the stream ran the golden stallion, Careless, racing with its head thrown high, canting toward its master. But now, both man and horse had ceased their play and each stood statue still, listening, intent. Sleeper turned, studying the brushes off to the left, alert. Then he shrugged, a slight, puzzled frown appearing on his tanned forehead beneath the brim of his battered hat.

He jerked his hand toward his head, and the chestnut came at full speed with his mane fluttering high and tail stretched straight by the speed of the gallop. Sweat polished that marvelous body; the sun flamed on it; he was as glorious as music, more stirring than a battle cry as he hurled himself toward his master.

From lip to lip, the creek was twenty-five or thirty feet across, but the stallion made nothing of it. He shot high into the air, struck well in on the farther bank, and then rounded breathing deeply to the side of his master.

Sleeper took a few pieces of sugar from his pocket

and fed them to the big stallion, one by one. Even that he should be able to offer his horse a treat as cheap as this seemed surprising, considering the ragged clothes in which he was dressed. The only things new were the good moccasins on his feet, true Indian work decorated with a bright patterning of beads. His hair was black, his skin was almost dark enough to give him the look of Indian blood, but the blue of his eyes told a different story.

The stallion whirled about and threw up its head. It made no sound, but its whole attitude was one of challenge. Sleeper, with a subtle gesture, brought a knife into the flat of his hand. It was perfectly concealed, the handle remaining up his sleeve, but a flick of the hand and wrist would throw that knife as straight as ever a bullet flew.

Again, from the brush he heard a light crackling noise, and presently there came into view a string of three mules, the first pair carrying heavy packs and the third bearing two wicker panniers. At the rear, stalked the peddler with long, slow steps. The bunch behind his shoulders looked less like a deformity than a knapsack—he stood straight enough. He carried a walking stick tall enough to be called a staff, and on this he leaned as the mules came into the open.

"Hi, Sleeper!" he called.

"Hi, Pop," said Sleeper.

"I seen you from the hill running Careless. How do you manage that, Sleeper?" Pop Lowry asked.

"A dog can do that . . . and a horse like Careless can do anything that a dog can manage," said Sleeper.

"Stand up and beg, f'r instance?" suggested the peddler.

Sleeper made a sweeping gesture—the stallion reared instantly and struck a balance by beating at the air with its fore-legs. Another gesture brought him back to all fours, and Sleeper affectionately rubbed the stallion's muzzle.

"Well, damn my eyes!" said Pop Lowry. "What else have you been teaching him?"

"To catch a rope in his teeth and pull . . . to slide back the bar of a gate . . . to kneel down or lie down . . . to come to a whistle when he can't see me . . . to go through brush without making a sound . . . to walk a log like a circus performer . . . and to fetch my clothes or shoes or anything else I point out. Like this!"

His hand flicked. The knife, like a line of light, left his fingers, shot past the head of the peddler with hardly an inch to spare, and lodged in a narrow sapling, where it stuck humming like an angry wasp.

"Confound you, Sleeper," shouted Pop Lowry. "I thought that steel was aimed for my brain!"

"Go fetch it, boy," said Sleeper.

The stallion went to the knife, gripped the handle of it, and worked it up and down for an instant to free it from the wood. Then he tugged the knife out and brought it back to his master. Sleeper palmed the knife with a motion of the hand too swift for the eye to follow.

"Always wasting time, eh?" growled Pop Lowry. "Foolin' around with a horse, playin' with a knife like a kid. When are you gonna grow up, Sleeper?"

"When I get through working for you, Pop. But here's two days of my three months used up, and you haven't asked me to do a thing. Couldn't you think of anything hard enough?"

"There's eighty-eight days left. You'll be busy," said Pop.

"Busy or dead," said Sleeper. "What's the first thing you want me to do . . . since I'm the slave?"

"Kind of a queer job," said Pop Lowry. "You wouldn't guess what it is."

"To get a man in the Diablo Mountains," suggested Sleeper.

The peddler straightened suddenly, and his long jaw dropped. Pockmarks made his face hideous at all times, but suspicion made it even more ugly now. "Who've you been talkin' to?" he asked. "How'd you know that I want you to get a man in the Diablos?"

"You looked south at them in a queer way when I asked what you wanted me to do," Sleeper answered mysteriously. "And what else could I fetch for you from the Diablos? There's nothing but rattlesnakes and men down there."

"You got a funny brain in your head." Pop Lowry scowled. "But it gets results, and those are what count. Yeah . . . I want you to get me a man in the Diablos . . . one of Gil Fanwick's outfit."

"How many gunfighters are you going to send along with me?" Sleeper asked.

"Nobody," said Pop Lowry. "Gil is a kind of a friend of mine, and I don't want no killing."

"I walk right into a bunch of outlaws and come out with one of them? Is that all?" Sleeper wanted to know. "Fanwick has the meanest crowd of man-killers that ever rode on leather. They chew lead instead of gum."

"It's a job that needs a right cool head and a steady hand, maybe," said Pop. "That's why I come to you, Sleeper!"

"Who's the fellow I have to catch?"

"By name of Stan Douglas . . . son of Champ Douglas."

"Has he gone wrong?"

"Started that way. Gets into a ruction with his old man because old Champ won't pay a gamblin' debt of the kid. Stanley pulls up and quits home. He runs away and joins up with Gil Fanwick. And the idea is to get him away and take him home before he rides with Gil on some damn' raid. The old man is pretty nigh crazy."

"He'll pay big for that, Pop."

"I dunno," said Lowry. "Mostly I'm interested in seein' the kid taken home safe and sound."

Sleeper smiled. "What's he paying?" he asked. "Fifty . . . sixty thousand?"

Pop answered, scowling: "You ain't hired to ask so damn' many questions."

"All right," said Sleeper. "How long have I got to make the clean-up for you?"

"About two days," said Lowry. "If the bunch starts anything, you see that the kid don't take a part in it. Understand? Go up to the town of San Miguel. Somewheres near there is where Fanwick's gang hides out. They don't hide much, neither. They own the folks around there because Fanwick believes in payin' for the beef and the horses he uses. He pays double the market price, and those hombres down there all swear by him. Which is nacheral and right. Like a wise dog, he don't foul his own kennel, and he leaves his dead men a long ways off. If a posse starts up through the Diablos after Fanwick, every mother's son on that range is out to help the crooks get away."

"That makes my job look easy," said Sleeper. "Everybody in the range against me, and Fanwick's gunmen on top of the rest."

"Why, kid," said Lowry, "you never was cut out for easy jobs. You'd go to sleep, sure, if you was to try your hand at an easy job. I've just picked out a little thing that'll keep you stirred up and on your toes."

"Thanks," said Sleeper. "How's Bones, these days?"

"He's doin' fine. Layin' low and puttin' on flesh. He swears that he'll die for you if you ever as much as lift a finger for him to come. And the poor gent don't know that you sold yourself to me for three months in order to help him out of trouble."

"I don't want him to know," answered Sleeper, "but I could use a fellow like Bones on this kind of a job."

"Numbers won't help you. Brains is all that you can use . . . and maybe a fast hoss like Careless. But you can't take him with you."

"Why not?"

"A hoss with the looks of Careless? He'd be stole in five minutes by the Fanwick gents."

"I'll have to take my chances," said Sleeper sourly. "Careless stays with me. He goes off his feed when I'm not around."

"Do it your own way," answered Lowry. "What'll be your first step?"

"I won't know till I get on the spot," answered Sleeper. "So long!"

San Miguel Town

In the town of San Miguel in the Diablo Mountains, the largest building next to the church was the hotel that was run by Carlos Oñate. That is to say, the hotel was owned by him, but it was run by his wife, Rosita—because she was a bigger man than her husband.

It was she who woke on this night, and heard the voice of the *gringo* calling from the street below: "Hello! Hello! Hey, landlord! I don't want to spend the night in the streets! Let me in, will you?" Then the cry changed to very good Mexican, and the call was repeated.

Rosita hoisted herself upon one elbow and kicked her husband with her knee. He woke hastily, with a grunt, between two snores. "Ah, Rosita!" he said as his eyes were open. He seemed to know that touch.

"Listen, Carlos," she said. "You hear the *gringo* dog howling in the street? It is true that we are in the United States, but may my blood change to water before I ever take from the *gringos* anything but money . . . a curse on the air they breathe! Now we have the hotel full to the last room. There is a good excuse. Go down at

121

once and tell the dog to go and howl at another door. We have no room, and we have no wish for him here."

"That may make bad feeling, if the thing is repeated," said Carlos, nevertheless obediently getting from the bed to his feet, because he had long ago learned that it was best to begin to obey, even if the cause were worth an argument.

"We have the house full," said Rosita, "and, as for bad feeling, that devil of a Gil Fanwick is our friend, at last, and what else do we care?"

"Do you think," said Carlos hesitantly, "that I could dare to open the door of the patio and go out to him? Do you think that I could dare to kick him down the street?"

"My dear," said the wife, with an unusual tenderness, "I shall go to the window and watch you. Kick him as far as you please, my own Carlos, my sweet."

Carlos stepped into heavy shoes, pulled on a pair of trousers, and jammed a big sombrero on his head. Even in the middle of the night, he felt undressed unless he had that sombrero over his eyes. In order to clear his eyes and rouse his spirit, he found by sense of smell the string of onions that had been hung across the room to dry. Taking one of these, he began to eat it like an apple as he descended the stairs.

"The fool has a step like a work horse," said Rosita to herself. "He will rouse all the guests."

But since nearly all of these were Mexicans who would appreciate a good joke at the expense of an *Americano,* she got her bulk out of bed and leaned her full bosom against the casement so that she could peer down into the street.

The moon was not in perfect position to show all the picture. It glowed on the whitewashed walls of the old adobe church up the street and it showed to Rosita a slender, ragged youth in front of the big patio gate. As for the horse, it was lost, almost, in the shadow nearer the wall, like something deep under water.

Presently Carlos cleared his throat in the patio and clanked open the great iron bolt of the patio gate. Then Carlos stepped forth. He had grown a little heavy in the belly, of late years, and he was a stout man. His forward-leaning head gave him a bullish appearance.

The *Americano* began pleasantly to ask for quarters. Carlos replied like an angry watchdog. More words passed. The *Americano* seemed to shrink away. Big Carlos, following, launched a kick that was famous all through the Diablo Mountains. And then something strange happened.

Rosita rubbed her eyes. She could not believe what they told her. But it seemed certain that Carlos had been hurled backward through the shadows of the open patio gate! She held her breath. But as the *Americano* took his horse and started to lead it through the gap, there was the sound of the gate being slammed, and the heavy bolt being driven home. There followed the groaning murmur of Carlos from the court. He had been badly hurt, but he managed, like a prudent host, to get to his feet and secure the gate.

Rosita breathed very hard, so that her nostrils flared. Her great hands opened and closed again into fists. She wished that she had been present in person at that scene down the stairs, and she was about to descend to the battle as the voice of the *Americano* arose, again speaking quite good Spanish: "Landlord! Landlady! Am I to sleep in the street?"

Then she remembered her three tall sons. Each was taller than his father. Each feared nothing under God, either with knives or at wrestling. So she stepped to the inner door and pulled it open. Three snores, all deep, all resonant, greeted her from the darkness.

"Miguel! Pedro! Juan!" she called.

Three musically intermingling snores answered her. She leaned, found a heavy boot, and threw it at the nearest prostrate, dusky figure. A long and rippling Mexican oath, embracing the names of half a dozen saints, answered her. The figure sprang up.

"Down to the court!" said the mother. "Go down, Miguel. Waken your two brothers, the snoring pigs. An *Americano* is beating the life from your father. Go down and break him into little pieces. I give you permission."

She went back to her window in the front room with a certain balm of expectation already warming her heart. Behind her and beneath her, she heard the rumbling of three pairs of feet that were descending to the battle.

When she thought of her three sons, she thought of three great notes on a trumpet—she thought of angels in blue and gold—she thought of three great and strong gods.

She was in time, at her casement, to see the patio gate flung open, and, in a close body, the three strong men issued forth. She heard them snarl, not over loudly, but like dogs each about to take possession of a bone. Almost, in her heart, she pitied the slender, solitary—*Americano*. They swooped upon him. They rose over him, like a great stampede of bulls over a tethered calf. They closed upon him.

An obscurity of whirling followed. She could not see very well. A great form, she saw, had hurled grotesquely through the air and descended face down with a mighty flop in the dust of the street. It looked like Miguel, and Miguel did not rise again.

Another bulky figure began to stagger, like an athlete running backwards. It crashed almost head on against the wall beside the gate and then pitched to the side. This form, also, did not rise. The third man, tearing himself clear, turned and fled through the open gate like one with wildcats on his back, and disappeared.

Then the slender *Americano* took his horse and led it out of view into the patio. Rosita Oñate rubbed her eyes twice, took a great breath, and went straightway to the second room that opened off the sleeping quarters that she occupied with her husband. She threw the door open and stepped into an atmosphere flavored with a delicate aroma, as of flowers.

It was the chamber of Anna, her daughter—Anna, tall, graceful, lovely as a single rose in a a garden of cacti.

"Anna, child," murmured the mother.

"Well?" Anna said sleepily.

"There is a man in the patio," said Rosita.

"Ah," said Anna, and was instantly out of her bed.

For her, while her mother lighted a lamp with a badly smoked chimney, it was the work of a moment to don a dress, slip her graceful feet into straw *huaraches*, thrust a rose into her hair, practice one smile at the dazzled mirror, and then seize the lamp from Rosita's hand.

"Your poor father . . . and then all your three brothers," said the mother tenderly. "I fear that they may have broken bones. But it's a long time since we've been certain that there was a man in the house."

"Only last Sunday," said the girl, "I burned two candles as an offering . . . and this is my answer, no doubt."

She descended the stairs while the lamp cast a smoky glory about her dark young head. Then Rosita went back into her room as a groaning figure dragged itself across the threshold. It was the voice of poor Carlos, saying: "My leg is almost broken at the hip. The devil, the *Americano*, turned himself into three men. While I kicked at one, the other two both hit me behind each ear. My skull is fractured. Call for the doctor, in the name of God!"

"I might send for the veterinary," said Rosita, "but only a fool will spend money to mend a pig. There was only one *Americano*, but you were only a third of a man. I saw it all."

Rosita now set open the door of her room, opening on the main stairs, and she heard voices rising, and saw the loom of a light that was mounting. The voice of a man sang softly an old Spanish song:

> *The sea was of mountains;*
> *The mountains were thunder;*
> *The way had no ending*
> *When I journey from Anna.*

> *The sea was of silk;*
> *The mountains were meadows;*
> *The road was a step*
> *When I came home to Anna.*

Here the song and the noise of steps ended. The knocking at a door broke the brief silence, and a sleepy voice asked what was the matter. The slender stranger offered to wager five dollars against the bed of the guest—and the bet to be decided with the guest's own dice.

"In this," said Rosita, sighing and shaking her head, "the *Americano* proves himself to be a fool." But a little later, still, she heard a sharp, bright exclamation from

Anna. And, still later, she heard a voice hissing soft Mexican curses, and a dragging step that passed down the stairs.

Only a few moments more and Anna came back up the stairs, laughing, singing to herself. When she saw her mother, she exclaimed: "Even luck is the servant of a man!"

"Is he as small as I thought he was?" asked Rosita curiously.

"He is not an inch taller than I," said Anna. "He is not ten pounds bigger. He has an eye as soft and blue as the color of a mountain pool. He has a smile like a sleepy child. A hand faster than a cat's paw. When he stands still, he looks like nothing. But whatever he does makes him seem bigger."

"Where are your brothers?"

"Juan has locked himself with a gun into the granary. I can hear him calling on the name of his saint. Pedro I saw running, flopping his arms like the wings of a bat. I saw Miguel crawling on the stones of the patio and begging for mercy because he cannot walk."

"It will do them all good," said the mother. "Some are born to be masters and some are born to be men."

"The pity of it that he is only an *Americano!*" said Anna.

"Sweet child," said Rosita, "real men are of no nation. So long as they speak Spanish, do not look the gift horse in the mouth, but thank God for your good fortune!"

"Speak Spanish? He can sing it, also," said Anna. "He must be from the opera. And into an old song he puts my name as if he were a poet, too. But, Mother, he is in rags."

"Every caballero may be caught in a thorn patch," said the mother, "but what sort of a horse was he riding?"

"Such a horse," said the girl, "that Gil Fanwick will weep blood with envy when he even hears of it. A golden stallion that follows the hand of its master like a sheepdog."

"Now, by the name of kind San Miguel," said Rosita. "If I were ten years younger and ten inches less around the hips, I would forget the world for a man like that."

"But the rags, Mother!"

"Money buys clothes, and men spend money," said Rosita. "A wise woman could coin the whole treasury out of one man like this *Americano*. But say your prayers, wash your face clean, and never stop smiling. Who can tell what may happen? What is his name?"

"His name is Sleeper, he says. That is a strange name."

"Men who have strange names have strange stories," said the mother. "Thank God for him and go straight to bed."

Into the Diablos

Operated by fat Carlos Oñate, the cantina on the ground floor of the hotel served patrons who came to sit at the little tables on the side of the street under a row of pepper trees. Carlos served Mexican beer that was cooled by a running spring that pooled its waters in Oñate's cellar and then came out sparkling to run down the gutter of the street. Almost the only municipal effort of the town of San Miguel had been to enlarge the gutter to a trough, here and there, so that horses and mules and goats and cattle could be watered up and down the street. At a table under a pepper tree sat Sleeper, on this bright, hot morning, listening to the trickle and chiming of the spring water and sipping his glass of beer as though time mattered no more to him than it did to the sailing buzzards high over the town. They seemed to think that San Miguel was dying, and Sleeper appeared willing to be included in the death.

When he lifted his dreaming face from his drink, it was to look through the branches of the trees toward the upper peaks of the Diablo Mountains, glimmering slopes of gray stone on which streaks of dull foliage appeared like thin clouds.

A man rose from an adjoining table, a tall, elderly man with a fat puff of a face and deep blue pouches beneath the eyes. He had legs so long and a body so short and thick that he looked like a great blue crane, and, as he rose, he tossed his newspaper aside. It fell at Sleeper's feet, and Sleeper picked it up and seemed, in his mild way, to be offering it back to the older man. Instead, he was saying softly: "What is it, Colonel?"

"Read the paper. The job's off. Douglas is in hell. Lowry wants you back," muttered the colonel, and strode away to his horse, which he mounted, and rode off down the street.

Sleeper unfolded the paper thoughtfully. The news he wanted was spilled across the front page of the little countryside journal:

STANLEY DOUGLAS ACCUSED
OF TRAIN ROBBERY

The story ran for columns. Sleeper slipped his eye over it rapidly. Four bandits had stopped the Overland, forced the fireman to flood the firebox of the engine, kept the passengers in the coaches, and then cracked open the safe in the mail coach. The theft was nearly seventy thousand dollars. The thieves were unknown with one exception. That exception was very odd, because one of the criminals had actually addressed a companion as Stan Douglas.

The man so addressed had the height, the bulk, the apparent youth of Stanley Douglas—and, since his mask was badly arranged, some blond hair showed, like the hair of Stanley Douglas. To make matters certain, it was discovered that Stanley Douglas, after quarreling with his father, had left home. He had turned, apparently, straight to a career of crime.

No wonder Lowry wanted Sleeper to return from this lost cause. For even if young Douglas were returned to his father's house, now it would be as a dodging fugitive pursued by the law. Stan Douglas must be left to fulfill his own fate, it appeared.

Sleeper, with calm eyes, continued to dwell on the paper long after he had mastered the details of the account. One of the instructions of the peddler had been to keep Douglas away from crime, and in that he had failed. It hardly mattered to Sleeper that it had been impossible for him to prevent the hold-up. The impossible was exactly what Pop Lowry expected of him—otherwise why should Pop have sent him to the Diablo Mountains, a single man, to execute such a mission?

He knew, in his heart, that Lowry hated him with a profound loathing and that he would almost sooner hear of Sleeper's death than of a coup that won him a million for his hoard. Sleeper had given himself into the hands of Lowry for three long months—his pledged word made him a slave of the pseudo-peddler—and yet now he continued to brood over the paper and gradually dismiss the thought of obeying commands and returning at once to Lowry.

It was not the written account that troubled him. It was the large photograph of Stanley Douglas that filled the center of the first page of the newspaper. It showed a fellow no older than Sleeper—in the early twenties, at most, with a fearless eye and a fine, open, handsome face.

This was the man who had thrown himself to the dogs. He had gone downhill like a rolling stone from the moment when his father refused to pay that trifling debt of honor. The success of the first crime would make the second attempt more callous. There might be bloodshed in that affair. Then Stan Douglas would be hopelessly outside the law.

Anna Oñate came hurrying out and stood before Sleeper with frightened eyes. "How can I tell you, señor? The devils have broken into the stable through the back door that hasn't been open for years. They have taken away your beautiful horse. . . ."

"Well," said Sleeper, "if they've taken the horse, bring me another beer, will you, Anna?" And he sat for another hour at least, slowly sipping the cool beer and thinking.

Swift, thoughtless action is like blind charging in a fight. It brings many broken heads and little else. He had known from the first that Careless could not be exposed with impunity to the air of such a place as San Miguel. Now he was stolen as Pop Lowry had warned—but that was exactly what he had expected and wished—because he was reasonably certain that the prize would, before long, find its way into the hands of Fanwick's outlaws.

At last he paid his bill, gave Anna a tip that made her blush, and went back to the stable.

"As though," she told her mother, "to lose such a horse was a nothing, as though he had a whole herd of better horses at home."

"A real man," said Rosita, "knows that his feet can carry him where no horse will go. Things will soon happen around San Miguel."

Behind the stable, Sleeper easily found the trail. Among other hoof marks, those of Careless were as recognizable to him as the faces of friends in a crowd of strangers. The trail led straight across the hillside, into a shallow draw, and thence up the stony bottom, out across a rock plateau where almost all sign disappeared. He ran all the way with a swinging, smooth Indian gait that devoured the miles with little effort. Where the trail grew dim, he did not decrease his pace but merely bowed over until his head was hardly higher than his hips. So he read the dull print of the trail left by Careless.

That trail had been laid with care. It doubled back here and there, and finally topped a small hill not two miles from the town of San Miguel where it had started. Over the top of the hill, Sleeper saw a picture that halted him at once. He never could have expected such a sight among the naked Diablo Mountains. It was rare as an oasis in a desert—a narrow little valley thronged with trees, the thin gleam of a stream running through the center of the slope, and fine, open-faced meadows that offered excellent grazing. Hobbled horses stirred here and there. Canvas tents appeared under the trees. He marked a group of men, small with distance, gathered to watch a horse that was fighting its rider, flashing like bright gold in the sun.

That was Careless at work, and they would be good riders, indeed, if they were able to sit on his back.

Sleeper lay down in the shadow of a rock and drew out a spyglass. It was small and light but the lens was excellent. It picked up the distant picture and enlarged it wonderfully. Features of the men were dim, but the whole course of the action was perfectly plain. One rider went off, sailing sidewise. A second followed, a moment later. A third went the same way—a fourth. And yet Careless had hardly opened the box of tricks that his master had taught him. He had not galloped under trees that had low branches. He had not hurled himself to the ground, half risen, dropped back again. He was merely executing some ordinary maneuvers that Sleeper had taught him to go through with the whirling speed of a fine dancer. As he watched, Sleeper laughed a little.

Then he left his place beside the rock and moved rapidly down the side of the valley. High above the middle of the secluded place rose a huge pinnacle of rock on which a single watcher sat turning ceaselessly this way and that. He was a sufficient sentinel to keep guard over the entire crew, except that he was watching for horsemen and not for creatures that moved with the snaky subtlety of Sleeper from shadow to shadow.

When Sleeper was within a hundred yards of the group of men, he paused in a thick clump of brush and, worming his way through it, crouched again to make observations. He could read every face, now, with his glass. Three or four men sat about or reclined, badly knocked out by the falls they had received. Careless, sweat-blackened, still shone brightly in the sun—and now there was a pause in the struggle.

It continued until a tall young fellow stepped out from the rest. A shout greeted him, the sound tingling up to where Sleeper waited in concealment. Studying the face of the newcomer with care, he made out the features that he had seen in the newspaper. It was big Sam Douglas.

A little, thin-faced man stood at the stallion's head, steadying Careless before the new attempt was made. When he spoke and made gestures, other men hurried to do his bidding. It was no doubt the famous man, that infamous criminal, the great Gil Fanwick.

As Douglas mounted, Sleeper gave the signal. It was a whistle high and shrill and thin, such as one hears when the scream of an eagle is blown down the wind. The pitch was too high, at such a distance, to run more than the slightest thread of sound through a human ear, but Sleeper could be sure that the stallion's pricked ears would hear it.

The great horse was whirling the instant that his head was released. Instead of using efforts to pitch Douglas from his back, he bolted straight across the floor of the valley toward the source of that whistle— and a yell of triumph came up from the outlaws. They took it for granted that Careless at last was mastered.

Douglas seemed to feel the same thing. He was laughing with joy and making no effort to take a hard pull at the reins. Perhaps Fanwick had offered permanent possession of the horse to the one of his men who could ride it.

But as the chestnut headed straight for the clump of big brush and whirled around the side of it, Careless made one sharp pitch in the air that sent the surprised Douglas out of the saddle. He landed with a heavy *thud*, sitting on the ground almost at Sleeper's feet.

At the Hoot of the Owl

The impact stunned Douglas for a moment while Sleeper lifted his two guns. But the first shock did not endure. Stan Douglas came off the ground like a flame and, since he had no better weapons, went at Sleeper with his hands. He leaped in with a boxer's long, straight shooting left, the most unavoidable of blows, in which the arm strikes out like a long rapier.

Sleeper met this attack with his hands open and a thoughtful expression on his face. His head swayed a little to the right—the driving fist whirred over his shoulder as he stepped in and struck with the edge of his palm. It is a little trick that has no use unless one knows where to find nerve centers. This blow fell on the strained side of Douglas's neck where all the tendons were stiffly drawn. If the shock had been delivered with the edge of an axe, the effect could hardly have been more complete. Douglas's head dropped limply on his breast. He lunged straight ahead, but with buckling knees, and would have fallen on his face if Sleeper had not caught him. Then Stan Douglas, staring helplessly at the gun in the hand of the stranger, was at a loss for words.

"Sit down," said Sleeper.

Douglas shook his head. "Who are you?" he demanded.

"Most people call me Sleeper," was the answer. "Sit down, Stan, and be easy. I'm not an officer of the law, and I don't want you for that Overland robbery."

Douglas blinked, then drew in a long breath. "Then what the devil are you after?" he demanded.

"You," said Sleeper. "You're going home. Home to your father."

"The sheriff would have me the next day," Douglas growled. "What are you driving at?"

"When you held up the train, nobody was killed? There wasn't any bloodshed?" asked Sleeper.

"I'm not talking about the train. I don't know anything about it," said Douglas. "I wasn't there. Somebody else that looked like me. . . ."

"Quit it," urged Sleeper, without heat. "I haven't got the time to argue with you. I could take you in the way you are and get the reward. They've got a reward on your head now, Stan. You know that?"

Stan Douglas said nothing. He could only stare. The big stallion, coming to Sleeper, began to nip cautiously at the brim of his master's old hat. Sleeper put up a hand and pushed the sweating head away.

"You're the man that . . . ," began Douglas.

"They stole the horse from me," said Sleeper. "I could follow any trail that Careless left, and I thought it would bring me to Fanwick's gang . . . and here we are."

"It was you that called him a minute ago?"

"Yes."

"What else can the stallion do? Read books and talk French? I thought I was breaking him," Douglas muttered ruefully. Suddenly he grinned at Sleeper with a fine flash of his gray eyes.

"You know where the loot is that was taken from the train?" asked Sleeper.

Douglas was silent.

"That's all that stands between you and a cleaner record," said Sleeper. "Return that stuff to the railroad and explain that it was just a foolish practical joke. You know . . . fool kids running wild. They'll even see a point to the joke if they get the coin back, I think. Or do you want the life down there in the valley? Fanwick and his gang of thieves . . . do they look good to you?"

Douglas's mouth twisted with distaste. He could not help breaking out: "I've been a damned fool! I've been the biggest fool in the world!"

"Why not wash your reputation clean again, then?"

"You mean, go down on my knees and beg the old man for enough money to pay the railroad back? I'll go to hell first."

"That's where you'll go, all right, if you don't get the money back. Stan, nobody beats the game. You can't beat the law."

"A fellow can have a few free years, anyway," growled Douglas. "Instead of being kicked around over the map of the world. . . ."

"What kind of freedom?" asked Sleeper. "Taking orders from Fanwick? Is that freedom? Doing his dirty work . . . is that better than taking orders from your father?"

"I'll never beg for a chance to go back," said Douglas.

"Don't beg, then. Take the chance."

"Take it? How?"

"Have they split up the Overland loot? Is it all together?"

Again Douglas hesitated, staring, but Sleeper's eyes were wide, friendly, and steady. Finally Stan Douglas broke out: "The stuff is still crammed in the saddlebag. Two of the boys haven't come in yet."

"Then get that saddlebag," said Sleeper. "Get that and make the run home."

"Get the saddlebag? Out of Fanwick's tent? Hell, even if I were a ghost, I couldn't wangle that!"

"I'll help you."

"Look here, stranger. What do you get out of this?"

"Not a penny, if that's what you mean."

"Did Father hire you to ride this trail?"

"Your father never heard of me. I never saw him."

"Well, it beats me," said Douglas, frowning. "I don't make you out."

"Stay in the dark till you're home . . . with your hands washed clean."

"And where will you be at the finish?"

"Fanwick will be one down to me."

"You hate Fanwick?"

"Mister Murderer Fanwick? He's not a friend of Sleeper's."

This implied motive seemed enough to satisfy Douglas.

"But the saddlebag is inside Fanwick's tent, and he never leaves that tent, day or night. He keeps a couple of his best men handy, too. Sawed-off shotguns are lying around."

"Shotguns are never a joke," agreed Sleeper.

"And they're ready to use them," said Douglas. "Every man on Fanwick's inside ring is wanted for more than one murder. They'll shoot to kill."

"It looks a little tough," agreed Sleeper.

"Nothing could be done . . . unless you had twenty good men. Even then I don't know how the fight would go."

"Numbers won't do it," decided Sleeper. "A crowd would be heard on the way, and the birds would be off. It'll take a light touch and no noise to do this, Stan. What I want to know is this. Will you be with me? If I come down to the camp and try my hand, will you be ready to help? Help steal the money and help make the getaway?"

Douglas turned pale. He pulled out a fresh bandanna and rubbed his face with it. He looked down to his freshly polished boots and studied them.

"Yeah," he said finally.

"Are we shaking on it?" asked Sleeper.

He held out his hand, which Douglas, after a bitter inward struggle, forced himself to take. Gradually he lifted his head until his glance held level with Sleeper's. "I'll be with you," he said at last.

Sleeper said: "If you double-cross me, Stan, I'll manage to live through anything that happens . . . and get at you!" He waved a hand to dismiss the subject, and abruptly held out Stan's guns. "Take these back," he said.

The significance of the gesture could not be missed. Douglas, taking the guns, flushed deeply. "All right," he said. "I don't understand you, Sleeper, but I'm starting to appreciate that you're not like any other man."

"God help me, then," answered Sleeper. "When I show up near the camp . . . where'll I find you?"

"On this side, in a tent under two trees. Spotty sleeps with me. Be quiet."

"Who's Spotty?"

"A French-Canadian with a long record north of the

border. Knife work is his specialty. He says it makes no sound. And throats cut easier than beef."

"If you hear an owl hoot . . . two times, close together . . . like this. . . ." Lowering his head, Sleeper brought from his throat two softly mournful sounds. Although he stood close, the noise seemed to be coming from far away. "If you hear that, come out and start for the sound, will you?"

"I will," said Douglas. He repeated the words, sternly, to himself. "I *will* come!"

Sleeper eyed him narrowly, in doubt. "You've got the right blood in you," he said, "and you'll certainly do better than you think, when the pinch comes. That's when the good blood counts, Stan."

"If I quit on you, I'm the worst skunk in the world!" exclaimed Douglas. "My God, Sleeper, how can you tackle a thing like this for a stranger? And even if you get into the camp, what's your plan to get at the money?"

"I haven't a plan in the world," admitted Sleeper. "I'll try to do some thinking . . . but remember, day or night, when you hear that old owl hooting, you come for the sound of it."

"I'll come," repeated the other.

"You've got to ride the horse back, or people may come out chasing him . . . and pick up my trail."

"Nobody can ride him . . . except his master," insisted Douglas.

"I'll make it easy for you to ride him. Give me your hand." He placed Stan's hand squarely between the eyes of the big stallion. The horse's ears flattened. He winced back from the touch but slowly straightened again as his master spoke.

"Swing up into the saddle," directed Sleeper.

Douglas obeyed. The chestnut shrank under the

weight like a great cat, a green-eyed danger. Gradually the horse relaxed beneath the voice and the touch of his master.

"You can ride him now," said Sleeper. "Give him a light rein. Talk to him till he gets used to your voice. Talk a lot. He's in your hands, Stan." Saying that, he stepped back, and watched Douglas ride the stallion slowly out from behind the brush and toward the center of the valley.

Splitting of the Loot

Anna, starting up suddenly from her place at the window, cried: "I see him!"

"Who?" demanded Rosita.

"I see the señor! Señor Sleeper! I see him walking across the patio, and now through the gate. He turns up the street."

"There's nothing in that," said Rosita.

"Why should he be going out now, in the dusk of the day?" asked Anna. "And at the very time when supper is nearly ready?"

"Men are like cats," said Rosita, "and they must walk out in the twilight. They must walk out and smell the night and bristle their whiskers a little . . . the devils!"

"Señor Sleeper is walking up the street," Anna continued. "He comes to the lane . . . and he turns down it. Why does he turn down that lane? Is it because he has seen that little fool of a Dolores with her loud, squealing laugh and her painted mouth?"

"Girls have the meaning that men choose to give them," said Rosita. "Is he going straight down the lane toward her house?"

"He has come to the bend of the lane . . . no, he is walking around it. He stops and looks about him . . . then he slips into the tall brush."

"I knew, when I first saw him, that he was a hunting cat," said Rosita. "What bird will he catch in that bush?"

"He has gone through it. He is on the farther side. He looks stealthily about him. He thinks he is alone. He cannot tell that I can look down on him from this height like a bird from the sky."

"Poor bird!" said Rosita. "You are in the sky and yet you are caught if he whistles."

"He begins to run!" exclaimed Anna. "He disappears into the shallow draw. Now I see only his head as he moves to the west. I am going."

"Where?"

"After him. How do I know where?" She turned hastily from the window.

"Don't be a crazy thing," said Rosita. "A woman never can run fast enough to catch a man . . . it is better to sit still . . . they run so far that they end up where they begin."

Anna, instead of making an answer, threw open a chest that stood in a corner of the room and snatched out a big new Colt revolver.

"What are you doing with that? Put that back . . . it's your father's finest gun!" called Rosita.

"If Señor Sleeper needs help, he needs more than my bare hands can give him. Mother, pray for me."

"*Ai!* Anna! Wait . . . listen to me!"

But Anna was already off down the steps. Her mother puckered her face and tilted back her head to scream. But she thought better of this and took her stand at the window, looking out over the dim, sunset landscape. She saw Anna cross the patio, turn up the street and into the lane.

At the bend of the lane, the tall girl slipped through the brush and appeared on the farther side of it, running like a deer. In fact the slim body of hers was no weight to carry, and there was enough Indian blood in her veins to make her as fleet as a rabbit. She ran with a long, easy stride that the short skirt did not impede, and in a moment she was out of sight in the shallow draw. Her head did not appear. But her mother knew that the girl was running to the west.

Rosita went back to her sewing and heaved a single sigh. She began to mutter what might have been a prayer—at least, she was naming many of the saints.

In Gil Fanwick's camp the darkness had fallen, and Fanwick himself had started a pleasant little ceremony. His tent was a fairly comfortable affair with a center table and canvas chairs about it. A bright lantern shone in the center of the table and cast its light over the faces of the four men who Fanwick had called in. It also gleamed on the canvas side of a saddlebag that reposed on the table, and threw a shadow from it against the faintly luminous wall of the tent.

"This job," said Gil Fanwick, "was one of the smoothest that was ever worked. We should have got away without a trace if Turk Malone hadn't gone out of his head and called Douglas by name. That was simply too damn' bad."

"What's to become of that fool, Malone?" asked one of the men.

"You'll never see Malone again," said Gil Fanwick. "Nobody else is ever gonna see him. He and I took a ride through the hills, and I came back alone."

The men shifted their glances toward one another. There was no comment. Young Douglas had grown a little pale.

"The rest of you all did well," went on Fanwick, having closed the other subject. "But the rest of you were old hands. Stan Douglas was a green hand. But I take it that he did his stuff."

"He was right on the job," said a red-headed man.

"Cool as steel from the start to the finish," added another.

"He had the hardest part, and he played it well," said Fanwick. "I'm going to give him an extra thousand out of my share."

There was a murmur of hearty agreement. Douglas flushed.

"You know how we have to split this melon, boys?" asked Fanwick. They waited, and he explained: "For the inside tip, I have to pay twenty percent. You know how it is. We can't work in the dark, and we have to pay high for the sort of news that we want."

"Sure," said Red, "we know that news has to be paid for. But how much is in the sack?"

"Fifty-five thousand," said the chief.

There was a groan at this. "I thought they said seventy thousand in the papers!" said the youngest of the crew, a kid of nineteen.

"It's a wonder they didn't say a hundred thousand," said Fanwick. "Newspapers live and breed on lies. That's all they are . . . lies and lies!" His very color changed with his emotion, but the same senseless, meaningless smile kept twitching his lips. "Twenty percent to the inside," said Fanwick, continuing, "and one third to me. Does that still hold with you boys?"

"Yeah," said Red. "Or a half. It's equal by me. We'd never make a nickel if you didn't plan the job for us."

"Twenty percent . . . that's exactly eleven thousand goes out of sight . . . to a fellow who may have a chance to give us another tip worth twice as much.

That's why he has to be paid on the nail. Well, then, that leaves forty-four thousand. A third to me, leaves about twenty-nine. That gives a shade over seven thousand to each of you. How does that sound? Douglas, you get an extra thousand out of my split."

"It sounds small," growled Red. "Here we take and haul in around seventy thousand . . . according to the papers and what the railroad says. Split that five ways and it would make fourteen thousand for each of us. Now we get down to seven thousand. It looks damn' thin to me."

"How about the rest of you?" asked the chief, turning his eye around the circle.

The others shrugged their shoulders. "Let's make the split, chief," one urged.

"Not a penny," said the leader. "Not till we've talked the whole thing out. I don't want any bad feelings. I won't have them. Either we get along smooth, or we don't get along at all."

Douglas spoke, slowly: "As far as I'm concerned, I don't want any extra cut from the chief. I need thirty-five hundred dollars. As long as I get that much, it's as good to me as though I had thirty-five million."

"Because you have a thirty-five hundred dollar debt to pay," said the chief. "Forget that, Douglas. They know your name now, and they'll slam you in jail for twenty years if they catch you. Forget your debts. You've washed your hands of the old life, debts and everything."

"I can't wash my hands of those things," said Douglas. "They're on my honor."

"Honor! Hell!" said Fanwick. It was plain that the devil was up in him. "Honor is what men fight for . . . that and hard cash. The honor goes up the chimney, and the hard cash remains. The crooks that cheated the public two generations ago founded our aristocracy, the fellows that play it big in the headlines today. Honor be damned. Money is what counts in the world. And money is what you boys are going to get. You forget that debt, Douglas."

Douglas said nothing. He was looking steadily into the face of his leader, and it would not have been hard to find words to explain his expression.

"Well, let's make the cut and have it over with," said Red. "I had to say my say, but I'm satisfied. Every man that works with Gil Fanwick gets plenty of coin. There's no doubt about that. By the way, chief, how much do you lay up in a year?"

Fanwick's face withered. His eyes blinked rapidly before he said: "I pay for horses, chuck, and all sorts of things . . . guns, ammunition for you to blaze away with. That all comes out of my third, and what I get at the end of a year is a damned sight less than you boys think. But I'm waiting till I get you all ready for the big stuff. The day's coming, boys, when we'll all be taking in hundreds of thousands, instead of tens. There's millions to be had, and we're going to have them."

He said this with such a fire of conviction that every face lighted except the gloomy face of Stanley Douglas.

Then, very softly from the distant night, came the double hoot of an owl.

Stan Douglas stiffened suddenly, with a quick intake of breath. Only one eye noticed the quick change in him, but that eye was the leader's. He snapped: "Douglas, what the hell does that mean?"

Strange Capture

Douglas, when he heard the challenge, looked casually over his shoulder. He felt that he was calm all over except in his eyes. He dreaded letting the chief penetrate his mind through those open gates. "Nothing," he said. "Sort of surprised me . . . that was all . . . hearing an owl just then."

"It doesn't mean anything to you?" asked the leader.

"No. Of course not," said Douglas, and he turned with a frown. He could feel all eyes on him, prying at his mind, but Fanwick was the only one he feared.

"You're lying!" said Fanwick.

"You can't say that to me," answered Douglas, his fighting blood instantly hot.

Metal winked swiftly into Fanwick's hand. He laid the revolver muzzle on the edge of the table. "Wait a minute, everybody," he said. "Don't move. Listen!"

A moment went by. Then the long drawn, double note of an owl sounded again.

"A damn' funny owl that sounds off twice from the same place!" said Fanwick. "Boys, get out of here and walk toward that call. If you sight a two-legged owl on the ground, blaze away with everything you've got." He stared at Douglas. "This is too damned bad," he said. "Don't move a hand, Douglas. If you stir, I'm going to slam lead into you!"

On the verge of the camp, sheltered vaguely behind a small bush, Sleeper had given the signal twice. Now he saw a man coming slowly toward him through the dark. Not one man—for two others moved at a little distance behind the leader.

He had been double-crossed, then, by Douglas, who had betrayed the signal to the bunch! Well, this made it easier, far easier. If Douglas were a skunk, then Sleeper could wash his hands of him and go back to answer the next command of the pseudo-peddler, Pop Lowry.

But for now, he had to get out of the way of that trio who moved watchfully, carefully forward. There was not much cover to take. A snake could hardly have used the little irregularities of the ground and the brush, the stones that Sleeper put between himself and the three. Softly, rapidly, on hands and knees, with some wriggling flat on the belly, he drew away. He gained larger brush. He could stand up now and run, but he had a better thing to do than to run. With his whistle he could bring the great stallion to him. No matter how they had tethered Careless, it would be strange if he could not break away at the call from his master.

Before that whistle shrilled from Sleeper's lips, however, he heard a slight outcry, a scurrying, and then the three pounced upon a figure that had risen out of the ground not far from the place where Sleeper had been lying. Then he heard the voice of a girl, the rich deep voice of Anna Oñate, from the village.

Already they had her far back toward the tent from which they had come. As the flap of it was thrown back, he saw the light come out and meet her tall body and her high-thrown head. He had hardly seen her before. Now he saw her as though the light shone out of her own mind and body. Why was she here? Why was she being hauled back before the men in the tent? Who were they? Douglas, it appeared, had betrayed a new friend. What part had the girl to play in this business?

Sleeper came rapidly back toward the tent. He rounded it to the rear, at the same time hearing a voice that called out loudly: "What's this girl got to do with it, Douglas? Is she the one that came and made the owl call for you? Why don't you answer?"

That remark told Sleeper a great deal. He closed in toward the tent. The other men of Fanwick's band—perhaps a dozen of them—were lounging here and there, near their own tents that were scattered under the trees in a sort of oval shape. The tent to which the girl had been brought had, at the front of it, a hitching rack to which four saddled horses were tethered.

Sleeper aimed for them. He untied the ropes that bound them, hearing Douglas say: "I'm not talking. You can think what you want!"

"This is likely to make a hell of a lot of trouble for you!" said the sharp voice of the man who asked the question.

Sleeper, walking slowly, making small whispering noises that caused the horses to prick their ears and come willingly, led the horses around the tent and tethered them to the nearest tree up the slope. As he returned toward the tent, he heard the inquisitor inside exclaiming: "I'm not going to keep on asking you questions all night long! Will you talk, Douglas?"

There was no answer. Sleeper could feel the strain of the silence. Then, as though rising like a spirit from the ground, a figure appeared suddenly before him, a man with a rifle held at the ready. The fellow had stepped out from the rear of the tent, and Sleeper could understand his own peril and the reason for it. This must be the tent of the leader of the gang, and the leader had chosen to have the back of his tent guarded rather than the face that was exposed to the eyes of all the rest of the band.

"Well?" said the voice of the guard.

Sleeper brought into his hand, with a subtle gesture, the weight of his hunting knife. "Hello, partner," he said.

"You ain't any partner that I remember," said the other in the same subdued voice.

"Wait a minute," said Sleeper as he stepped closer. He seemed to be thrusting his face forward, so that it might be seen more clearly. With the point of the knife he could do his work easily, infallibly. But that would be, in his judgment, murder, even if it were no more than the killing of an outlaw. Therefore, he struck, suddenly, for the temple, using only the butt of the knife.

The blow hit the soft of flesh and yielding bone. The guard slumped forward and Sleeper caught the rifle from his hands, lest there should be clattering of metal. He thrust out his knee and broke the fall of the dropping body, also. Then the man lay still, and Sleeper, on his knees before him, rapidly tied the hands and feet together and worked a gag inside the teeth.

He was hearing the men inside the tent as this preparation went forward, and, above that, the dominating voice that finally called out: "I won't have any of these damned mysteries. If the girl means something to you, tell me what it is, Douglas."

Sleeper got to the rear of the tent and applied his eye to a very thin rent in the cloth. The scene within was perfectly clear to him, then. He saw the thin, hard face of the leader—he saw Douglas with Fanwick's gun pointed at his breast—he saw Anna Oñate and three men who were watching intently everything that happened.

Douglas said: "I don't know the girl."

"No matter what happens to you, you don't know her?" sneered Fanwick.

Suddenly Anna said: "You do know me, señor. He does know me, Señor Fanwick."

"I thought so," said Fanwick, nodding. "You tell me about it, Anna. You thought he was a pretty fine-looking young fellow, eh?"

"I still think so," said Anna.

"And you let him know that?" demanded Fanwick.

The girl looked at Douglas, and suddenly her glance rolled up and a sort of agony came over her face.

"She's ashamed," Fanwick said with a sneering laugh. "But I'm about to get to the bottom of this. We're going to find out that Douglas has invited women to come up here . . . that he's showed the natives where we live. By God, that means that we've all been minutes away from having our throats cut. Murder . . . that's what it means! Go on, Anna."

But Anna said: "I meant to help him, Señor Fanwick. I didn't mean to do him any harm!"

"Well, tell me the truth, then."

"Will it take away trouble from this poor young man?" asked the girl.

"We'll see about that," answered the chief.

"I never saw the señor before," said the girl, nodding at Douglas. She was panting with excitement, and her eyes flashed—they were like the eyes of a deer, big, gleaming, accustomed to danger and the escape from it by flight.

"If you never saw Douglas before, what brought you up here?" asked Fanwick.

"Another man," she said.

"Ah-ha! Which one?"

"Señor Sleeper," said the girl, blushing very red.

"Sleeper? Who the devil is that?" demanded Fanwick. "Is that the nickname of one of my men?"

"He is the man with the red stallion," said the girl.

"Ah, that man. Wait a minute! You say that he came up here?"

"Yes, señor."

"When?"

"There's no use trying to follow him. He's gone far away, by this time," Anna said. "And God forgive me! Every man suffers because of what I say."

"You followed him up here . . . this night?" shouted Fanwick.

"Yes, señor," said the trembling girl.

Sleeper's pulse struck a note like a drumbeat through his ears. He could hardly believe the thing he heard. But it was spoken under circumstances that could not lead to anything but the truth.

"Get out of here!" Fanwick shouted to his men. "Douglas, stay here because I've got to talk to you damned straight. The rest of you scatter. Find me this Sleeper and bring him back by the ears, dead or alive!"

Sleeper, lifting the rifle, aimed it carefully through the small gap in the side of the tent. Now, as the men rose hastily, he pulled the trigger, and with the *boom* of the gun there came an answering crash of glass, and the lantern went out.

Master of Five

One sweep of the hunting knife divided the back of the tent with that razor-edge of sharpness. Inside, there was a swirl of figures, a rapid clattering of exclamations, and from the distance came the shouting of the men who had heard the rifle shot and seen the light extinguished in the leader's tent.

"Douglas!" called Sleeper. "Anna!"

His first answer was a spitting red flame from the muzzle of a revolver. He slashed back with the edge of the knife, and the keen edge slashed through flesh and grated on bone. A screech answered the stroke, and two swift figures darted out of the rent in the back of the tent, past Sleeper who had gained the table and seized the saddlebag.

He was after them like a greyhound. "Straight ahead!" he called, panting. "The tree . . . the horses there!"

Behind him, glancing over his shoulder, he saw a tumbling knot of figures spilled out from the tent. But they were well behind, and the two ahead of him ran well. Douglas—he noted with a keen and approving eye—would not race on ahead of the girl but kept steadily at her side. Then out of Sleeper's lips came a long, shrilling whistle. That signal would be heard by sharper than human ears, and it would be answered unless the straining ropes were very strong, indeed.

They were at the four horses, now, slashing the lead ropes instead of pausing to untie them. In the rear, the sharp, barking voice of Fanwick raved madly. More distant answers proved that orders were being heard and obeyed. The whole number of these men would soon be on horseback, of course, and they would sweep like so many hawks in pursuit of the fugitives.

The girl was first in the saddle, leaping to her place like any active lad. Big Stan Douglas followed. Sleeper was the last to gain a place and take the spare horse on the lead.

Now he saw that there was no further pursuit up the slope. Instead, Fanwick and his men, dropping to their knees or lying flat, were taking pot shots at the flying shadows as the fugitives went off at full gallop. Other horsemen were mounting in the hollow of the valley, dimly seen.

Suddenly a form rushed rapidly, as though on wings, up the slope, overtaking the three. "Go on, the two of you! I'll take care of that one!" called Douglas. He was reining his horse in, poising a gun, when Sleeper saw a glint of starlight on the pursuing figure.

"Don't shoot!" Sleeper cried. "It's Careless coming . . . and there's no man on his back!"

He came straight on to the second whistle of his master. Sleeper, swinging out from the saddle, was instantly on the naked back of the stallion. It did not matter that there was no saddle, no bridle. A touch of hand or voice would guide the big horse.

So they gained the ridge of the hills, while behind

them a roar of many hoofs swept up from the floor of the valley. As the three poured over the ridge, outlined for a moment against the stars, a rattle of gunfire rose behind them. It ended as they dipped on the farther side of the hill.

Sleeper rode close beside the girl, leaning from his place. As he leaned, he called: "D'you hear, Anna? Turn left! We'll take the right . . . they'll follow us . . . they won't follow you. . . ."

She merely looked up and shook her head. She laughed. "This is the best part of the dance, Señor Sleeper."

The noise of hoofs mounted the ridge. Sleeper looked helplessly down at Anna. He was aware of Douglas, riding just ahead, and of the big saddlebag flopping clumsily at the side of one of the led horses.

Two or three gunshots rang out together—and the girl suddenly was struck double, over the horn of her saddle. A bullet had surely found her. She began to slip to the side. Sleeper, pressing the stallion closer, held her in place with one straining hand.

He called: "Douglas, take the saddlebag and that led horse! Go on! Ride like the devil! The girl's hurt . . . I'll stay with her. If you ride ahead, they'll probably follow you. It's you and that saddlebag that they want!"

But Douglas was not to be deceived by such talk. There was plenty of manhood in him, and he showed it now. He reined straight back beside the girl and with his powerful hand helped to right her in the saddle.

She recovered from the first shock of the impact and pain. "Sleeper . . . señor!" she gasped. "Mother of heaven, I am dying! Señor Sleeper, I cannot sit the saddle. I cannot. . . ."

"You have to!" commanded Sleeper. "Where did the bullet hit?"

"I don't know . . . I don't know . . . here . . . in the shoulder."

He touched that shoulder and his hand felt the hot wetness of the blood. But there was no great flow of it. The horses were speeding down a shallow valley. Now they were turning onto the broad slope that led down toward the village of San Miguel, far away.

They could not get to the town, he knew, before Fanwick's men would overtake them. He and Douglas— yes, they could escape, but not with the wounded girl to set pace for them. There was no way of dodging. It was all a straight run and the only way of crossing the sharp-sided ravine that ran along the slope of the mountain was to take the bridge that arched the chasm a mile above the town of San Miguel. Toward that point they had to run their horses with the men closing the gap every moment.

It was a matter of moments. The rising wind that blew on their backs seemed no help to them—it was assisting the pursuit only.

"You *can* ride, Anna," Sleeper said. "Set your teeth hard. Can you move that left arm?"

She tried and nodded, with a groan.

"Then there are no bones broken," he said. "It's a flesh wound. And you can stand it?"

"I can stand it," she answered insistently.

He had snatched off his shirt, and now he caught this around her body and knotted it behind, so that the wounded arm was pressed close to her side. That would keep it from swinging and would leave one arm free for clinging to the horse. The reins he took himself.

They made slightly better speed, now, but still the outlaws were gaining. The tall, dead grass made a rustling sound, like water, about the sweeping legs of the horses.

Douglas called: "There's nothing to do, Sleeper! They've got us before we can reach the bridge. On the other side of the bridge, they'll run us down. We're done for. Let's send the girl on and try to hold them back...."

If that was the stuff that Douglas was made of, Sleeper was glad that he had risked all these chances for the sake of the man.

"We can't leave her... because she won't go!" called Sleeper in answer.

"Then there's nothing to be done... and we're lost!" cried Douglas. "By God, Sleeper, I've dragged the two of you down into hell!"

Sleeper, glancing desperately around him, saw the whirling bright faces of the stars overhead, listened to the noise of the hoofs in the grass, and heard the shrilling of the storm that was whipping their backs. Dead grass and a high wind right on the course toward San Miguel....

"There's a chance!" he shouted.

Leaning from the back of the horse, he caught up handful after handful of the tall, brittle grass. He twisted it hard into a tight ball. Then, holding it down before him on the saddle, he fished a wooden match from his pocket, snapped the head with his thumbnail. Dry as the grass was, it took four matches before he managed to ignite it—and then, instantly, it puffed flame into his face, so powder-dry was the old growth. Quickly he flung the ball of fire into the long grass behind him and spurred on.

A thin column of smoke rose, and a dark red tongue of the flame. The flame spread. The wind caught a billow of it, tossed it far ahead, and a fresh fire burst out violently.

Fanwick's men reached the point of ignition. The

flames rose from it in a cloud of sparks and luminous smoke and fire. As fast as the wind, that fire blew and spread. The height of it increased, the noise of its roaring reached the ears of the fugitives, and the red sparks began to shower over them.

Fanwick's men were spreading out to the right and to the left to round the course of the fire, but it smouldered still farther out and drove them back. Straight behind Sleeper and his two companions, the sea of flames rolled down for the bridge that crossed the chasm.

They crossed that bridge, the three of them, not half a dozen jumps ahead of the front of the wall of flame. As they rode on, they could see torrents of crimson light flooding their path—and all sight and sound of the outlaws was lost well behind them.

They were safe. The crowd in San Miguel would give them a sufficient protection once they reached that haven. Beyond it, they could ride on, once the girl was safe at her home again. When they looked back from close to the town, they could still see the red inferno raging behind the cañon. It had done its job well.

Then they were in the still street of San Miguel, hushed as sleep at this time in the night. They came to the hotel, and Sleeper rapped on the patio gate. Behind him, big Stan Douglas was holding the girl in his arms, because she had fainted dead away.

A window screeched up. The voice of Rosita called: "Who is there?"

"Sleeper!" was the answer. "And your daughter. . . ."

A wild cry of excitement answered him. The window slammed down. Footfalls rattled on the stairs. They clattered on the stone pavement of the patio. The gate was unlocked and wrenched open.

"Your daughter's hurt . . . wounded in the shoulder,"

said Sleeper. "But she'll get better, well enough. Don't doubt that. There's no man in the world with a better nerve or a truer heart."

"Ai!" cried Rosita. "Anna . . . you hear me?"

"Faster," murmured the girl. "Faster. Ah, God, they are turned back by the fire . . . even fire is his servant. . . ."

Sleeper took her from Douglas and carried the slim body up the stairs.

Satan's Treasure

The doctor came at once, and at Anna's wound he merely laughed. Two days in bed and a nourishing diet would make up for the blood she had lost.

"She was no nearer death than thinking of it," said the doctor.

Outside the bedroom door, in the dingy hall lit by lantern light, Sleeper was saying good bye to big Stan Douglas. "You've had enough freedom," he said. "Go back and square yourself with the railroad. Call the thing a joke. They'll laugh and pat you on the back."

Douglas nodded. "I'll do that," he agreed. "And if my father wants to kick me in the face . . . why, that's what my face is for. But what about you, Sleeper? What are you going to do after this?"

"Whatever the devil tells me to," said Sleeper.

"The devil? The devil never was inside your mind, old fellow."

"The devil is the one who sends me out on the trail," said Sleeper. "I have ten weeks of his special hell ahead of me. If I live through that. . . ." He made a gesture and whistled. Then they shook hands.

Afterward, Sleeper sat beside Anna's bed. He held one of her hands and looked straight into her eyes.

"Have you ever heard of the town of White Water?" he asked.

"I know where it is," said the girl.

"If there's ever a time when you need help . . . you or your family," said Sleeper, "send to White Water and find an old peddler called Pop Lowry. He'll know where to find me."

"And you," said the girl, "are you going there now?"

"Yes," said Sleeper. "I'll write to you soon. I'll have news for you, Anna."

"You'll never come back," said the girl.

"I? Of course, I'll come back," said Sleeper.

"Go . . . quickly . . . ," said the girl. "Before I begin to cry."

And Sleeper went—quickly, silently in his moccasined feet.

Rosita said, when he had left: "You might have held him longer than that, Anna. Where was your tongue? Suppose that he had seen a few tears? Men like to remember them."

"I'm glad he's gone," answered Anna. "You, Mother, are a wise woman. You know a great deal more than any three men in San Miguel. You should be glad that he's gone, also."

"Why?" asked the mother.

"Do you remember what you told me . . . that hawks caught wild fly better than tame ones?"

"I remember."

"Why did you say that?" Anna asked.

"Because they're used to living on the wing."

"That is true of Sleeper, also," said the girl. "All other

163

men are tame. They have weak wings. They are nothing. But Sleeper has flown so high that he'll never come down to earth to a girl like Anna. So I'm glad that he has gone away forever."

"Nevertheless," said the mother, "you'll hear from him at least once more."

They did hear from him, and by something much weightier than a letter. A week or more later a muleteer brought to the hotel a loaded mule and left it in the charge of Anna herself as she sat in the cool of the evening at the cantina. She was already forgetting Sleeper—the lads of San Miguel had such bright eyes, such charming smiles.

But when the pack was taken from the mule's back—when on the tables were unloaded muslins, silks, laces, and bright slippers, and figured cloths, and packets of feathers for hats, and strings of brilliants and rare beads—when she saw these things and gradually realized that they were all meant for her, Anna's heart overflowed and she wept with joy.

"So you see," said Rosita, "that a mother's eye is the sharpest. I knew that good would come out of him, after all. The blood you've lost has only been enough to wash the wish for him out of your heart. Look . . . there are even rings and bracelets. Mother of heaven, the cost of that mule load must be two, three thousand dollars! What a price among young men. What a hero! What a good man!"

Anna opened the little note that came with the great gift and read, merely:

When all that the mule brings is worn out, I shall still be remembering you.

"There," said Rosita, "is the speech of a gentleman. To love a man like that . . . it is much better than the reading of a good book."

Anna agreed.

Far north of San Miguel, near the town of White Water, at that very moment Sleeper was reading a newspaper that carried, not on the first page but toward the center of the news, this item:

> *Railroad robbery was joke! Stanley*
> *Douglas returns money taken from overland!*

Sleeper looked up from the page.

"But it's not a joke . . . not the money Stan's father paid to you, Pop?"

Pop Lowry was on his knees, arranging the stuffs that he was putting into one of the panniers for his trade among the ranchers.

He said: "A joke? The money I took from that man was given to me with a smile and a handshake. Old Douglas tells me that his son has given him the whole story. Old Douglas wants you to come and stay at their home. He says that Stan is a new man. It is all owing to you. That is what they say. But what about Pop Lowry, who gave you the news and the opportunity? What about me? I get no thanks, only money!"

"How much money?" asked Sleeper curiously.

"Well, he's a rich man," said the peddler. "It was to have been twenty thousand dollars . . . but after Stan became a robber . . . why, I boosted the price several notches."

"To what?" asked Sleeper.

"What do you care?" snapped the peddler. "I gave

the mule load of nonsense to the Mexican girl for you, and that's all you asked for yourself."

Sleeper sighed.

"And tomorrow," said Pop Lowry, "I have new things for you to do. Go to bed early tonight. You'll be riding Careless in the morning."

Jokers Extra Wild

"Jokers Extra Wild" first appeared in *Short Stories* in the October 10, 1926 issue. It appeared under Faust's Max Brand® byline, and was one of twelve short novels to appear that year. Twelve serials also were published in 1926, all but one finishing before year's end. Although Faust rarely employed a first person narrator, he did in "Joker's Extra Wild" with humorous effect.

I

There was a couple of yards of me stretched out toward the fire, and there was another section laid out on the pine needles, and the upper chunk of me, including the head, was resting on a mossy stump like an old song.

Take it all in all, I never felt better, or sleepier, or more comfortable, or lazier in my life. There had been just enough work in that lumber camp to peel the fat off me and get my muscles hardened. The soreness had gone out of my hands and I could swing an axe all day long as light as a toothpick. They used to give me a big cross-cut all to myself because nobody else in the camp had a stroke long enough and strong enough to team with me. Altogether, I was in shape. Although I realized that the roughening up of my hands would make it hard to break in on the cards again, and, although I hadn't had a chance to practice running up a deck for close onto three weeks, still I felt that I had beaten the game and that no matter where they might be hunting for me, they would never think of hunting up here.

So, all in all, you can see how much I was enjoying the warmth of that fire. We'd had a cold snap. Those mountains was colder than Iceland for a spell, but then the wind fetched around into the southeast and the thaw come on so fast that it would have made your head swim. The snow sluiced off of the ground. The rivers you could hear bumping and bumbling over in the ravine, and the spring was coming up so fast that it seemed like the ground was quivering and stirring with new life.

So it was pretty sweet to lie back there. It was only the second night that we had bunked outdoors, and I was just beginning to shake the smoky, greasy smell of that bunkhouse out of my brain and nose. It was slick to keep one eye half open while the yellow of the firelight swarmed over my face, and to look up, now and again, past the big black pines to the stars and thank God that we was not as cold as them. A little spell back, I can tell you that the stars had looked hot to us, compared with those white mountains.

After a time, I heard somebody let out a screech from the bunkhouse, and Chivvers came out, raving and raging. He said that somebody had stole his wallet, and I forget how many twenties was in it. Anyway, Chivvers made a speech, which I would put down, except for printing it would have to be chiefly dashes. Chivvers had a talent for talk when he got really worked up. Between muleskinning and punching cows and lumbering, he'd picked up a lingo that would have filled the pack of Papa Christmas, you bet.

Well, he unlimbered on that whole crew, and he told them what he thought of them until one of the boys got a chance to say that he thought they ought to lay their heads together and decide who the thief might be.

I didn't hear their talking and decision-making. All

that yelling had just drifted into my ears no louder than the mumbling of a honey bee that is loaded with pollen, but still keeps hanging about for more. That was how fine and sleepy I was feeling.

I sank a hundred fathoms closer to a drowse now, and I had just took a good slow, deep breath of pine-filled mountain air, when I heard a voice chanting something at me faint and far, like a poor stiff that heaves the lead in safe waters and sings a song that nobody don't listen to.

Then somebody leaned over and bellowed right above me: "Hey, Daisie! Will you wake up?"

Well, I closed my eyes to think it over.

"Fetch your hand through his pockets, and see for yourself, Chivvers!" sings out somebody.

Then I felt a hand go slithering down into my pocket. I just reached out and gathered in something that squawked and wriggled and hollered for help. Then I opened my eyes, and there was Chivvers himself, Chivvers the gunfighter, Chivvers the bad actor, Chivvers the cardsharp. Believe me, he didn't look so hard or bad or sharp, just then. He was fighting to get my grip off of his shoulder and neck. Well, I just give it a little more of a squeeze, and he stopped struggling and blinked and gasped and stuck his tongue out. Like a little boy that has swallered something that he oughtn't to have.

I let up on him a little. "Why can't I sleep?" says I.

"I'll tell you, Duff," stutters Chivvers, "the way of it is . . . this . . . some swine has copped my wallet. We thought that maybe, by mistake, you might've picked it up not knowing . . . and so. . . ."

"Now what the hell do you think?" says I.

It made me so mad that I pretty near woke up, but I was feeling too good to get any pleasure of tying Chivvers into knots. So I let him go, and I sank back into a thousand cables of weariness and got the taste of the pine trees fixed firm and fair in my mind again.

After a time, I heard off on the horizon of things that there was a ruction starting up again, and I heard how that somebody was yapping like a dog that is heading for home, but don't know the way, and there was a roar behind that yapping. All that I made out like a murmur in a dream was the yelling to "Kill the chink! He done it!"

Then there come a trampling and a rushing around me and somebody shouting: "Hey, Daisie Duff, get out of the way before we step on your face. . . ."

Well, I closed my eyes and smiled a little. I couldn't help thinking how funny it would be, somebody to step on my face. But nobody done it, so I just lay there and kept on smiling and listening to the humming and the roaring and the yapping, that went winding about through the trees, and around the bunkhouse, and then past the fire again.

Then, dog-gone me, if somebody *didn't* step on me. Not on my face. But on my shins.

It bothered me a good deal. I got up on one elbow, and just then I seen Wong, the cook, with his hands stretched out in front of him and his pigtail stretched out behind. He wasn't white. He couldn't get white, but he was like old ivory, you might say, with a queer look carved into it, and froze there.

You could see that he had been playing tag with hellfire for ten minutes or so, so that he'd almost got used to being scared to death. You've maybe seen a hunted rabbit come and run between your legs to get away from the dogs? That Chinaman was spent and done. He had throwed off one slipper, and his eyes was glassy from the speed of his own running.

When he seen me, he took a long header, like he was diving for water, and he fetched up under the shoulder that I had just heaved up off of the ground. There he crouched. He was shuddering so hard that it fetched tickles through me, and he was so winded that he couldn't draw a breath without groaning, and his larynx worked like a gate on rusty hinges.

The lumberjacks was pounding along as fast as they could leg it, and, when they seen that the Chinaman had halted, they got a look in their faces like the last day of school with a whole dog-gone lazy hot summer to spend ahead of them. They just licked their chops and come whooping.

Well, I reached around and took Wong under my arm and pulled him across my lap. He give me one look. God never worked overtime in the making of my face, and seven days of whiskers didn't improve it particular. Wong gave a last groan, and then he rolled his eyes up at the stars.

I seen the boys coming, and I picked him up in my hands and hefted Wong to chuck him to the dogs, as you might say. But just at that minute, by a taste on the back of the root of my tongue, I remembered the beans he had given us for dinner that night. They had been baked with molasses *and* mustard, like I had particular requested a couple of days before. So, instead of chucking Wong away, I changed my mind and held up my hand, and the lumberjacks that was hoofing it in the lead, they stopped themselves so fast that they raised a regular smoke.

Wong belonged to them. I could see that. But me being in the wrong, I seen that the only way for me to do was to put them in the wrong, if I could.

"Now, what in hell might you mean by kicking the dirt in my face like this?" says I.

"Aw, Daisie," says one of them, "hand that chink over, will you? You ain't gonna spoil the party, are you?"

"As for the Chinaman," I says, "I ain't interested"—which was true, because it was the beans he cooked that I was thinking about—"but as for the way you been walking on my shins, that I am interested. Who's been doing a clog dance up and down my frame is what I would like to know?"

I seen Chivvers come shouldering his way to the front of that mob. He was slavering with meanness and with hunger to get at the Chinaman. His fingers was working and wriggling like they was already fixed in that pigtail. And I got to admit that pigtails make me feel just that same way.

Says Chivvers: "Will you be a sport and give us the chink, Daisie? Or are you gonna sit here and kid along with us . . . ?"

I let out a little holler at that. Says I: "Do you call it kidding for a gent to lie down and get all peaceful to sleep, and then to have him wake up and find that gents have been jumping up and down on him while he was having a dream, and to have them kick dirt in his face when he opens his eyes? Is that your way of making a joke, Chivvers?"

"Aw, Daisie!" says Chivvers. "Be reasonable, will you? Aw, Daisie! My God, won't you just loan us that chink for a minute?"

They was all hopping around on first one foot, and then on another.

A voice yaps back in the crowd of them: "What have you got to do with Wong? What is that damn' sneak thief to you?"

"How do you know that he is a sneak thief?" says I.

"Chivvers has got his wallet stole," says somebody.

"Is the Chinaman the only gent in the world that likes money?" I asked them.

"Look here," said Chivvers, counting out his ideas on the tips of his fingers, "my wallet is stole. That's that! Somebody done it, then. That's clear. Does any white man step up and say that he done it? No, nobody claims to have done it. What is left but the chink that stole it? I ask you, ain't that logic, Daisie?"

Of course, it was. I thought it over and seen that Chivvers was right.

I looked down to the yellow face of the man, and I says: "You damn' little monkey-faced runt, now how did you get the grit up to swipe a wallet from a growed-up man?"

Wong didn't seem to hear me. He was still walling his eyes at the stars.

"All right," says somebody. "I guess that settles it. You better hand over that chink, Duff. We've tried reason with you. . . ."

It sort of disturbed me, the way that he said it. I got up and tucked Wong under my arm.

"You tried reason," I said. "Now what would you be trying next?"

They all looked up to me, but they didn't answer. Teacher hadn't taught just what to say.

Chivvers said: "But, aw, Daisie, wouldn't you please listen? What is the damn' chink to you?"

Now, you maybe know how you can get worked up about nothing at all. Of course, Chivvers was right. But I tell you that partly I was thinking about the taste of those beans. And partly it was just because I had started arguing the point, and I didn't want to be downed. And partly I was so stubborn just because I felt that I was all wrong.

"What have I got to do with this Chinaman?" says I. "Why, I got everything to do with him. This Chinaman,

175

he belongs to me, by a way of speaking. As long as you start arguing about that, why, I got a lot more to do with Wong than any of the rest of you."

I took Wong by the neck and set him down, real gentle, and held him while he stiffened his knees.

"Now you go right on back to your kitchen and finish with your cleaning up," says I.

"Mlister Daisie, ah, god damn, please save poor Wong!"

"I am saving you," I said. "You are all saved, and you don't have to worry about nothing, because nobody would hurt you. I tell you, that you would be surprised, Wong, was you to know the kindly feeling that is percolating through that crowd of lumberjacks and bohunks. They would rather burn their hands right off at the wrists than to lay them on you. So you step along and get on about your work, will you?"

I sat down, and the Chinaman backed up a little toward me, but, when he looked back, I waved him away because he was standing right between me and the fire.

He sort of caught the idea, then. And he begun to weave along through that crowd. None of them would move for him. They just stood like posts, and he sidestepped around, asking pardon of everybody and thanking everybody, and shaking so much you would think that he would fall to pieces. But nobody touched him, and I seen him get across the clearing to the edge of the firelight, and head for the kitchen door. Then he spilled forward out of sight.

The rest of the boys, they still stood around like posts, and stared at me and studied me, until I laid hold on a log and chucked it into the fire, and it sent the sparks washing out like water from a tub. But they just brushed the sparks over their clothes and their faces and damned a little, very quiet, by which I could see that they was real mad. However, I couldn't help that, so I lay down and closed my eyes again.

II

That was a gloomy night for the rest of the gang. But I rolled down my blankets and admired things in general until I got to sleep. When I woke up, the sun was sliding through the trees and a couple of the boys was calling for coffee. But there was no sign of the bucket of coffee that was always put outside the cook house door at daybreak. There was no sign of any smoke out of the chimney of that house, either. They busted open the door, and then we found out that Wong had cleared out. Five minutes later, half the crew was listing up the number of things that Chinaman had swiped. To have taken all that junk and carried it away, he would've had to be a cross between a sleight-of-hand artist and a mule. But, of course, a Chinaman is always handy to be blamed. If he didn't actually do you dirt, you feel that maybe he might have, and that amounts to about the same thing, somehow.

There wasn't much of a breakfast. Somebody volunteered to make coffee, but the stove smoked, and the water didn't really boil, so we got a mess the color of tea and the taste of boiled shoes. We had moldy bread to eat along with it, and, while the eating was going on, one of the boys says: "Daisie's chink made all of this here happen."

They all looked at me very dark, and you could see by the silence of them that I was the goat.

When things go wrong, you got to have a goat, because if there ain't a Jonah handy, you would have to blame yourself, and that would be walking in a circle.

So when the rest went off to work, I sat down to think and to listen to the cook they had elected damning to himself while he soused the breakfast tins through lukewarm water and calling them clean.

I was the Jonah, although I hadn't done anything worth mentioning to make the boys blue. Besides, I was a little tired of that camp. I had done enough work to get fit, and now the smell of the spring made me remember the lowlands, where the plains would be turning pink and white with wildflowers, about this time of the year. Also, maybe this was too far south for what I had done last autumn to matter.

So I went out and saddled Mary. She was a mule that looked enough like a moose cow to get herself shot, if she had started out across the range alone, but there was more sense in that big head of hers than you could shake a stick at, and two Montana sheriffs, the fall before, could tell you how she could shift the mileage when she ambled up a trail.

She had been living easy long enough to be sleeked up, only she was the kind that didn't sleek. Her head and neck and shoulders and quarters and legs was always the same, except in winter they was covered with goat's hair and in summer with sun-faded moss. She had a camel's hump with reverse English, as you might say. Hard fare made her skinny all over, but an easy time fattened her belly and nothing else. After those weeks in the camp, a head-on look at Mary was like a view of a potato stuck up on four matches. However, I could see that she was in good shape, because, when I came up with the saddle, she dived at me with her teeth, and then tried her heels. Mostly she never bothered about anything but biting. There was a tiger strain in Mary.

I took a half hitch in her upper lip and held it till she groaned, then I saddled her and put on her bridle.

At the cook house I stopped and called out the new cook. He was all over flour, including his hair, and there was a swab of grease and soot across his chin and cheek.

"The boss owes me twenty-eight dollars on the book," I said. "He ain't paying off till noon, and I've decided to start along now. Just lemme have that for an advance, will you, Harry? Here's my order for the chief to pay you."

I give him the slip of paper entitling him to collect my wages, but Harry read it through, and then turned it over and looked at the back. He seemed to keep right on reading where no words was wrote.

He said: "Daisie, there's nothing I'd like better than to please you. But the fact is, I'm busted. I been. . . ."

I didn't want to argue, because it might've heated him up and hurt his feelings. But I seen an edge of leather peeking out of his vest pocket, and so I reached out and gathered in his wallet. There was sixty-two dollars in that purse. So I took my coin and gave him back the rest and went on down the trail, feeling pretty good. Not that I had robbed Harry, but somehow money you take is always a lot sweeter than money that you borrow.

About two miles down, I opened a saddlebag to slip in my second Colt because I'm a one gun at a time man, and there a bit of red silk peeked up at me. I took it up by one corner like it was an insect that might sting, but it was sure red silk, and it was sure peppered with a little green embroidery. I unrolled it. It was a big handkerchief of the finest Chinese silk, and out of that handkerchief a golden dragon dropped. I mean to say there was a golden ring that Wong used to wear on his thumb when he was feeling pretty smart and big. It was the shape of a dragon with scales all enameled in green, and with two little rubies, like pinheads, for eyes, and a pair of wings curled up down its back. The work on that ring was so fine that a sparrow hawk would have had to use a microscope to see all the points of it. When Wong wore it, you better believe that he always kept the thumb that had it on turned up.

It tickled me a good deal. Slipping that into my saddlebag was so sort of modest and grateful that I felt that maybe Wong was pretty near human. Because usually when you do something for anybody, you hang around afterwards and try to look bored and say: "Aw, hell, that's nothing."

I tried that ring on my little finger of my left hand, and it was a pretty tight squeeze, but I managed to work it over the first joint by wetting the skin a good deal.

So we sashayed down the side of the mountain and came out after a little onto a place where we could peek at the southern valley. I had never been that direction before, but it all looked good to me. It was a big country, and I like room. There was just a streaking of mist in the air, but not enough to hide the green spots up and down the valley along the river. Those were farmlands, and so were the black patches that checkered the rest of the basin. Summer fallow, of course.

It was a long time since I had worked farmlands. Mostly I prefer lumbermen first, and miners second, and cowpunchers third. They all have less money and more cash than farmers, and it hurts them less to spend it. At a card table any undersize in cowpunchers would make an oversize in farmers. However, there is more real pleasure in trimming a farmer, even if there ain't so much gain, and art is something, in this here life of ours. The extracting of a ten dollar pot from a gang of hay pitchers is like squeezing water out of a handful of quartzite—hard on the hands, but good for the muscles.

So I took the air of that valley and decided that I might visit yonder town for a while. It was shaped like a pear cut in two by the river. The little end of the pear was crowded into a heap on one bank, and on the other bank the good part went swelling out and crowding into the country with an acre of lawn and a couple of trees in every front yard. I could tell that by the look of the place, and I knew that there was concrete gutters and macadam pavement, even though I was too far away to see them glitter in the sun—an up-and-going Western town without pavement feels like a Sunday collar and tie and no shirt at all.

The whole valley was prosperous, as I could see while Mary and me went down the length of it. All the signs on the fence boards and on the telegraph poles was pretty new and fresh, and at every crossroads there was sure to be a set of big boards plastered all over.

I took my time down that winding river road and let the posters drift through my head—hair tonic, sub-soil plows, the well-dressed man for fourteen dollars a suit, the Jones Brothers and their pills, canned beans, ten percent down and rest easy, waterproof paint, the First

National Bank for investments. . . . But while those words ran into the hopper the information into which they turned was: This is a growing town with lots of money and lots more coming, why not take your share?

I got out a pack of cards and began to limber up my fingers with a few little tricks—simple, but, oh, how useful! But I felt pretty guilty because I had been wasting so much time and getting so out of practice. Once I even dropped a card.

By the time that I reached the edge of San Rafael, I knew that all my guesses had been bull's-eyes. I could tell by the number of trees growing along the streets and the size of the washings that flashed along the lines in the backyards.

So I got to a stable, put up Mary, and went out to see the sights.

There was three moving-picture houses where the girl was saved from the villain, and there was one theater where super pictures could be seen for a dollar a head. This week Lawrence B. de Mulvaney's masterpiece, *Society*, was laying bare the secrets of the upper set.

I decided that I would have to shave and buy a new tie before I began to play my hand in this joint, otherwise I would be asked for references. But the farther I walked along those streets, the cleaner I could see myself leaving San Rafael with a pair of trunks and a suitcase, wearing a moniker and patent leather shoes to worry my poor feet. In a word, San Rafael looked good to me!

In front of the courthouse, a gent without a tie and with his shirt open was working up a sweat telling about how God made all men free and equal and particularly the working man, and a lot of gents and ladies, too, was standing about and saying: "How true!"

I listened to that lingo for a while, and then, as I eased away, I reached into my pocket and found that my money had been swiped. Even in San Rafael you couldn't go to sleep in the street.

III

While I was still smiling down at the sidewalk, I saw a shadow slide up and stop at my feet, so I raised my head and saw a tall, thin, brown-faced man with a pair of twinkling eyes.

"How do you do?" says he.

I picked him at once for a good poker face.

"Why, hello," says I. "I ain't seen you for a long stretch, have I?"

"No," he said, "this is the first time. I'm Bert Moonie, and I want you to remember me."

"Thanks, Bert," I said. "I'm Charlie Lang from. . . ."

He smiled a little. "I'd rather know you are Daisie Duff," said Moonie. "What are you doing in San Rafael?"

"If you're running the town newspaper," I said, "lemme see your card."

"No," said Moonie, "I run a free hospital. And here's my card."

He twitched open his coat a little, and I could see the flash of a sheriff's badge.

185

"Thanks," I said. "I hope I won't have to drop in on you before I leave town."

"I can tell you how to keep healthy," said the sheriff. "It's advice that I give to my patients over and over again, and it usually works. Fresh air and exercise, lots of exercise, is what I advise. And of all the exercise that I know of, the best is horseback riding down any of the roads leading out of this town."

"A change of air is often good," I said.

"It is," said the sheriff, grinning. "But sometimes my patients get so set in their habits it hurts them to change. What way are you thinking of traveling?"

I looked him in the eye, and I seen that he was polite but steady, very steady. "I'm traveling to some joint in San Rafael where I can get a twenty-cent meal. Where can I find the place?"

"Twenty cents?" he repeated. "Twenty cents?" And he measured me up and down and around.

"I had my money pinched back there," I explained, hooking a finger over my shoulder.

"Yes," said the sheriff, nodding. "He's a good worker. Quiet but earnest. He hypnotizes the crowd, and then his pals go through them. Maybe the three of them will be invited to my hospital for a little treatment pretty soon, but I never like to take a case until I can find the symptoms of the disease right on them."

"Well," I said, "they must have a temperature, by this time. But what about the twenty-cent restaurant?"

"There's nothing on this side of the river," said the sheriff. "But if you go over into Chinatown, you'll find three or four places where you might almost fill up on rice and such. However . . ."—he lingered for a minute and drew his eyes over me like a gun—"however, you'd better take fried potatoes and steaks. Here's my prescription . . . you could have it filled out right across the street." He wagged his head at a chop house, and then passed me a five spot.

I spent a minute studying it.

"So long, Daisie," he said.

"Wait a minute!" I called to him. "If I start this treatment, I'd have to continue with it, I suppose."

"Yes, that would be better."

"Change of air, exercise, and all that?"

"Exactly," said Moonie.

I handed back the five spot. "Thanks, but I always liked Chinese cooking."

"Are you sure?" said Moonie.

"Yes, I've made up my mind. Suppose that we shake hands before I start, old-timer?"

"Be careful of my hand," said the sheriff, "because it's the one I use for feeling pulses."

He turned off up the street with a sigh, and I went the other way, chuckling. It is always pretty comforting to meet a white man, but I wondered how long my game would last with the doors of that "hospital" standing open for me. And I wondered, too, where would I get the stake to start the game.

I crossed the bridge and walked down into Chinatown, through alleys so narrow that I was scraping a shoulder on each side of the passageways. At the first smell of food I turned into a doorway and sat down at a table. To the Chinaman that came bobbing and grinning toward me, I said—"Rice and tea."—and then sat back to wait.

But things started fast in that shop. The Chinaman just then looked down at my hand with Wong's ring on it. He gasped and padded to the rear of the restaurant. Then I heard a crash of dishes, and voices sing-songing high and low. It looked like trouble, more particular when the waiter came back and told me that the cook was sick, and there was no more rice, and, besides, the fire was out—good bye! I had a mind to ask more questions of that Chinaman and at closer range, but, when I started up, something whispered behind me. I turned around in time to guess at somebody drawing back into the shadow of a little niche in the wall and a wicked shiver went through me like quicksilver.

I decided that backing out of that restaurant would be the right way to make an exit, so I waded out of the door and stood in the street for a minute, wriggling my shoulders and letting the sun bite home between my shoulder blades. The curtain behind the restaurant window wrinkled back and around, a mean-looking Chinaman peered out at me. He gave me a stare and disappeared.

It was irritating, as you see for yourself. On top of being hungry, and losing my little stake of money, this treatment was a bit too much, and so I decided that I would pull the paper stuffing out of that place and find out why it had such a funny face. I went for the door, but when I tried the knob, bolts groaned and clicked from inside. They had fastened up shop against me.

I considered a minute about kicking the door in and going on with my investigation, but decided that maybe it was better not. Particularly in a town where Moonie's hospital was so open and free.

So I stepped back and went off down the street, feeling eyes knife me from both sides and behind.

It wasn't me. It couldn't be me. It had to be the ring. One half of my brain told me to get out of that net of twisting streets and shadows and whispers and singsong talk as fast as I could get, but the other half told me that something rare was in the air, and I had better try to get at the bottom of it.

So when I turned a corner and came straight at another eating house, I walked in again. I didn't want to make any mistake. I went in with my left thumb sticking through a buttonhole of my lapel, and my little finger wagging in full view, but the wooden-faced Chinaman that took my order didn't blink an eye. It seemed by this that Wong's ring was only poison here and there.

I hadn't a long wait.

When the waiter came back, he brought another wooden image that must have been his brother. Chinaman Number One spread out a piece of fine white silk over the top of my table. Chinaman Number Two, he fetched out a handful of punks and begun to light them, so that a dozen little worms of smoke were pretty soon wriggling up through the air and making a cloud of smell against the ceiling. That wouldn't do, though. He lighted a sort of hanging lamp, too, and walked up and down the place a couple of times and then hung it against the wall, where it poured out a brand new sort of smoke with a smell that made the punks as faint as a single rose compared to a bottle of perfume.

In the meantime, a silver dish came in, and I found that there was soup in it.

"Look here, John," I said. "I asked for rice and tea."

"Yes," said John, "rice plenty quick."

I watched him out of sight while I sipped that bowl of soup. It was warming, but not filling, but then John came back with half a dozen chops done brown and a siding of rice and half a dozen dishes filled with pickled sweet things, and bamboo shoots fried crisp, and ginger, and so much other stuff that I can't half remember it.

Besides all of that table load, there was a sort of an

air of waiting about that room, and a noise from the kitchen that made me think that more was coming.

I decided the fool Chinaman couldn't understand English. When I told him "rice and tea," he must have thought that I said "everything in the shop", so they began to light the wicks of lamps that didn't have any oil in them, and bring on the flock of food.

Maybe this would end in Moonie's hospital, but it tasted too much like a happy dream for me to worry about that. I stowed everything that was in front of me, and then I let out a link of belt and waited for the next crash on the cymbals.

This was what happened. In comes the pair of wooden faces packing big bowls in each hand, and in front of them comes traipsing along a Chinese girl with a marble face and lips painted orange-red and the biggest pair of black eyes that ever looked at the world. She was all done up in slimpsy silks, trousers, coat, and all, with a coil of jade beads flecked with gold around her neck and her slippers worked over with what looked to me like topaz and gold brocade.

"Hello, parade," says I, "are you the landlady?"

She fetched up close to my table and smiled at me a queer little smile that looked like it had been taught to come into the corners of her lips and never dared to get a spark into her eyes. She crossed her hands at her breast so that I saw the pink-stained tips of her fingers, and she gave me a little bow. Then she took the first bowl from the first Chinaman and put it on the table.

I recognized chicken and mushrooms, but the other twenty things in that dish was beyond me.

She took the other bowl and put it down.

Everything else that's good to eat was in the second bowl.

The first Chinaman had scooted out and come back

carrying a tray, and she took off of it a little ebony box with pearl scrollwork, and she fetched out a pair of silver tongs, not much smaller than her own white fingers, and took out a pinch of tea from that ebony box, and dropped it into a pot. Then from the tray that the waiter held, she took a pitcher of boiling water and poured it slowly into a pot, and the tea fumes and the steam rose up in a mist before her face, like incense across an idol.

IV

What all of this meant, beat me. I had a first idea that maybe it was the proprietress coming to be nice to a gent that had ordered everything in the restaurant. But now I seen that was wrong, and that I would have to make a tack around in another direction before I fetched to windward of the right solution.

But she was just a picture, and not a girl at all, and everything that she did looked as though she had been trained to it and done it by second nature, without thinking. She never hurried, but she got things done quick, and I noticed that there was never any noise. The little silver tongs didn't clink against the edge of the tea box, and the bowls didn't jar against the table, and she put on the top of the teapot as though it was a piece of felt.

Yet what made her more like a picture than anything else was the color of her skin, which was strange in the first place because I never had heard of a race of white Chinese. Her little round throat and her face was all carved of one white stone, and like stone they never changed color. The steam of the tea fumes didn't make her eyes dim, and the smoke of the punks and the incense didn't make them blink. In a minute I was feeling that she was more machine than human.

It sort of irritated me. Mostly ladies notice me. Which I don't mean that they like me particular, but they know when I'm around, and, when I meet a girl, she usually holds her breath as if she was wondering whether it was a man or a grizzly. However, just to be noticed is a comfort, and now I was a little peeved.

She was making herself useful, passing me the bread tray before I could reach for it, and filling my cup when it got low. So as I finished that second bowl of fodder, I reached out a thumb and forefinger and took her hand. It was soft beyond believing, and almost too cool to be flesh and blood, and made out of crystal that a light could shine through.

"Are you real?" I said, and looked up into her face.

Why, there was not a touch of pink in her cheeks, not a stir of nostrils, not a quiver of her lips, but the long black eyelashes went gradually down and covered her eyes.

I let go her hand, worse beat than ever, and just then somebody turned the knob of the door. It didn't open. I looked over my shoulder and seen that they had drawn the curtains and shut the blinds so that it looked as though the chop suey joint was closed for the day. But even that wasn't the crown of this queer place. Because now the boss of this place come in.

He was so fat that he had to lean backwards, and the front of him wobbled up and down as he walked, while the end of his long pigtail snapped like a whiplash at his heels. By the embroidery on his coat I guessed that he was quite a man, and, if I'd been in any doubt, the jewel work on his slippers would have made up my mind. He came along to my table, shoved his hands into his sleeves, and made as much of a bow as his stomach would permit.

Says he: "I am Shih Nung. You are welcome for your own sake and for the sake of that, also." He pointed a long-nailed claw at my ring and bowed again.

I could see that he was something special by the brand of English that he talked. He was perfect in it except that it bothered him a good deal to chop off the words, and, while he was talking, a sort of humming came out of his throat and filled in between words and ended the sentences with something like a groan.

Then he sing-songed something to the girl, and she give him a bow and give me a bow and turned herself around and floated out of the room. She could have walked through a field of standing grain like a cloud shadow, without no sound.

I watched her out of sight with the tail of my eye. "Look here, Shih Nung," I said. "There is some sort of funny business about this. I come in and ask for rice and tea, and the whole works are trotted out for me. Now what is the main idea?"

"A man cannot talk while he is hungry," said Shih Nung. "I shall have a roast of pork. . . ."

I watched to see him smile, but he seemed to be in earnest.

"This little lunch," I said, "is enough for me, because I hate to load up in the middle of the day. Now tell me what's what, because the first thing for you to know is that to pay for this spread, I've got twenty cents in my pocket."

"That is a pity," said Shih Nung, "but I have enough for both of us for a little while, and you are very welcome. Will you come upstairs and smoke with me?"

Even if it was a dream, there was no use turning my back on it. I unfurled myself from behind that table and followed him, out of the restaurant, down some steps, around a bend, through a hall, along a twisting flight of stairs, past an incline, and up to a door where Shih Nung turned a big key twice around and waved me into the room.

I was turning my wits more times than the key to unravel in my mind the trail that I had followed to this hang-out, because I hate to be lost. I hate it worse than a Yankee hates Saturday without beans.

There was something to see in that room, however. It was rather low and narrow, but it was long, and it was packed from one end to the other with comfort and color.

There was the girl before us. She was just slipping another cushion into the back of a big couch, and she stood back with another of her little bows to me. That was to be my place—that couch. I settled back into it, little by little. It was as soft as a cloud, and no matter how much I settled, there was always a few yards of me that kept on sinking, it seemed.

"It is a little warm," says Shih Nung, "but Feema will keep you cool."

That seemed to be the girl's name. She sat down cross-legged on a hard bench beside the head of the couch, and she worked a fan back and forth, showing me a black mountain against a silver sky on one side of it, and a dragon eating himself, tail first, on the other. The soft little *whish-whish* of the air kept whiffing across my face, and it was pretty comfortable.

"Now, Shih Nung," I said, "the way I was raised, the men do the fool things and the women make themselves easy. I feel sort of silly with this girl laboring over me."

"Does she bother you?" says Shih Nung.

A little green devil went snicker-flicker across his

eyes as he looked at the girl, and in the white of her wrist, as she turned the fan back and forth, I saw a bit of a tremor. It was the first suggestion I'd had that she might be human, but it was hardly proof, because that look in the face of Shih Nung would've made a wooden statue do a hundred yard dash.

"Oh, no," I said, "she ain't bothering me any. Only, I thought that if we were talking, maybe it would be better to be alone."

"She understands no English," says Shih Nung, "and, as for the rest, she is my daughter, and therefore is it not her duty to serve me?"

"By way of speaking," I admitted, "I suppose it is."

"Therefore," says Shih Nung, "how much greater is her duty to serve those who are greater than I."

He leaned back in his chair and nodded his head a little at me and went on grinning as before, as though he was tickled to death with the neat little way that he had ended off the argument. Because his face was always smiling and the yellow cheeks puckering back from his loose mouth, the wrinkles gathered around his eyes until they was only glints of light. Except when he sobered, and then you could see the smoky whites of his eyes.

I decided to let the girl slide. If she was raised to this sort of business, it might not do her any harm, and, besides, there was a scent like tea, or tea flowers, maybe, hanging about her. I was always partial to good smells. Besides, there was a couple of other things the China-man had said that started me thinking. He had said that I was greater than him, but what did he know about me except a guess at poundage, and even in that I wasn't half a hundredweight more than that big round tub of a man. But the next thing he had to say stopped me more than the greatness idea.

"Is Feema your daughter?" I asked him.

"Yes," said Shih Nung.

"Six days a week maybe she is," I said. "But on Sundays whose girl is she?"

"I don't understand," said Shih Nung.

"All right," I said, "if you don't want to talk about that, we'll try something else. What shall it be?" I took another look at the white hand of Feema, and then at the face of Shih, which was the color of my forefinger where nicotine has stained it.

I rolled a cigarette while Shih was saying: "Talk, my friend, of whatever pleases you. When your good time comes, you will tell me what commands are brought to me."

What commands I brought to him? It was plain that the ring still bothered him a good deal, so I decided to take him out of his haze with a straight story.

I simply said: "My name is John Duff. People call me Daisie. I was working up in a lumber camp a few days back, and the cook by name of Wong got into a ruction with the boys. I helped him out, and, before he slid out of camp that night, he put this ring into my saddlebag. Now, Shih Nung, there's the whole truth about the ring."

He didn't leave off smiling, although you never could tell what was tickling him.

"It is as much as you care to tell me," says he. "And that is well, Daisie Duff."

"It is the truth," I said. "Where do you poke a hole in it?"

"Ah," grunted Shih, "if you know nothing, how did you happen to go to Shien Tu's to frighten them before you came straight to me?"

"You mean the other chop suey place? I was hungry, Shih Nung. That's the short and the long of it. I have nothing to do with any Shien Tu, if that's the name you call them. But I know that they're a mean set. Ask something more, Shih, if you can't believe me."

But he just leaned back in his chair and kept on smiling and nodding. "I understand," he said. "Some of us must know, and some must not know. This is wise."

I lit my smoke and blew out a haze through which I could study Shih, but it was clear that he was serious, and just then a little silver bell clinkled and a hand came tapping at the door.

"It is Sing Lu," said the Chinaman, "and he wishes to marry my daughter. He is a rich man, but he is not one of us, Daisie Duff."

He looked at my ring with a sort of an apologetic air. And then he waved Feema to the door.

V

She let in the most whopping Chinaman that I ever seen. The floor creaked under him, and he ducked his head to avoid a hanging lantern. After he had been introduced to me and had told me in good English that he was glad to know me, he sat himself down crosslegged on a mat, and even sitting on the floor he seemed as tall as Shih.

If marrying was in his head, you would never think that Feema was his girl. His big square block of a face was never turned toward her for a minute, while he sing-songed in deep bass to Shih, and Shih Nung sing-songed back in his groaning baritone. Feema brought tea, and poured it for all of us, but Sing Lu took it without giving her a glance. He went on with his talk, and after a while he fetched out a silk purse, slipped back the rings, and began to count out gold pieces. He made three little stacks of them and passed them across to Shih, and Shih forgot to smile just long enough to let me see a look on his face like a man on the desert when he sees water ahead.

It was over very quickly. Sing Lu got up and told me

that he had been very happy seeing me, and that maybe we would meet again, he hoped, and then he sashayed out of the room.

I forgot to say that he was dressed exactly like any other Chinaman up to the chin, but above that point he'd graduated. He'd bobbed his hair, and he wore a broad-brimmed hat that he didn't bother to take off when he was indoors. However, his hair being short, I could study the back of his neck as he went through the door, and I knew by the set of it and the size of the cords that he was about the strongest heman that I'd ever laid eyes on. He looked padded all over, but his silk coat hung in a crease between the shoulder blades and fat isn't laid on that way. It was spread even, like butter on bread. It made all the punching muscles along my shoulder get hard to see the power in that Chinaman.

When the door closed on him, I said: "You've got other daughters, Shih Nung?"

He said that he hadn't, and, when I asked him if Feema was the one that was to marry Sing Lu, he said that she was. It made me turn and take another look at her.

"Does she like him?" I asked, with my eyes still on her face.

Shih Nung looked at me, a little dazed, and took the pipe out of his mouth.

"I do not understand," said Shih. "He is paying a good price."

It was my turn to blink. "A good price?" I repeated.

"Fifteen hundred dollars," said Shih, "is more than most girls can bring. But Sing Lu has American eyes. He wants a pretty face."

The idea simmered down to the solid parts. What I had just been looking at was a Chinaman paying earnest money on his wife-to-be, and, while I've rode or sailed over a good part of the world, I never grounded on anything that shook me up as much as that. Because it would be like taking down a picture from the wall of my own house, somehow the idea of Feema had sunk into my head so far, and I knew that I could never smell tea in my life without seeing her again and the nightmare of knowing she was sold to that block-faced Chinaman, Sing Lu.

"Shih Nung," I couldn't help saying, "is it right?"

Well, he opened his eyes again, as though the right or wrong of it was a question to be asked on Mars, not here on the earth.

"Is it wrong to sell a horse?" said Shih Nung.

"Why, no," I answered.

"But is a horse born in your family?" said Shih.

It stumped me. I rubbed my chin and thought the thing over for a while.

"Also," explained Shih, "she has not been easy to sell. For years I have been trying, but other men come to look at her, see her, and are frightened. Because men do not want a wife who thinks."

"Does she think?" I asked.

"Every woman who is silent thinks too much," said Shih Nung, holding out his pipe for Feema to fill.

I looked at her again. I would never have accused her of being anything but a picture, but her own father ought to know a bit about her.

"She's older than she looks, then," I said.

"She has been on my hands a long time," said Shih Nung with a sigh. "She is eighteen."

Eighteen! I looked at her pink-stained fingertips and her red-painted lips, and all at once I felt a good deal like my first trip at sea—mighty lost and unhappy.

Shih Nung was talking again. He was telling me that,

while I would stay in the house, he would be the happiest Chinaman on this side of the world, and would I do him the honor of seeing my room?

I would do him the honor, right enough. Because, somehow, I felt that there was things in my head that needed thinking over. About the world in general and about Feema in particular. So Shih showed me a little room all done up in pink and blue and yellow and violet. The two wooden-faced waiters were just putting a second bed along with the first one, and making it one for one. So it was plain to see that I could be comfortable here.

When we come back into the other room, Shih Nung asked me again when I would be ready to tell him the commands I brought him.

Just how far I could go, I couldn't tell. I fixed my eyes on a big picture at the end of the room, done of paper, and showing a big fellow with a pair of horns growing out of his head, and a long, narrow beard like a black spider sticking out of his chin, and his trousers tied around above the ankles, and a big curved sword in each of his hands, and his lips grinned back from his teeth. He was on one foot and looked like he was dancing mad. But it helped me to think, watching the face of that Chinaman in the picture. I wondered who it was that had ever wanted to look like that.

"There's only one thing, first off," says I to Shih. "But maybe you've guessed it already. Feema can't marry Sing Lu."

I could see a fire of suspicion and anger and doubt flare across his eyes.

"Feema?" says he. "Do they even know that I have a daughter?"

Whoever "they" might be, it was plain that I was supposed to have my marching orders from somebody. I looked the fat man up and down, trying to think of something to say. I wanted something mysterious, and I didn't know what to say.

Finally this came out of me of its own accord: "You wouldn't marry your girl to a dead man, Shih Nung?"

Shih Nung wobbled a little. "Sing Lu is marked!" says he. "And what . . . ?" He stopped himself so short that he almost bit off his tongue. "I do not ask," says Shih Nung, and busted into a sweat, as though his asking why Sing Lu could be "marked" was about the worst thing that he could've done in the world.

By the drift of all of this chatter, I gathered one thing for sure—which was that Wong must have given me the ring of a Chinaman from some strong secret society that had a little habit of checking off its enemies, now and then. I had hit the spot by luck.

"However," says Shih, "if the money is paid to me, could not the thing be done before they are married?"

He looked hopeful and sort of expectant, the old scoundrel. It was the same as crying: "Can't I collect all of the coin of Sing Lu, and then, before the marriage, won't you have him knifed . . . as long as the job has to be done someday." He was a cool one, was old Shih.

"These here things," I says, "are all done when the right time comes. Feema don't marry Sing Lu."

He thought it over, getting whiter and whiter. "I have taken twelve hundred dollars from Sing Lu," says he. "And I have only this three hundred and a little more with me. . . ."

"You blew in the rest?" I asked.

"I have gambled against devils," says he.

"All right," says I. "Give me that last three hundred, and you can pay him off the whole slice tomorrow."

Now, no matter what the society was that this dragon ring belonged to and no matter how much this Chinaman respected it, he respected hard cash just about as much. There was never a slicker man in the world than old Shih Nung, but he handed over the gold, and I let it chug down in my pocket.

Then I went outside, with Shih trailing along behind me to the head of the last flight of steps, with his hands stretched out a little after me, like he still had something to say but couldn't quite find the right words for it.

So me and three hundred dollars walked out into the street, and the minute that I felt the bright white sun in my face and took a breath of the open air, Shih Nung and Sing Lu and the Shien Tu and Feema turned into nothing like a spider web, all shining one minute with the dew on it, and lost sight of the next with the dew shaken out.

All that I had with me as I walked down the street again was a rounded-out feeling in the stomach, and the weight of the good gold in my pocket. My conscience always worked on hinges. Blood money that a Chinaman took from selling his girl it was almost rightful to hook. So I put the whole crowd behind my back and started back to the last ideas that had been crowding through my head before I found that my wallet had been pinched.

I got to a clothing store and found something that would do for me in the way of shirts, as long as a slit was cut from between the shoulders of them. I got a white collar with a splice put onto the buttonhole in front, and a big black necktie to cover up the gap. There was no hope of finding shoes that would fit, but I got my boots polished while I waited for my clothes to be cleaned, and, when I stepped out at last with a good Stetson on my head, I looked good enough to sit at a table with the most respectable kind of crooks.

Before the day was turning into shadows, I found them.

VI

The minute that I seen them, the only thing that I worried about was would my fingers be fast enough to keep up with my ideas? They were stacked to the gunnels with money, and they were crooked as eels. I knew they were by the first look that I laid on them, and in a minute or two they were inhaling my story about how I owned most of the good timber in Oregon and how I had come back to my old cowboy home to get away from the financial burden of having to sign checks and the miserable grind of raking in the money with both hands.

They were mighty sympathetic. The way that a man could be hounded by terrible business pressure was a sad thing. It turned out right away that one of them was an oil man from Oklahoma that owned about everything except what the Indians had staked out, and the skinny, white-faced one was from Wall Street, where the finance kings bumped their heads on the sidewalk every time this bird walked by, and the good-natured one had most of the cotton fields of Alabama under his thumb. So here was four tired businessmen gathered by luck in San Rafael and too weary to do anything but shift the cards.

I played very large and simple. I couldn't help grinning and laughing a good deal while I took in a couple of five dollar pots, and I began right away to boost the betting into the hundreds.

They told me that this game was only for fun, but the good-natured boy from Alabama, he said that if I wanted to spread myself, what did it matter. And wasn't it a crime to stop me when I was in a winning streak?

Yes, they had me all wrote down for some big money, and they didn't miss letting me get a hundred or two before they started trimming me.

I saw after the first couple of rounds that I would have to work fast. In my own little way I'm not bad with a pack of cards, but these fellows was dyed-in-the-wool. With the sky for a limit, I made eight hundred in two rounds—and then I lost five of that at the next turn, and got six back in another minute. But here I knew that they were playing me for something real, and, as the cards came to me for my deal, I made up my mind to make my clean-up on the spot. Those crooks were too fast for my company.

I was mighty liberal. I gave out three queens to the New Yorker, and two pairs to the Cotton King. And in the draw I let the Alabama man fill and handed him from New York a little sneaking pair of deuces. With two full houses up, I thought that a bit of betting might be in order, and it was. I got my whole wad of cash up. When it came to the showdown, I laid a straight flush on the table and collected.

When they saw that flush, they knew that they hadn't picked a sucker, and they looked a mite sick. They looked still sicker when I pushed back my chair and stood up. Over in the corner, the little Chinaman, who had just brought in the cigars, flicked his eyes over their faces.

Up to that time, it had been me that he was watching, and it hadn't been hard for me to figure out that he had had a word from Shih Nung. No matter what sort of a ring I wore, Shih Nung wasn't trusting me to expose his three hundred to the open air too long, and, if I tried to leave town, I would have some Orientals on my trail. However, that didn't worry me because I'm not of a worrying nature.

When I stood up, I simply said: "Close air bothers me, gents. It's about time for me to take a turn outside."

They looked at each other, and the little white-faced runt from Manhattan laid the barrel of a mean-looking automatic on the edge of the table.

"Sit down, Oregon," he said. "Sit down and we'll talk it over. We don't play with pikers, y'understand?" He had some reason on his side, and that automatic was a good deal in his favor.

I said: "All right, Wall Street. I see that you don't trust me. But if you want to take more chances with my winning streak, I'm with you!"

So I dragged up my chair and leaned over as if to sit down. Well, it wasn't a very big table, and, when I leaned, I was in easy reaching distance. I just closed my fingers over his gun hand. The pistol said *rat-tat-tat* under my arm and blew three little round holes in the wall behind me, but that wasn't where New York had aimed, and he would never aim again for a long time. I felt the bones give under my grip, and he screeched like a wildcat in a trap.

They were active workers. Alabama had draped himself around my legs, and Oklahoma had heaved up a chair to bash across my head.

So I picked off the cotton king by the nape of the neck and the seat of the trousers and held him up for the chair to hit. Then I threw the remains of him in the face of the oil baron and left, just stopping to lock the door behind me.

The hotel proprietor with a gun in each hand came down the hall at me, and a couple of his boys behind him. I told him that there was a ruction in the card room and that I'd nearly got myself killed and I would have his hotel sued for breach of peace.

He just give me a snarl and charged on past, so I went out and took the open air in my face.

They hadn't unknotted the tangle back in the hotel by the time I turned the first corner, but I seen over my shoulder that a shadow was slipping along behind me. I put on a bit of speed, rounded down the next street, and back-stepped into a doorway. The shadow came by, running soft and low, so I reached out and gathered him in. It was the cigar-holding Chinaman, right enough.

"Where are you hurrying to in this here dark night, son?" I asked him.

Well, he didn't waste time. He worked a slungshot out and slugged at the side of my head with it, so close that it knocked my hat off. So I gave him a squeeze until he stopped moaning, and then sat him up on the doorsteps to come to. After that I headed for Mary.

Right and left of me, I could see mighty shapely horses standing, asking to be took, but I am mostly a hundred pounds extra for horses, and even if Mary didn't have the foot, she had plenty of stomach and she would never stop going until she was as gaunt as an archway. So I headed for Mary down back alleys, and so it was that I come past an open kitchen window and peeked in at two old folks sitting down for a late supper.

I backed up and looked again. They was so old you would have to count in tens to reckon them up, and they sat at a table covered with red oilcloth. She was eating crackers and butter. He had a chop.

"But I couldn't eat no meat," I heard her saying. "I got no appetite this hot weather. . . ."

The old boy lifted up his head and looked at her with the youngest, bluest eyes you ever seen. He didn't say nothing, but I knew that he understood, and tomorrow *he* would lose his appetite.

I got out a handful of greenbacks and stuffed them under the edge of the geranium pot on the windowsill as the old woman tipped the teapot and the fragrance of it come drifting out to me as dim and small as the voice of a dead pal out of your mind.

But when I walked along again, I was seeing Feema pouring my tea. With just this difference. That when I took her hand, her eyes flashed at me, blue as the sea. It gave me a queer twist inside. It stopped me in the dust of that alley, damning a little.

Did she have blue eyes? *I'll go back and make sure,* I said to myself.

If you go back, you're going to find a Chinese knife stuck in your back before morning, said myself to me.

I will only have one squint at her, said me to myself.

You are a lyin' fool, said myself to me, *and you know it.*

It's only to make sure about the color of her eyes, says me to myself.

Old son, said myself to me, *the way this little old world is made, there are worse things than knives in it!*

But when you get into an argument like that with yourself, the first idea is the one that mostly wins. I told myself that I was not going to be a fool, and that I would stop the nonsense and go straight to Mary. She was a sure cure for day dreaming, was Mary.

So straight to Mary's stable I went. But when I got to it, me took charge and walked myself right on past and down the next alley and toward the hump-backed bridge that went across the river to Chinatown.

I leaned for a minute against the rail and looked at the little red and yellow snakes of light wriggling across the water, and I listened to the black river come hushing through the piers of the bridge. It was worse than poker.

Over ahead of me, Chinatown stepped up against the sky in heap on heap, with a thousand dim little lights in them. There was so many folks in that heap that you couldn't shoot a rifle bullet through a single house without killing a couple. It was worse than poker and automatics, too. But, thinking about Feema, I got myself in hand and felt strong enough to walk up and bust open a block of those buildings like a pack of matchboxes.

So I went through Chinatown. The little scuffling shadows gave me room on either side, but, as I passed along, I could feel them turning around behind me to look.

But there was never any voices talking very close at hand. Only, far off in the distance, you could hear somebody sing-songing, and nobody answering, and nobody caring, and everybody with lots of time for everything.

It was a fine atmosphere for sleeping, but in that section of the town I could guess that sleep wouldn't be healthy for either myself or me.

VII

The door of Shih Nung was open. I saw no bell for ringing and no need of rapping, so I just walked up and found Shih sitting cross-legged like an Indian in front of a tray. Back-breaking work for him to reach over and help himself from the floor level, you would say, but he didn't have to. Feema sat on her heels and did the reaching for him.

When he turned his fat smile on me and his eyes wrinkled out of sight, I nearly forgot about the cigar boy. It's a grand thing to be happy and it's not so bad just to look happy, so you might say that Shih was born with money in the bank. He asked me had I had supper, which I hadn't, so I sat down opposite him and tried to be comfortable.

Maybe Shih thought that I wasn't coming back with his gold, but, anyway, he had served up dinner for two. He worked largely with a pair of little wooden sticks and done pretty good, but I made out with a horn spoon—Feema handing the things around. It made my fingers ache, to watch her sitting on her heels that length of time, but she was a machine where the

211

hinges never got rusty and there was never any sign of pain in that stony face of hers.

I set me to watching, but I couldn't make sure of the color. Mostly her looks was fixed down. She only guessed what a man wanted, but she always guessed right. If her eyes raised for a flash, what with the length and the blackness of her lashes and the shadows they threw, I could never be sure.

After eating, I had one of Shih's cigars, which was prime, and he sat back and smoked his pipe. It was three feet long, but the bowl at the end of it only held a pinch of tobacco at a time, so Feema was busy every minute or so knocking out the ashes and filling it again, and holding the light.

"Has she eaten?" I asked Shih.

"She will eat when her time comes," he answered. "Now I wish to speak to you about Sing Lu."

It was quite a piece that he had to say, at that. He told me how Sing Lu was the son of a rich man who had come over from China and gathered in some good bottomland down by the edge of the river, and how he had pumped water, by hand, to irrigate his vegetable patch, and then he had carried the hamper of vegetables into San Rafael and peddled the stuff about the streets. After ten years or so, he saved enough money to expand a little, and he kept right on expanding until he had the vegetable trade of San Rafael sewed up and put in his pocket. He still kept right on branching out. He made money so fast that he had to loan it out, and his money loans gradually worked all through the folks of Chinatown. He wasn't a bank. He was better than a bank. Banks was held down to six percent, but old Lu asked twenty without blinking an eye, and he got it. Sometimes he lost interest and principal. But mostly he collected, and, when they couldn't pay, he took over the shop or the house or the land, or whatever it was that was security. Finally he had Chinatown in his hand. Shih showed me by stretching out his fat fingers and closing the long claws as though he was squeezing a throat.

I followed all of this, because any newsboy-to-president yarn is interesting, but I didn't see what it all had to do with Sing Lu, except that it showed how he could afford to blow fifteen hundred dollars for a wife. I told Shih where I was in the dark, and he put me right.

It seemed that the point was that Sing Lu was like his father but extended in every way a good deal. His father was a strong fellow, but Sing Lu's hand closed just as fast, and it gripped a great deal harder. Where old Lu had one man under his thumb, Sing had two. Old Lu had just dealt in bodies and houses and lands and negotiable stuff like that. But Sing Lu dealt in souls, too. He had folks that was willing to jump in the river for him.

Now it happened that Sing had gone along for years and years and had never looked at a girl to make his wife in Chinatown, except that once he had gone out and made a dicker to marry a white girl, and it was at that time that he had cut off his hair. But he had come back from the deal with a couple of bullet wounds through his body, and after that he gave up the white wife idea. But finally he saw Feema, and he had gone off his head about her.

"It seemed to me, Shih," I said, "that Sing Lu kept hold of himself pretty well, the only time that I ever seen him with Feema in the room."

"Sing Lu is not a boy," said old Shih, and grinned at me.

There was a good deal in what he said. There was

still more around the corner of his words, as you might say, and, as I looked at his glinting eyes, I gathered what he meant. Sing Lu was not a boy. No, he was reasonable deep, and he kept his feelings out of his face.

Now all of this led up to the main point, which was simply that, if young Sing missed Feema, he would start a ruction that would tear the yellow part of San Rafael into bits, and he would never stop until he got the girl, or his money.

When I heard that, I reached into my pocket and counted out the whole story of fifteen hundred into Shih's sweating hand.

I have never seen a man so thoroughly surprised. He was shaken right down to the roots of him. The smile went out and left his cheeks hanging in flabs, while for the first time I got a fair and open look into his eyes, and there I saw one flabbergasted Chinaman.

"Are you rich, Daisie Duff?" he said to me at last.

I smiled back at him and thought it a good time to tap the green dragon that I wore on my little finger, and Shih blinked again. Still he didn't seem to make it out, and I had to count out the idea to him with gestures. That fifteen hundred was for paying back Mr. Lu. It was to shut him off from the girl.

Finally he swallowed the whole line of thought, and, as he gripped the money, he said: "If Sing Lu will take the money back. . . ."

What he left unsaid was to the effect that if Sing Lu didn't want to take the money back, and held Shih to the contract, then what would happen to Shih? What would happen with the big hand of Lu ready to grab him and toss him, for instance, into that black river that never told tales?

"As for that, Shih," I answered, "I'll stay on here long enough to see that Sing Lu stays quiet. Will that do?"

Now I expected to see that Chinaman show a little relief, and he did, but not as much as I thought was coming. He measured me up and down and nodded his head, as though I might be a comfort to him, but still he seemed to think that he might have to fall so hard that even I couldn't break the shock.

So I leaned over and tapped fatty on the shoulder. "Shih," I said, "you don't know me, but take my word that you'll have no trouble."

His mind twisted back to something else. He wanted to know, and he wanted to know bad, if it was really the desire of the society to stop this sale of his daughter to Sing Lu, and wasn't it a fact that it was all an affair of my own?

I could see that my opinion didn't count, so I told him that everything I did was dictated by the society.

Even then, Shih wasn't happy. He went to the window, mumbling to himself, and looked out over the roofs of Chinatown. Then he came back and showed me a face looking sort of streaked and flabby. He was so upset that, when some footsteps came padding in slippers to the door, he fairly jumped.

Feema went and listened to a string of Chinese lightning that sung high and low. Then she came back, and I heard her voice for the first time. It was small as the voice of a child, and pitched rather low, and the sound of it stuck in my mind and percolated through me, little by little, and kept on seeping inwards and downwards.

Shih Nung translated, and I was more than a mite interested.

The message was all about some trouble that had happened over in the bigger half of San Rafael. Four men had sat down to a quiet game of cards, and that game had only gone a little while when three holes was drilled through the wall by a pistol, and, when the

215

boys broke in to see what was wrong, one of the four was gone and the other three was all apart. They carried them to the hospital and pieced them together and got some sort of a story out of them about a man from Oregon, and now the sheriff was looking around for a quarter of a ton of man by name of Daisie Duff.

"They thought," said old Shih with a twisting-around-the-corner look at me, "that my friend would be glad to hear about these things."

I admitted that I was, and I told Shih that, after all, it might be a fairly good idea for me to start right out of town without stopping to ask any questions.

Shih said: "You have no fear of Sing Lu?"

"Old-timer," I said to Shih, "Sing Lu is a good deal of a man, by the look of him, and, if he has as many friends as you say, he might be able to make a lot of trouble, but even if he had as many limbs as a centipede, he wouldn't make the half of one side of the sheriff of this here county."

"But," Shih said, "there are places where the sheriff may not think of looking."

When I remember back to the way that a man had to go to get to this room of Shih's, I was ready to agree. Part of those stairs was above the ground, but part of them was below, and, wherever you went, there was doors opened and shut, and there was glimpses of more passages right ahead.

I couldn't help laughing at the idea, but I put a good deal of faith in that Chinese puzzle, and I said: "Keep the sheriff from me, Shih, and I'll keep the hands of Sing Lu off of you."

"That will be done," said Shih Nung. "I have places where you and your woman will both be safe."

"My woman?" I said, very empty of ideas.

"Yes," he said. "Your woman." And he nodded at Feema.

"*My* woman?" I yelled at him.

He held out both hands and shrugged his shoulders. "Is this not your money?" Shih Nung asked. "Have you not paid my price?"

Well, myself said to me, *I'm damned!*

VIII

Why, of course, you could see how Shih had worked it out. He was too good a businessman even to hope that he could get something for nothing. He had fifteen hundred dollars paid him for his daughter, and a bang-up price he considered it. Since the payer wasn't the other Chinaman any more, but me, why he transferred her over to me with a wave of his hand.

I mean it is easy to sit down at a distance and think the thing out the way it must have gone through the head of Shih, but, right then and there, I was flabbergasted. I looked at him and then at her stone face, while Shih chattered a bit at her, and she said a little song back.

"It is finished," said Shih. "I was afraid that she might not wish to change from Sing, because, as I have just been telling you, he is a very great man, but it seems that she *will* change, and she says that she knows how to obey." He rolled back and nodded at me, until his fat jowls wobbled. "I have made her a good daughter," he explained, "and therefore she will make you a good wife."

I was reaching out on all sides of me, as you might say, trying to get hold of some sort of ideas that would be useful for explaining to Shih. There was no use to tell him that, take me by and large, I had as many faults as any two men, but still I hadn't sunk down to the level of having a Chinese wife. I would sooner have been a squaw man. No, I couldn't start talking to him about ideals, and such things. But I hit on something shorter and straighter.

"Look here, Shih," I said, "traveling around the way that I do, from pillar to post, y'understand, how could I manage with a wife? There ain't anything wrong with Feema. She's as pretty as a picture, and all of that, and she sure acts useful, but what would I do with her? Put her in a saddlebag?"

Shih Nung glinted his eyes at me and waited.

"So," I said, "you take this here girl back. You could use her fine around your house. So you take her back, and all I say is that she isn't to go to that scoundrel of a Sing Lu. I don't like the looks of that Chinaman."

Shih Nung gaped a minute at me, but then he looked like a man trying a brand new kind of drink and mighty pleased with it. He babbled something at Feema, and then he turned back to me and told me how grateful he was, or tried to tell me, but I was so relieved at getting out of this mess that it made me sleepy and I couldn't help yawning.

Having had fifteen hundred dollars presented to him as a gift, old Shih was a pretty attentive host, and, when he saw me yawn, he said that it was time for me to have a good sleep, and he added that, being where I was, maybe I would be pretty wise always to keep plenty rested so's when I was awake I would have my eyes open.

I was beginning to think the same way, what with the

219

sheriff on the look-out for me on one side, and Sing Lu about to be turned loose on the other, that section of San Rafael was apt to begin to hum, as far as I was concerned. So I got up and said good night and started for my room, and the minute that I got started, Feema got up and snaked along behind me.

I turned around and said: "Shih, what's the meaning of the parade?"

It seemed that she still thought she belonged to me, and you can lay your money that Shih didn't sit quiet and let that idea keep in her head. He busted into some high-powered talk and worked for a minute or two, but, when he got done, she said just two words. I didn't know what they were, but I did know that they meant she didn't understand. When I turned for the door again, she kept right on after me.

I hollered to Shih for help, and he busted up and stepped in between me and her. He had done himself proud before, but it was nothing compared to the way he worked now. He must have distilled pounds and pounds of blubber, the way that he laid down the law to her, and finally he grabbed her by the arm and dragged her across the apartment, and pitched her in the direction of the opposite door.

She nearly stumbled and whacked the floor, and, if she had, I would have taken the head of Shih off his fat neck, but she was as neat as a cat on her feet, and she got her balance back and started right back for me. Shih made a pass at her, shouting, but her footwork would've done credit to any light-weight champion the way that she passed him up and came straight to me. She stepped up against me and turned around to face Shih, as much as to say: "This here is where I belong."

"Shih," I said, "can't you do nothing?"

"She will not talk," said Shih, sweating and looking black as murder. "Will you order her to explain?"

"Feema," I said.

She turned around to me, when she heard her name, and tipped her face to me. So I scowled and pointed a stiff arm toward Shih and waved her away.

She began to talk, then. There was no more expression on her face than there had been before, and her voice was wonderfully pleasant, but lifeless. It went along like the noise of a brook on a hot sunny day. You think that there's a lot of variety and change in it. But when you listen close you find out that it's repeating the same bubblings and humming and purrings over and over. It was the same with Feema. Press a button and she could walk like a fairy. Press another and she would wait on the table like a dog-gone angel. Press another and she could even talk.

But still she was just a machine.

She finished up, and Shih done a little translating.

The way he put it, Feema said that she had been honorably bought by an honorable man. That instant she ceased to belong to her father. She belonged to her husband. She had not harmed her husband. She had done no wrong. If she had done wrong, I could explain what it was, but, in the meantime, she did not understand how she could be sent away.

While Shih translated, that girl stood there and watched my face with her big eyes, dead black in the shadow that fell on them. She watched me the same way that a sleepy kitten watches its mama, or the way that a fat trout with a belly full lies on the bottom of a gravel bed and lets you trail flies across the surface of the water.

I mean it was dead easy to see that she knew she

was right and that nobody with good sense could possibly find anything wrong with her position.

"Damnation, Shih!" I said. "Ain't there anything more that you can do?"

"I have done my best," said the old skinflint. "She was once mine. I have sold her. Everything now must be done by you."

Well, I hung my head a minute, but no inspiration come to me. So I turned toward the doors. And *slip-slip*—along come her feet behind me.

So I whirled around and let out a roar that made the ceiling rattle. "Get out!" I bellowed at her. "You're not my wife! You wooden face, don't you understand? I don't need you! I don't want you. Marrying chinks is not my way. Exit. Finish. Beat it. Vamoose. On your way. Lead off. Forward march. Can't you understand plain English? Damned if I ever seen such a sap!

"Shih Nung, you tell her that the reason I been eating so light today is that yesterday I had a good square of real meat. Tell her that I eat it *raw!* Raw, y'understand!"

I made this here little speech with a few more additions, and, while I talked, I waved my hands a bit, until I barked my knuckles on the ceiling, and I made the most ugliest faces that I could think up. But that wooden image stood there with her hands crossed on her breast, and the pink tips of her stained fingers as steady as though she was carved in place, and her head bowed a little so's I could look at the back of that uncommon well-rounded neck.

When I had heated myself up a good deal, I flung out of that room and crashed the door shut behind me.

But when I got to my sleeping room, dog-gone me, if a shadow didn't come right in at my heels. I couldn't hardly believe it, but, when I turned me around, there was that girl. Yes, sir, you wouldn't think it was possible, but there she was. For the first time in my life, I was pretty near staggered by any one person. I leaned against the wall until I got my wind back and my brain stopped whirling. Then I opened the door and picked her up under the armpits and lifted her into the hallway. I took her chin between my thumb and forefinger and tipped up her head, real gentle.

"Honey," I said, "you are mighty sweet to look at, you are the best looking China doll that I ever laid eyes on, but you won't do. The Chinese way ain't my way. When I marry, I marry white, even if I've lived black. Besides, this here ridiculous slave business has got no meaning to me. It ain't right. Marriage, girl . . . why, marriage . . . why, hell!"

There was no use. Her face never changed the least mite in expression. I might as well be the wind blowing as a human being speaking to that picture lady. I dropped my hand, and she dropped her head, with the two little pink spots, one on each side of chin, where I had been touching her.

Then I went back into my room and locked the door and closed all the bolts, and lay down on that bed. But I was plumb nervous. I never felt so shaky and done up in my life, hardly. There seemed to be a weight leaning against that locked door from the outside, and, when I finally couldn't stand it any longer, I jumped up and tore the door open.

Why, you may have guessed it already. There she stood with her hands shoved into her sleeves, waiting and never complaining. Never seemed to come into her fool head to whimper, any more than it ever come into her brain to understand the plainest talk in the world.

I looked at her, and I knew that for the first time in my life I was beat.

IX

What was I to do? What would you have done?

I felt a whacking big need for some womenfolk to come along and take charge of this numbskull. But if I called in some Chinese ladies, most likely they would draw as blank as her.

Somehow what done me up worse than anything else was that the pink spots on either side of her chin had turned into little faint purple shadows. Why, I hadn't meant to hurt her a mite, only to explain. She seemed to be made like one of them flowers. Camellias, I think. They lose color when you touch 'em.

Well, all I could think of was to open that door wide, and prop a stool against it. Then I wrapped me up in a rug and lay down on the floor, and damned the Chinese and Chinese ways, quiet and steady, until I talked myself to sleep.

When I woke up with the light prying at the dinky little window of the room, there was Feema sitting on the stool against the door, asleep, with her head fallen on her shoulder and her hands folded in her lap.

It give me a wrench to see her. I picked her up, very

careful under the knees and under the shoulders, and, as I hefted her, she murmured something against my breast, but she was sleeping as sound as a child, and shivering a little all over with the cold. So I laid her on the bed, and, as I covered her up, she give a little sigh and dropped a thousand leagues deeper asleep.

Then I leaned out the window and seen the good, honest sun streaming over the top of Chinatown and making the river burn like white-hot steel, and covering all the morning fields with silver, and, Lord, Lord, how I hankered to be on the back of Mary and footing it up one of the out-trails from San Rafael.

However, I had to do a mite of thinking before I could vamoose. I went out into the big room and sat down with a cigarette and tried to work the puzzle out, but, no matter where I started, I always come out at the same end. Feema!

Later on, the town woke up—there begun a rattling in the streets, and sing-songing like the humming of bees far and near. Then Shih Nung come in, and Feema a little later, carrying tea and things for breakfast, and looking as fresh as though she'd slept on a featherbed all night long.

No, sir, there was no way of beating that girl. There was nothing else like her, and, when I watched her sitting on her heels and handing things out, I sort of despaired worse than ever.

Old Shih was a bit thoughtful, too, and after breakfast he said he was sending for Sing Lu to tell him that the deal was off and to give him back his money. And if Sing happened to take things the wrong way, would I mind listening in behind the next door?

No, I wouldn't mind. Because, of course, that was my duty, after letting in the old Shih for this deal. I sat down behind Shih's own door and hoped that there would be trouble, because the head of steam that was worked up in me had to get some outlet or else I would explode.

After a time I heard Sing come in, with the floor squeaking under the weight of him, and Shih turned loose his song, ending up with the chinking of money. Sing Lu hadn't said one word up to that time, and now he let out a *woof!* like a bear, and I heard a squeal from Shih no louder than a whisper.

I tossed the door open and seen Sing quietly throttling Shih and rapping his head on the floor. When he seen me, he threw Shih away and came at me with a bound. For a big man, he could move wonderful fast, and what gave a point to his speed was a knife a yard long that he had uncorked as he started for me.

I ducked at the flash of it, and it nipped off my scalp lock as it slithered past. That was how sharp it was. If Sing Lu hadn't been so blind mad, he would have chopped me in two, but, as it was, my shoulder hit his ribs so hard that he grunted like a horse when it settles into the collar and the knife rattled on the floor behind me.

Him and me spilled across the floor. I wasn't in any hurry, because I felt that the game was mine, and that was where I made my mistake, because wrestling is one of the games that Chinese learn, and anything they learn, they learn right. In the time it takes you to say damn, he tied a stranglehold on me, and I was lying face down, with him on top.

Altogether, it was plumb awkward. He was an India-rubber Chinaman. There was nothing but hard muscle in him, and there was tons of that.

All I could see, as I was going blind, was a spare knee. I gathered that knee in, turned it around, back to front, while Sing gave a moan and changed his hold.

He peeled my grip off like I had hold of a bit of slippery elm, and, as we rolled over on the floor, I seen a flash of Feema standing by with that great knife of Sing's gripped in both hands over her head, and her loose sleeves falling away from her arms. Even though I had only a glimpse of her, I couldn't help wondering at the mask of a face she wore.

She was making herself handy to kill Sing Lu the first chance she had of fleshing that steel in his body, but her face hadn't changed. Her lips were as still, and her eyes was as quiet as though she was pouring tea—or saying her prayers.

No, sir, there was never nothing else like her. She stood in a class by herself.

Then Sing and myself got loose from one another, and a lucky thing for him that I came up on the side nearest to the girl or that would've been his last minute on earth.

He was all fight. He came in reaching for another grip and left his head wide open. I hefted my right up and weighted it to smash every bone in his face, but it seemed a shame to go outside of a game he liked so well and knew so much about in order to kick him. So, instead of hitting him, I stepped inside of his arms and laid hold on him. Wrestling tricks was not very plenty with me, because I never had much use for them. But I pulled Sing Lu in and just gently squashed the breath out of him. When he went limp and his chin come down with a bump on my shoulder, I stepped back and let him slide onto his face on the floor.

And Feema handed me the knife! Cool as a cucumber she was. It gave me a quiver, though, to look down the length of that murder tool and think that she wouldn't have batted an eye while driving it home in Lu. Now she waited for me to carve Sing like a goose.

However, I chucked the knife away and turned Sing on his back and worked his arms for him to help him get his wind back. He had a hard fight of it, before his face turned from black to red. But finally he was nearly all right again and lay trembling on the floor with one big hand clutching at his throat, and his breath coming with a chug and a rattle. So I helped him to his feet. I had to buoy him up for a while, because his knees had turned to pulp, but finally he could manage, and he walked off like a drunk, putting out both hands to feel his way along.

I steadied him down the stairs and to the front door, and, as he stepped out into the sun, he turned around and give me a smile for a reward. It was a pretty smile.

Maybe you have seen a wolf laugh or a snake grin? The smile of Sing Lu was like that. He went waddling across the street. Two or three Chinamen scattered out of his way, scared to death by the look of him, then they scurried back to help. When I seen him go around the next corner, his big arms was draped over the shoulders of two or three men on either side of him.

I went back to Shih to find out how things stood. He was busy putting medicine on his throat, because Sing had nails, you understand, and they'd drawn the blood from Shih's throat. I was scratched up a bit myself.

However, when he was fixed up and Feema had wrapped a bandage of silk around his throat, the old scoundrel sat down and lighted his pipe and closed his eyes.

I knew that he was doing some useful thinking, so I didn't interrupt him none. I waited until he had finished off a couple of pipefuls.

Then he opened his eyes and pointed at Feema. "She is too beautiful to bring good luck," said Shih.

Beautiful? Why, by the Chinese way of thinking, I

suppose she was. But she fetched a white man about as much as a fashion dummy set up in a window to smile at the street. Except that this Chinaman dummy didn't smile. However, after the hardy way she had nipped onto that knife, there was no doubt that there was *some* blood in her.

"Ask her if she would have killed Sing?" I says to Shih Nung.

"She is not a fool," said Shih, "and also she is my daughter. Therefore there is no need of asking."

It was simple, you see. Yes, from their way of thinking, it was as simple and as straight as a song. But I gathered that there was more to come. Shih Nung at the end of his thinking didn't say more than what he had spouted about Feema. Then he called the servants and distributed arms. By which I mean that he turned them into walking forts. That fat old cut-throat had enough revolvers and shotguns and knives and crooked Oriental swords to stock an army, and he padded out his waiters and his servants with that supply. He was right, too, and I couldn't help admiring the directness of him as he went about these things, because that Lu meant murder, and he meant it wholesale.

"Only," I said to Shih Nung, "what would he do if he got Feema, now, knowing that she tried to knife him?"

Shih didn't have time to think. He answered right off. "He would tie her up by the thumbs and build a slow fire under her feet."

There was a sparkle in his eyes as he said it, and it was plain to see that Shih didn't speak by guesswork, but right from the heart. I couldn't help wondering when and where he might have tried that same trick himself.

"Shih," I asked, "how long ago did you come from China?"

Even Feema couldn't have looked blanker than him. "Time to an old man," he said, "is like water on a river. Does the water know how many bridges it has flowed under?"

Very slick, but not slick enough. Because that thief wasn't more than fifty.

X

Just on top of this, word come up that somebody had arrived, and by the gesture of Shih I knew that he was inviting the new gent to come right along in.

He explained to me right away that it was Wu Tsi, who was one of the best young men in the world and who was terribly in love with Feema, except that he didn't have any money to buy her.

I was sort of curious to see Shih's idea of one of the best young men in the world, and pretty soon in come Wu Tsi. I had to sit up and take notice. Change the color of his skin and fix up his eyes a mite and there was the likeliest-looking young chap that you ever seen. He give me a smile and a bow as cheerful as you please, and then said a few words to Shih, which Nung translated. He said that Wu Tsi had heard about the ruction in the rooms over the restaurant, and he had come right over to investigate. Shih said he would explain what had happened.

Now while Shih was talking, I saw Wu slide a glance toward Feema. She wasn't paying any particular attention to him, but, when his eyes fell on her face, I could see him wince. There was no doubt about this chap being in love. He was hit and he was hit hard. But he stood up to himself as sassy as you please.

In the meantime, there was Shih doing a pretty good imitation of what had happened. Mostly folks carry on about the Chinese being pretty wooden. But they ain't. They're as talkative and gay as you please, and, when they get lit up, they sure do flare. Shih was particular good about the way that Sing had collared him. When he showed how I came in, he had to snatch up the great knife and do a great jump into the air to tell how Sing had tackled me. He pretty near rolled himself on the floor, describing how Sing and me had fought, but the best thing of all was when he put his arms around a figure in the air and slowly squashed it, so's you could see the pleasure in his face and almost count the ribs of the other fellow popping. He wound up by showing how Sing had slumped to the floor and lain there, all in.

It was a good piece of show acting. Wu Tsi listened till it was all over, and then he give me another bow and he made me a little speech. He was a gentleman, that boy was. Shih translated the lingo, which was to the effect that Wu Tsi was glad that the kind gods had given Feema a husband worthy of her.

I glanced at Feema. There she stood, stifling a little yawn and paying no attention to what Wu intended as a very neat compliment to both of us.

But I started thinking. That ain't my long suit, and I usually wind up my figuring pretty pronto. Finally I said: "Shih Nung, I want to say something to Wu Tsi. You translate."

He nodded, and I began. "Wu Tsi, Feema isn't really my wife. She just happened by accident to be put into my hands. She is a fine girl, as you can see for yourself, and she ought to make the right man happy. But I ain't the man. I'm a wanderer. Never know where I'm gonna lay my head at night when I wake up in the morning. No sort of a person to have a wife, especially a home-making body like Feema. It seems to me, besides, that she ought to have a husband out of her own people. That being the case, I got to say that I never seen a more upstanding young Chinaman than you, Wu Tsi. If a man can buy a woman among you folks, he can certainly give her away. So I give Feema to you, Wu. Treat her kind and don't work her too hard."

Well, in the first place there was no doubt about this being a ten strike with old Shih. His eyes flashed, and his grin became real while he repeated my lingo in sing-song.

I thought that Wu Tsi would faint. He stood up, stiff and pale, and stared at me. Then he said through Shih Nung that this was a thing that was hard to believe, but that, if I meant what I said, he would pray for my happiness every day of his life and be ready to pay blood for me whenever I called on him.

"That's all right, Wu," I said, "all I ask is that, when you think you understand this girl, you can come around and let me know what she's like, because she has me beat."

Wu allowed that there was only one thing to stand in between the new idea. Would Feema want to come to him?

That was a white way of thinking about the affair, loving her the way that he did. I told Shih to put things in the best sort of light to Feema, and he certainly did it. I didn't need any interpreter to explain that shaky voice and the teary eyes of Shih was because he was telling his girl that she had got a whale of a husband in Wu.

But when he got all through, she just turned to me

and said two words, and stood looking at me with her big, dark, say-nothing eyes.

"She says," interrupted Shih, "do you command her to go with Wu."

That was a devil of a way to put it, but I answered that I *did* command it.

There wasn't another word out of Feema. She just started for the door behind Wu, and it was a wonderful thing to see her wait for him to go through that door, and then to see him step back and beg her with both hands to go first. Then, as she went through, he turned around, gripping his heart, and told me that I was the king and that he belonged to me forever and ever.

"That's all right, son," I said. "But you stop thinking about me and concentrate on her, because though you may not know it, you are starting out on a man-size job."

So Shih and me watched them down the stairs, and, when they was out of sight, we turned around with one impulse and shook hands.

Yes, I was considerable glad to see the back of that girl and wash my hands of a Chinese wife, but my gladness was just nothing compared to Shih's. Perhaps those big, quiet eyes and that wooden face of hers had been eating on him for years and years. Perhaps for years and years he had been waiting for her to turn human, until he'd given up hopes. But now she was gone, and the old rip went around rubbing his hands together, and he got out some spicy Chinese gin, and we had a drink of it together.

Altogether, it was a great send-off on the part of Shih and me, but right in the middle of the celebrations, the sheriff turned up.

One of the waiters come slam through the door, yipping something that turned Shih pale. Behind the waiter, we seen the cause of the trouble—half a dozen gents wading up the stairs. One of them yelled out: "He's straight ahead, Sheriff! He's right in that room!"

I didn't need to ask who they meant. They had spotted me, and, if I didn't want to spend some time in the sheriff's free hospital, it was time for me to get a change of scenery. I made for the window that gave into the back alley, and, as I leaned out, I looked down into the muzzle of a rifle in the hands of a rough-looking 'puncher who sang out: "I got you, Daisie Duff. Stand where you are . . . !"

He had me. It was foolish of me, because you never can tell how straight a man will shoot, but I couldn't resist thumbing my nose at him before I ducked out of sight.

His bullet whished past my face close enough to burn the whiskers of a bee.

Shih Nung had grabbed me by the arm. "Not that way!" says he. "Come with me! It is Sing Lu! He has sent for the sheriff when he saw that he was not strong enough to handle you."

That seemed logical. But damning Sing Lu wouldn't help now, and Shih was the first man to realize it. He took me to the picture of the gent with the two swords, turned a peg in the wall, and swung the whole section in on neat little hidden hinges. I seen before me a narrow passage as dark as the throat of a wolf, with the beginning of a ladder. The main question was: was that place big enough for me, even supposing that I was willing to trust myself to where it might lead?

Well, I was willing to trust myself to it. I got in, while somebody was hammering at the door and yelling that they would be let in or else that they would bash the door down. The section of the wall was closed over me, and then I heard old Shih hotfoot it to the door and turn the lock and open it. A bunch of men came stamping in. They run through the other rooms when they couldn't find me, and then they came back, cussing a good deal, and demanded to know what Shih had done with me.

He said that he didn't know. I had just disappeared.

Here the sheriff cut in, his voice was cold as the biting edge of a saw. "Shih Nung," he said, "don't pretend to be nervous, because I know you too well, you damned old smuggling scoundrel. You've put Daisie Duff into your underground railroad, and now you're going to fetch him out again. We saw him come in here. Do you think it would wash in any court in the land if we told a jury that you didn't see what had become of him?"

I heard Shih break into a yell. "How could I know?" he said. "I would have held him and made him give himself up. But he took me by the throat. He knocked my head against the wall. See . . . here are the marks of his fingers on my throat!"

He must have snatched off the bandage while he was running to the door. Anyway, there was a minute of silence, after that. Finally somebody said: "That's about the size of the grip that Daisie Duff would have."

The sheriff put in: "Has Duff got nails as long as that?" Nobody answered, and the sheriff said: "I know you're lying, Shih, but at least this is the sort of an excuse that would serve for you in a court. Now, boys, scatter and try to get trace of him. He's probably a long way off by this time, but we'll try to get on his trail. Sound every inch of this dive . . . the floors and the ceiling and the walls. There's probably a dozen entrances to the underground railroad out of this here place. Now get busy!"

They scattered, making enough noise to imitate galloping horses as they rapped here and there. I figured that there wasn't much chance for them to find me. But all the same, there was no use taking risks, so I begun to feel for the rungs of the ladder and backed down into the blackness of that pit, swearing that I'd never leave the open sky again, if I could ever get back under it once more.

XI

Backing up is bad enough; backing down is worse. I was glad to get to a level beneath me. I lighted a match and found myself in a passage a couple of yards high and hardly a third that wide. It was mean work, trying to double over and shrink narrower at the same instant, but I scraped along those damp, rotting boards for some time. Maybe the slowness of my going made the distance seem farther, but that tunnel doubled back and forth and went downstairs and up enough to make a snake dizzy. Then, as I leaned against one wall to think, the wall gave way.

I had simply leaned against one of their hidden doors, and down I went along another passage, a bit roomier, but still cramped. I was a glad man when I seen the glimmer of a bit of light through a crack just ahead of me. It looked like the end of the passage, but the light told me that it must be a door. I gave that door my shoulder, and it went open with a *whish*. I walked into a little section of hell-on-earth.

The air was streaked with brown and black mist, and the place was so foul that one breath of it closed my throat like the grip of a hand. It was a room with a double deck of bunks built against three sides of it, and each of them six bunks was filled. The first I had seen was an oldish Chinaman, clean gone in the opium sleep, his mouth grinning back with his dream, and his eyes partly open like the eyes of a dead man. He wasn't far from death, at that. His face had as much green as yellow in it, and the cheeks clove to the bone.

He was the worst, and the sight of him sapped the strength of me a good deal. I could understand that what made Shih Nung so rich wasn't his restaurant. It was squeezing the blood out of the gents down here. Four more of those folks was asleep in their ratty bunks, with the drizzle of the underground water drip-dropping slowly around them, or on them. What did they care? The sixth man was lying on his elbow just roasting his pill over the flame of an oil lamp that was more smoke than fire. He looked up at me and squinted as though I was a long distance off. Then he went right on with his work, very careful, turning the pill and watching it.

I thought of backing out of that hell hole, and I should have done it, but, when I seen a door on the far side of the room, I started ahead through it. You would say that any growed-up man in that sort of a dive would've watched his step and looked about before he went through doorways, but the stench and the choke of that place was too rank for me, and I just stepped right through and got what was coming to me.

It felt as though the roof had dropped all at once on my head. I went down on one knee and a curtain of mist was yanked across my eyes, but through that curtain I could see the shadow of a man with his pigtail flying behind his head as he jerked up his club to let me have it again. And other shadows were coming on the run.

I gathered in Chinaman number one. But I was so weak and numb that he pretty near wriggled out of my hands. I reached for the rest of the gang and closed a hand on one of them and brought him down, but then they sapped me again and I pitched head first into darkness.

Part of my reason come back to me before my eyes was open. I braced myself to see the same slimy horror all around me, but, when I looked up, I found that I was breathing sweet air again, and the God-blessed sun was shining in a hot patch right across my face.

However, with the first move I made, I stopped giving thanks. I was wadded around with ropes from head to foot; all I could do was to raise my head and that showed me that I was in a little room furnished up in pretty slick style, Chinese fashion. Over at the end of the room there was a whopping big man on his knees in front of a little tongue of fire that sent a twist of incense smoke up above his head and across the face of a little gilded idol—a figure of a pot-bellied little man with a golden robe gathered up to his waist as he sat there cross-legged, but all bare above the hips, and, as the light fell on him, I could see his fat, pouchy, gilded cheeks, and he was looking right across the room to me with his green eyes.

He was a mighty fine idol, take him all in all, but he didn't interest me half as much as the gent that was kneeling before him, kowtowing. Because one glimpse of the big, thick, round, hard neck of that Chinaman told me that it was my old pal, Sing Lu. Between me and you, I would rather have been in the hands of about anybody else in the world.

Perhaps he was giving thanks to that idol for turning me into his hands, but he had better have been giving thanks to the gents that had carted me up to him. I could believe, now, all that Shih Nung had said about Sing having half of Chinatown in his hands. Well, I would rather let him have all of Chinatown forever, rather than me for five minutes. As he began to get up, I dropped my head back and nearly closed my eyes.

The floor squeaked with the weight of Sing coming toward me. Through my lashes I could see him heave into view. He grinned down at me and prodded me in the ribs with his toe. As he prodded me, he fingered the haft of a knife that was the blood brother of the carver that he had tried to use on me earlier in the day.

No, he wasn't particular pleasant to look at. I would back my view of Sing at that minute against any nightmare that ever walked into a bad dream when your knees turn numb, and you can't even holler for help. It seemed to me that he was only waiting for me to wake up before he let that knife drive into me, or perhaps he was reserving me for slower work, where he could taste my death, little by little.

There was nothing past Sing, I think. Anyway, when he seen that the working of his bare toes in my ribs didn't waken me up, he turned around and squeaked out of the room again, and I heard the humming and the sing-songing of several Chinese voices in the next room.

He had some of his pals in there, I supposed, thinking over what would be the best way to finish me off, and maybe they was taking a vote as to whether it would be better to bury me in the bottom of one of those damp passageways or just to wrap a few chunks of lead around me and drop me in the river one of these nights.

In the meantime, I had my head up and was taking a pretty sharp look around me. I could see no door into this little room. I couldn't see any window, either, except the little one high up on the wall, through which the arm of sun was reaching down and warming my heart. It was a grand thing to know that I was at least above the ground. There was only one living thing in that room, and that was the little wagging tongue of flame that sent the incense smoke across the face of the idol.

So I started wriggling toward it as soft as I could, and, all the way, the green eyes of the golden man followed me across the floor, until he was looking right down into my face and smiling at me and despising me because I thought that I was smart enough to get away from him. Well, I stuck out my arms that they had swathed all around with pounds of rope, and I watched that little head of fire flinch from the hemp, and then taste it, and then begin to struggle and work away at it until finally the rope caught fire and sent a bigger wedge of yellow fire up and bitter black smoke across the face of the idol.

It made a little crackling noise that almost stopped my heart until I had something worse to wonder about, and that was whether I could keep from sneezing, because the fume from that burning rope tickled my nose something terrible, and the first whisper from this room would bring in a brigade of Chinamen hungry for blood. The first strand and the second parted; the third went with a little snap, and then by an outward squeeze of my elbows the whole tangle of ropes loosened and fell away.

I held up my hands and looked at 'em, and thanked God for 'em, and then I started to work on the rest of the ropes that bound me. It was very slow, because the bonds had stopped my blood, and it only came back into my fingers a little trickle at a time with all the prickling pains of flesh that has been asleep and numb for a long time. But I got the ropes off my feet and knees. I stood up and worked my legs up and down and felt the power begin to come back to them by leaps. I wasn't ready to die now. I looked at the grinning idol, and his silly smile made me so mad that I couldn't help laying hands on him.

Well, sir, the minute I hefted him, I changed my mind and began to respect him a lot. Because gilt never weighed like that. There wasn't much of him in bulk, but that little chunk of metal must've weighed close to twenty pounds, and all at once I had an idea that it might be solid gold that I was handling so careless. And those slanting big green eyes—suppose that they was emeralds?

There wasn't much time for supposing, because just then somebody sneezed very hard in the next room, and I knew that the fumes of the rope smoke must have got out to them. The next instant, there was a clatter of voices and a shuffle of feet.

I waited, gathering up the heavy stand that the idol had been perched on. I held it steady above my head, and, as two Chinamen stepped into the doorway, I let them have it. They shot backward, one screeching and one dumb, and I dove out right after them.

I think those loafers was so sure of me that they must have figured the idol himself was making this fuss, because of half a dozen Chinamen there wasn't one that wasn't paralyzed, with the exception of big Sing, and he was so cluttered up, what with his pals toppling around him, that he couldn't even fetch out his knife. I leaped down from that short flight of steps, and I give Sing Lu the whole weight of my fist—the first time that I had ever hit with all my might since I was a boy.

I felt the bones spring and crunch under my knuckles. Hot blood spurted over them. The head of Sing snapped far back across his shoulders. I thought I had broken his neck as I made straight for the door beyond.

XII

When I got through that first door, I whirled around to slam the men as they piled through after me, but I seen that the only piling they was doing was around Sing Lu. They were extra busy picking him up, and with that face of his turned into a red wreck, he sure needed help.

I kicked off my shoes and went ahead, because I guessed that what I needed as much as anything was silence, and I was right. Down the first stairs that I come to, I ran into a bevy of women, and they crouched away from me, squealing like a lot of rats. I went on down, and around the next turn two men charged me, shoulder to shoulder.

They were more surprised than I was, and they were harder hit. So I pulled a fine new Colt out of the hands of each of them before they should do any harm with their guns, and after that I kicked them in front of me down the stairs. One kick apiece was enough, because, although that stairway was built winding, it was also built steep, and they rolled down like stones after that flying start.

They was in the street before me, but they didn't get up to make trouble. One of them lay sprawled out where he fell, and the other dragged himself away on his hands and knees. So I stepped out into the open air with the weight of the yellow idol making a comfortable sag in my coat pocket.

These things had heated me up a mite more than they should have. By this time I wanted fighting, and a lot of it, but all that I seen was the flying ends of pigtails disappearing into doorways. So I walked right down the middle of those twisting alleys in my stocking feet with a naked gun in either hand, hoping for action, but there was no action to be had. It was quieter than Sunday in Chinatown, just then. The squeaking of a mouse would have sounded like thunder, things was so still, but I headed back for Shih's place, sort of wishful to find that the sheriff and his boys might still be there— because they would give me a man-size ruction and ease me a good deal.

Well, there was no sign of the sheriff and his gang when I got back. The door was locked, so I kicked it open and went up the stairs, and announced myself to Shih. I thought I would be coming as a sort of surprise, but I wasn't the main event at all, because over in a corner of the room, sitting on a cushion as cool as a daisy, was Feema.

I held up my hand when Shih Nung came rushing for me, spouting English and Chinese mixed, he was so excited, telling me that he had heard that big Sing Lu was burning me alive.

I simply pointed to Feema and asked what the devil she was doing back in that house when I had just fixed her up with a husband. I stood over her and asked her what it meant. Well, she got up and made a little bow to me and said something that Shih translated.

"She says that she did not understand how she could have two husbands in one day. But this is a letter which Wu Tsi sent back with her." He took out a little scroll of paper that looked as though a chicken had stepped in ink and then started scratching for a worm. He read it out to me:

> *To my honored friend and father, Shih Nung, from Wu Tsi,*
> *The kind gods who gave Feema to me have also taken her away. This day was not meant to be remembered by me in happiness.*
> *So I send back Feema to you. May she make all your days like a song that has no ending.*
> *As for me, I am not well, but the doctor says that I shall recover. He has stopped the bleeding and now I rest and now I give thanks that my life was not taken from me. Farewell.*

Neat, short, and snappy. No whining, as you can see for yourself, and no dwelling on the facts. He just inferred that Feema had slipped a knife into him while he was welcoming her home, and, instead of having his servants tear her to bits, he sent her back to her father's house until a bigger size in men than himself should come along and claim her.

"And so," said Shih, "that is ended."

"It is ended," I admitted. "I thought I had her fixed for life, but I see that your daughter is a dove, Shih Nung, a regular homing pigeon. Tell me, Shih, do most Chinese girls act like this? Or will you confess straight off that you've made a mess out of raising her?"

Well, the look that he passed her would've curled up a brass image, but it didn't seem to faze that girl. She kept the same marble face, while she waited in the corner of the room for orders.

I sat down and turned the green dragon around and around on my little finger, wondering what deviltry it would get me into next, before this game was ended. And I listened to Shih Nung pouring out his heart.

He told me that he had given that girl the best training that was ever give since the days of Confucius, but that nothing could really be done for her, she was so dog-gone bad. He told me that he never closed his eyes at night without wondering if he would wake up in the morning with his throat cut.

And I didn't blame him. She was a regular pet, that Feema.

Shih kept right on. He was a steady-nerved old beggar, but he'd had enough to pretty near break him down, and he told me that now his life was ruined.

I thought about the opium hell underground, and I wished that he might be speaking the truth. He said that Feema had first started Sing Lu paying attention to that happy home, and that now she had brought the devil of a sheriff on his heels, and the end was rapidly coming.

That was a true thing, too. I hadn't spent much time with that sheriff, but I knew him fairly well, and I knew that once he got the scent of the trouble that hung around this house, he would never rest until he got at the bottom of it. By the time he was through, Chinatown would have the finest airing that had ever happened.

I listened until I was tired, and then I said: "You can stop worrying about Sing Lu. He is finished."

"Ah, God," said Shih Nung, staggered and happy. "You have killed him, my son."

"He ain't dead, but he's had a lesson," I told Shih. "You won't be bothered by him any more. Unless I miss my guess, if he starts a ruction again, all that you have to do is to say boo, and he'll run for cover. Besides, he ain't going to show his face in the daytime for a spell."

I laid out the facts of what had happened to Sing Lu, and, when I showed Shih my bloody right hand, he gaped and gasped and grinned and couldn't stare enough.

I was still holding that hand out and telling the story when along comes Feema with a basin and a cloth. She washed that big mitt of mine, and she rubbed some fine-smelling ointments into the cuts that the bones of Sing's face had made, and then she wrapped up my hand with a bandage. It was a pretty neat job, but when she got through, I found that I couldn't wriggle my fingers very free, so I took the bandage off again. It seemed to bother Feema a good deal, and she told me through Shih that poison might get into my blood unless the cuts were covered.

"Poison fights poison, sister," I told her. "I'm full of stuff that kills germs like nothing at all. I never've had time to get sick, Feema, and this ain't one of my idle spells."

This appealed to Shih Nung a good deal, and he chuckled as he passed the words on to her. But she didn't seem to understand. She *never* seemed to understand. No, she was depressing, that Feema was. Life around her was just like one long Monday morning.

Well, I explained to Shih the way I felt about things. I had put him in a bit of danger by getting Sing Lu on his trail, but now I felt that Sing was done with and that any lightweight could finish the job with him. That left nothing in this town that was on my conscience, except Feema. Yet I couldn't help feeling that I had done my work for her.

Balancing one thing against the other, all that I seen before me was to stay on here and waste my time on trying to settle this girl on a husband tough enough to handle her, while Bert Moonie got ready to gather me in. On the other hand, I could tear away and head for the tall hills.

That was what I wanted to do. These close quarters cramped my style a bit, and I was getting nervous. Every time that a door opened, I felt as though a gun was about to point at me. So I aimed to clear out of that house by the dark of the day, God willing, and never to see it again.

"And those who sent you?" says Shih Nung with a wicked smile.

I looked down at the ring, recollecting myself in time. "I have done my best," I allowed, "and things will have to rest at that."

It was a miserable day that lay ahead of me, what with listening to voices and steps and creakings and wondering why the damned sun had stuck in the sky and forgot to go down. But finally it disappeared in the west, and five or six hours later most of the color had faded out of the sky. So I got myself ready, and said good bye to Shih.

He was terrible glad to see me leave, although he told me that his heart wept to part with me.

I went up to Feema and pointed a finger at her wooden face. "Honey," I said, "the next time that a man comes along and claims you, you grab him quick or you'll have a lonely old age. You savvy? Catchum man plenty quick. So long, kid, and be good to yourself."

Well, she didn't understand a word.

I sort of had flattered myself that maybe she had cottoned to me a little bit and that was why she had knifed poor Wu Tsi, but now, when she couldn't help knowing that I was going, she just made her little bow to me and didn't bat an eye. But she got on that trained smile—look pleasant, ma'am, and hold steady.

Damn such a girl. There wasn't no soul in her. Of all the things that I was glad to leave in that Chinatown, I think that I was gladdest to leave her, not excepting Shih himself.

XIII

Shih followed me down to the street. There I laid a hand on his shoulder.

"Now that we're alone under the stars, Shih," I said, "I'm gonna tell you that I seen underground in your place, and I seen a lot more than you wanted me to. I seen it. You know that I seen it. And if I'd tried to spend this night in your house, maybe you would have took steps to make sure that I would forget. But lemme tell you, son, that you ain't through with your trouble. You can damn me good and you can damn me proper, and the reason is because it was me that led the sheriff to you. Because I tell you, man to man, Shih, that Bert Moonie won't stop until he's cleaned up this joint, and I hope to God that he uses dynamite for soap!"

Shih said not a word. But there was essence of distilled poison in his face and his smile as he watched me. I stepped back into the dark. I was really afraid to turn my back on that devil of a man. So the last that I saw of him was his grin as he stood there in the doorway with his hands shoved into his long, loose sleeves.

I hoofed it straight down the alley, and the big,

squashy slippers that Shih had given to me didn't make a sound.

I hiked across the bridge and looked at the red and yellow lights quicksilvering over the face of that oily black water. A shudder started in the middle of my spine and traveled both ways for my head and my heels. Oh, man, but I was glad that slimy river hadn't got me! And I hoped that I'd never have to see the face of it again.

I went through the white side of San Rafael, sticking to the back alleys. By this time, there must be a good deal of talk around the place about me, and I wouldn't have to be seen in broad daylight to be recognized. Through the dark of black clouds, stumbling against scrap cans and kicking noisy curs out of the way, I got alongside of the stable. It was the way that all stables are. There was just the light of a smoky lamp somewhere in the innards of it. The entrance runway was wore into ruts and the wood all pulpy with the pounding hoofs. A couple of loafers had their chairs tilted back against the wall, talking soft in the dark.

I took my way through the back door and soft-footed it along behind the stalls, but in a minute I stopped. Well, I could have guessed it beforehand that Bert Moonie would've done it. That stable was as mild and as peaceable as all stables ought to be, but right behind the stall where my Mary was kept a gent was walking up and down, humming to himself, with a long glimmer of something over his arm. I didn't need telling about what it was. It was a rifle.

Still, I couldn't back up unless I wanted to hoof all the miles to the mountains. But walking ain't a thing that I'm fond of. Something like a hundred pounds of me always starts complaining right away. I took off my coat, and, when the humming turned away, I slid up behind and dropped the coat over his head and arms. He struggled a mite until he felt the grip of my arms, and then I heard him gasp—"It's Daisie Duff!"—and he lay as still as a lamb while I trussed him up with ropes and gagged him. Then I laid him across the wall and went down the line of horses in those stalls.

It wasn't too dark for me to see the sketch of each of them. You can judge a weight carrier by his quarters, pretty well, and there was only one where I paused. He looked big as all outdoors, so I stepped into the stall and lighted a match. Ah, but he was a beauty. He was a he-horse, and no mistake, with legs that could catch an antelope and strength to carry a mountain, almost. Almost, but I was afraid not quite. He was just a wee mite lengthy in the coupling. Otherwise, I would have knowed that he was the horse for me. But I couldn't take chances. That bright bay with the black points looked terrible good to me. He had the speed that I needed to get away from that devil, Moonie. But he had just an inch or two too much, fore and aft, I thought.

It broke my heart to turn away from him to Mary. But, at least, I knew what she could do. If only I could get her dragged across the lowlands to the mountains, I would be safe with her. So I went back and damned her softly for a minute or two, so's she would know that it was her boss, come for her. Then I saddled her and led her out behind the stable and climbed into the saddle and drifted her quietly out of San Rafael.

On the first hill to the north I eased her up and looked back at the rows of lights that marked the streets of the white town and the heap of glimmer that sketched the yellow one, and I was a glad man to turn my back on it and head for the mountains. I watched them growing taller and taller and blacker and blacker until they hung like a straight wall just in front of me.

Then I went through the black mouth of a ravine and slacked up the reins. There was no good using my eyes. In the night and in the mountains, Mary had eyes enough for herself and me, too. So I let her drift, and she worked along very patient and smooth, twisting and climbing where I couldn't see the shadow of a trail, and lifting me always into colder, clearer air, so that every minute spelled freedom and safety to me.

She wound up in a snug spot. There was a grassy stretch of ground with a bubble of water trickling across it and a fringe of brush all around it to fence in the light of a campfire. Here Mary stopped, and I didn't ask questions. I just got down and stripped off the pack and the saddle and let her go. She never wandered far, but she hated to be picketed out.

The sheriff was a gentleman. Any other law-hound, of course, would have confiscated my pack the minute that I was wanted for arrest. But Bert Moonie wasn't that kind. He didn't go after the small potatoes. It was only the roasting spuds that he wanted for delivery to his hospital, confound him!

Among other things, my emergency rations were still in that pack of mine, and a few minutes later I was sitting on a rock in front of a mighty cheerful little blaze of fire, and I was toasting slices of bacon, partly in the pine smoke and partly in the blaze, because that is the way that I like 'em seasoned. I had camp coffee, too, than which nothing is so good. And I had some self-rising flapjacks that was out of sight compared even with the best Chinese cookery. Because, after all, there ain't anything that fits into a man's mind so snug and perfect as what he's used to.

And I was used to the mountains. I was raised climbin' 'em, damning 'em, and not particular loving them, but just plain needing them. You don't love the air that you breathe, but you can't do without it.

There had once been a time when I had tried digging gold out of those same mountains, but that was in the old days, before I discovered that fifty-two cards is a lot better than fifty-two picks and shovels, when it comes to making an easy living.

I slept that night as I never slept before, and I dreamed of Feema, and Sing Lu, and opium dens, and other nightmares. But when I woke up, one look at the roses in the sky washed all the tiredness out of my brain.

I traveled steady to the north that day, and along in the afternoon I dipped down into the valley. I never should have done it. I should have stayed to the highlands all the time, where there was no danger of meeting up with folks. But I was sort of too happy to be careful, and so I turned a corner of the trail and bumped right into a gent that was harder on my eyes even than Sheriff Moonie.

It was Uncle Dick. He reined up his horse, dropped a hand on his hip, and nodded at me. He says by way of a cheerful greeting—him and me not having seen each other in three years—"White men and Indians and greasers wasn't enough, Daisie. You had to kill some chinks for variety, I been hearing!"

Yes, the news had got that far already. There was no use me denying it. Uncle Dick had always made a practice of not believing me, no matter what I said. Well, I let him say it, and I didn't answer nothing. He hunted around to find some better way of hurting me.

Then he says: "Your mother has been waiting for you, Daisie."

Aye, that touched me up a little. "Yes," says I, "she would be remembering me, I suppose."

"Particular just now," says he. "She still thinks that you'll come home, now that your father's dead."

It really knocked me all in a heap. "Dead?" I gasped at Uncle Dick.

"But I tell her," said Uncle Dick, "that you're still too busy with your . . . er . . . work. You ain't got time to go back and see the folks. Well, I got to be getting on my way." And he rode past me up the trail with never another word.

A mean man or a righteous man—which amounts to the same thing—that was my Uncle Dick. He never in his life done no harm to any man—nor no good, neither. When he went to church, every Sunday, his praying must have been all for himself, because there was nobody else in the world that would say a word for him.

But I rode along that day in a trance, remembering till my heart ached. Women had always been shed off my mind very easy. But now the face of my mother and of the China doll, Feema, was fitted in side-by-side, and I couldn't see much of anything else. The meanness of Feema kept her with me, I suppose. And the kindness of my mother.

Because there was so much gentleness and love in her that, even in spite of the hardness of my father, I had used to sneak back to see her, now and then. So when I thought of her in that great big ranch house all alone, with the black of the night outside, and nothing inside but servants and furniture and remembering, why, it bowed me down a good deal. But what was I to do with Moonie on my trail?

Anyway, Uncle Dick had took the glory off the mountains for me. I headed Mary for a high place

again that evening, and in a wedge of the mountainside I made my second camp, cooked me a supper,
and went to sleep because I hated the world too much
to want to stay awake in it.

I slept like a rock until I dreamed that the little gold
idol had come to life and growed into a golden giant
and was towering over the fire and looking down at
me. I woke up quick, and looked.

There was Feema sitting cross-legged on a stone on
the far side of the fire, with her eyes turned down to
the rosy glow of it.

XIV

Now, when I looked through the fire glow at that girl, it was a queer feeling, like a dream had turned into flesh and blood, or like the day had commenced at midnight, or like midnight at noon, or anything else topsy-turvy that you could think of.

I stood up, and she stood up, also, and lifted her eyes with that made-to-order smile. That was odd enough even in a Chinese setting where you expect queerness, but up here on one of my own mountains, with the smell of the pines breathing around, why she was terrible out of place.

I walked around her, and she turned like a model on a pivot, always facing me very respectful. Yonder, in the edge of the firelight, I seen the white-starred forehead of a horse, and I led it up close. Strike me blind if it wasn't the same big blood bay that I had seen in the stable back there at San Rafael. It threw me into another whirl. She had followed me from Shih's house down to that stable. She had sneaked in there and picked out the best mount in the lot, and there was strength in those narrow hands of hers to swing the heavy saddle onto his back and lead him out and ride him across country. There was wits enough in her to follow a trail that I thought had been wild enough to beat even a wise old hand like Bert Moonie.

Now, the least thing of all that set me wondering was the fact that this fool girl had become a horse thief. That was the least bewildering thing of the lot. They would never blame her. It would be me that would catch it, and I would a lot sooner've been found with a killing on my hands than a stole horse. Because you can't work self-defense about horses that are found with you. However, as I looked over that fine gelding, what beat me was that in her education she had learned horses so well, and trailing, too. And how much else was there locked up inside of that little head of hers? What did she know about men?

I took her chin in my hand and raised her face a little and looked straight down into her eyes. They seemed as black as the night, and they was as steady and as blank as stone.

Well, she looked a bit pinched, so I cooked her up some chuck. And even while the bacon smoke was blowing across my face, it seemed unreal and sleep-like, and every time that I looked up at her, the sight of her was a start. She was waiting on me again.

She was sitting on her heels passing me things, and holding what I didn't need, and making the job easy. But when I got through and handed the chuck to her, she sat for a minute and looked at it, and then looked at me, as dumb as a trained dog asked to do a new trick.

Well, the idea sort of percolated into her head, after a time, and she sure did eat. I could see that she was starving, and I got an idea that maybe she hadn't touched grub since she started out after me. But the most wonderful thing was to see the way that she went after those flapjacks and the bacon and the camp coffee, as dainty as a bird, with tiny bites, and the firelight fair shining through the pink crystal of her fingers.

When I looked at those little hands, I figured that it was all right—she was only a child. She was like a sort of scared child, too, the way she wanted to stop, now and then, as though I had been bored long enough, sitting back and watching her eat. But when I seen the big, shining shape of the bay horse in the background, I knew that she was no child at all but a growed-up woman with fire and iron in her enough to do a thing that no man I knew of could've managed. She was a woman, and it was a poor Chinese girl that folks would accuse me of stealing away into the hills because she didn't have no better sense than to go.

I had to look up and take a breath, and the stars, burning so white and close around us, made me almost believe that there *must* be a God. Because it would take God to understand this here tangle.

Well, I made down a bed of pine branches, as soft and springy as wind, and wonderful fragrant. I used my coat and blanket and the blanket off the horse that she had stole. Then I waved her to it. Why, sir, she seemed a good deal beat by that. She tried to tell me with her hands that that was my place, until finally I got all my dummy talk used up and just picked her up and laid her in the blankets and wrapped them around her. She looked up to me with one of her trained smiles and a shivery little sigh, and in an instant she was sound asleep.

Aye, and I wondered maybe had she closed her eyes before, since she started after me through the mountains. Being without no blanket now, I was too cold to sit still, so I roamed up and down through the black of the night and thought my way a step or two through this tangle. But I always wound up by coming back and looking at the girl.

I kept the fire up uncommon high, so's I could have a better light, and it would've beat you to know how she took hold of me as she lay there with her lips parted a mite and smiling in her sleep. Because, all at once, it occurred to me that it wasn't really her fault if she was a mechanical sort of a doll. It was the fault of Shih Nung, the scoundrel, that had raised her this way, and trained her to be what she was. Yet she wasn't so dog-goned mechanical, either. Not as she lay there asleep. A pain begun to squeeze my heart and make me a little dizzy.

How queer I was and how much less than myself I'll explain to you when I tell you that as I turned around at the end of my beat, hurrying to get back and have another peep at Feema, I run my chest right up against a big, shiny Colt revolver, with a brown hand holding it perfectly steady, and behind the hand some rather narrowish shoulders, and above those shoulders the face, of course, of Bert Moonie.

I looked around him and past him, feeling very wild and lost because I begun to realize it little by little, just what Moonie had done.

"Why, damn your heart, Bert," says I to him, "you've gone and come up here all by yourself. You got no backing yonder down the mountainside."

The sheriff shrugged his shoulders. "I'm thanking you to poke your hands up over your head, old-timer," says he. "And don't you be too sure about what sort of backing that I have."

"Oh, hell, Moonie," says I, "do you need to bluff? No, the fact is that me, Daisie Duff, I'm took by a single skinny, second-rate, no-account sheriff. Me! Why, damned if I can believe it. There ain't any fighting and there ain't fuss . . . it's just over."

"Will you get those hands up, old son?" says he.

"I'm gonna sit down and think this over," says I.

"If you move, you're a dead man," says he.

"That's interesting, but it ain't important," I told him, and I turned my back on that gun, almost hoping that he'd blow a bullet through me and finish off the mess of things that I was standing in.

However, he didn't shoot. I sat there on a stone and stared down at the fire.

"Big boy," says he, "I hate to do it, but I got to have your guns."

"Moonie," says I, "I like you and I respect you and I sure admire you for nerve and for gall, but you keep your hands off of my gats."

"Are you making this a showdown?" says he, as cold as steel.

"You describe it in your own words," says I. "Now don't bother me, because I want to do some thinking."

He was an exceedingly reasonable man, was that sheriff, and he just stood there and let me think.

Not that he had any kind feelings about me. He adds in a minute: "I don't blame you, big boy. If you go down there and have this whole mess brought to light, and the woman thing as well, folks may be a little hard on you."

It made me raise my head and stare at him.

"Moonie . . . ," I began, but he chopped me off short with a gasp. He had seen my ring.

"My God, Daisie," he said, "is it possible that you're one of them low-down, throat-cutting . . . ?"

"You mean this ring?" says I. "Take it and eat it, if you want to." I chucked it to him as soon as I could work it off my little finger, and it was sort of amusing to watch him study that ring with one eye and me with the other, never turning the muzzle of his gun away from me. I would say the sheriff was playing me pretty safe.

But all at once he jumped again. "Why, the damn thing is a fake, big boy!" he said. "And who would ever think of you wearing an imitation hoodoo thing like this?" He laughed a little and threw the ring back to me—the tail of the dragon had broke right off short under his thumb.

All at once I remembered that little, sneaking Wong and his crooked eyes and his crookeder ways. It was like him to make a present of a lead ring to a gent. But still, I couldn't help being shocked.

"And the Chinamen was fooled, too," I said. "Sheriff, I only wish that you'd found this out two days ago. Because it would have got me free from a terrible lot of trouble."

"Including what?" says he, with his eyes glinting through me.

"This," I said.

"You been drove into this, I suppose?" says Moonie. He looked across at where the girl lay sleeping in the shadows, just a streak of darkness against the darkness. There was a wicked note in the voice of the sheriff, because, out here in the mountain desert, we forgive a gent for a good many things, but we don't forgive him for making mistakes in his treatment of the women.

"Suppose I was to tell you, Moonie," says I, "that she followed me up here of her own accord?"

He smiled. It wasn't a pleasant smile to see.

"Moonie," says I, "you're an uncommon white man. I'm going to try to explain this thing to you if I can."

"Are you?" says he, lifting his brows a little. "You better save something for the judge and the jury."

"If I can make you believe what I say," I said, "I *will* try it on a judge and a jury. But if I can't make you believe, then you and me will have it out right here."

"Wait a minute, big boy," says he. "Do I understand you?"

"Yes," says I, "you do."

"Me having you covered?"

"I don't think that one bullet will kill me," says I, "and you wouldn't have time for two."

Moonie backed up a little and sat down on another stone.

"All right," says he. "Lemme hear you talk. I don't mind saying that you have got me scared, old-timer, but I ain't bad enough scared to shoot crooked."

Of course, I could see that was right. The gun would never wobble in his hand, and every minute, as I talked, he had the mouth of his Colt gaping at me, and never a tremble in the highlights that run down its barrel.

So talking low, because I didn't want the China doll to get waked up—knife and all—I started right in with Wong, and I told the whole yarn to the sheriff.

When I got through, he said: "Is that what you intend to tell the judge and the jury?"

"Yes," I said.

"Including the gold idol?"

"Yes," I answered, "or maybe the idol would speak up for itself." I pulled it out and set it right down in the flare of the rose and yellow firelight.

XV

There was a wonderful change in the sheriff. The smile was wiped off of his face, and he sagged a little forward, and I could see his fingers work, he was so anxious to lay hold on that golden dummy.

"But that ain't possible, big boy," he said. Then he looks straight into my eyes. "Daisie, this here yarn is true!"

I grinned at him. The idea was catching him like fire in a stubble field.

"But," he says, "all of these here things is the facts, then! And you ain't. . . ." He stopped himself. He was all worked up. "Hold out your right hand!" says he.

I held it out.

"The marks of Sing Lu's face is still in it," he says to himself, and give a little shudder. He sat back again and looked me up and down. "No judge would believe you," says he.

"No," I agreed.

"No," says he, "no judge is about as foolish as anything that God ever made and put together and called men, even a jury wouldn't believe you."

266

"No?" says I, looking at him.

"No," says he, "and not even a newspaper reporter would believe you."

"But," says I, "you believe me, Bert Moonie."

He blinked a little and tried to shake his head, but he couldn't.

"You believe every word that I've said," I told him.

Says he: "If you could take that sleeping girl, and that horse, and the black of the night, and these here mountains into the courtroom, old son, you might have a chance. Or would Shih Nung talk for you?"

"No, he would forget that he had ever seen me."

"Because why?"

"Because I seen the opium den that he runs."

"Daisie," sighed the sheriff, "if that opium yarn is true . . . ah, man, if it's true!"

"Look here," says I, getting a brand new idea, "I'll tell you what I'll do, Sheriff. I'll give you my word of honor that every last syllable I've spoke is the gospel fact."

It stiffened him again.

"Will that go in court?" says I.

He sighed. "Man, man," says he, "not unless you could bring these stars in and them big pines and the flicker of that fire and my gun looking you in the face." He got silent again. "There is only one thing that busts it all to pieces," said the sheriff.

"And what is that?" says I.

"The girl," says he.

"*Humph*," says I. "I free admit that hell-raising is second nature to her. But would you like to have a peep at her?"

He said that he would. We sneaked across the firelight, with the nose of the sheriff's gun in the small of my back, and we leaned over Feema. He studied her long enough to have been able to make a map of her. Then we went back.

"You," says the sheriff, "might tell this yarn and get away with nearly everything, except for the girl. Folks won't believe that. She ain't possible."

"Go on and tell me why."

"Because an ignorant chink don't know how to trail a gent. . . ."

"I've wondered about that," I admitted.

"A chink that can't even speak a word of English," says the sheriff.

"No," I admitted, "it does sound awfully queer. But everything about her is funny. She ain't a human being, Sheriff. She's a mechanical doll."

He studied me for a mite. "Lemme see," says he, "the first thing that she done was to try to kill Sing Lu."

"Yes," I said.

"That don't have a mechanical sound," says he. "And when she knifed the gent that you gave her to . . . not particular mechanical, either. And then she followed you out of Shih Nung's house and stole a horse to trail you . . . which ain't exactly what we can train mechanical dolls to do. After which, she worked out a trail . . . oh, damn it, man, don't you see that it won't do? You and her . . . why. . . ." He stopped, and then he added: "You tricky hound!"

"Moonie," I said, "are you a mite dippy? How would you figure out that I have any luck in the world?"

He didn't seem to hear me, but he said after a while: "If she could speak English. . . ."

"Damn it, man," I said, "you make me tired. I tell you, she don't understand a mite of it."

"It's a shame," says he, "because if a girl like that was to stand up in a courtroom and testify for you. . . ."

It made me mad. And I snapped at him: "Easy, Sheriff. You're gonna keep her out of this. Would I drag her into a law court? I would not!"

He studied me again, like he wanted to remember my face for drawing. Then he said very thoughtful: "If she was to testify for you, do you know what the jury would do?"

"Well?" I said.

"The jury," he said, "would ask you would you want to run for governor, and would you please excuse them for taking your time in court! A jury, old son, would be twelve dizzy gents, if they looked at her face."

"Ah, Sheriff," says I, "that's what you look, seeing her asleep. But when she wakes up, there's nothing but a wooden face."

"Humph!" says he. "Big boy, you must be wrong. The facts are ag'in' you. She can't be a dummy. There ain't any way out except for her to have sense . . . and English sense!"

I sighed. "All right, Sheriff," I said. "There ain't any use, I see. You won't believe that she ain't got the language."

"If," the sheriff went on, "I was you, I would make her talk."

"Go on," says I. "How would you do it."

"Well," says he, "I would go over and sit down beside her, yonder."

"Go on," says I, yawning.

"And I would lean over and take her hand."

"Go on," says I. "I'm sorry to see that a smart man like you is sold for a China doll, Sheriff."

"And I would say . . . 'Feema, I love you.'"

"Go on," says I. "What next?"

"There ain't any next," says he, "because all that you'll have to do, after that, is to sit back and listen, and you'll hear plenty!"

"Well," says I, "if it wasn't that I hated to take your money, I wouldn't mind betting you a five spot."

"Son," says he, "this is a sure thing with me. But I'll steal five dollars from you on the strength of it. You go ahead."

I was too plumb irritated to let the thing go. I got right up, and I saw the muzzle of the sheriff's gun following me as I walked across. I sat down by her bed and took her hand, just as he'd told me to do, and watched her eyes open slow and look up to me. It staggered me for a minute, the idea of saying such a thing to a China doll, but I had made my bet, and I was going through with it.

"Feema," says I, "I love you."

Did you ever find yourself stumbling about in the dark, until your hand found the switch and all at once the lights flashed on?

She sat up into my arms, and she took my face between her two cold little hands. "Daisie!" she said to me *in English*. "Daisie Duff, do you mean it?"

That minute come the spring. The snows was gone, and the trees turned yellow-green, and the flowers flowed over the earth, and the rivers busted the ice away and went smashing and foaming through the valleys, and the air was sweeter than honey, and the doors was unlocked in me, and the voice of Feema went singing along through the halls and rooms in me that I never had knowed was there before.

I took her in my arms and stood up among the stars.

"I love you, Feema!" I said.

XVI

The case never come up for trial, by the managing of the sheriff, who didn't have to say much, except to let folks know that I was his agent and that I had been working real secret to expose the crookedness and the opium traffic in Chinatown. And what those Chinamen got was plenty, lemme tell you, except Shih Nung.

It was the sheriff himself that let Shih off in return for a bit of information, and that bit of information was the name of the folks from whom Shih had swiped Feema fourteen years before. Mr. Connover and his Chinese wife come all the way from Hong Kong to find if it was really their daughter, Anne. And I got to say that they were a lot gladder to see their daughter than they were to see their daughter's husband.

However, nothing mattered. What difference did everything make, because Feema and Anne Connover is simply two names for the same thing, and that thing is mine.

Not that everything is so dead easy. Skirts is a great nuisance to Feema, and, when she's alone, she prefers sitting cross-legged on the floor to the best chair in the house. However, as my mother says, time will take care of Feema, because time and love take care of most things in this here grand old world.

It has took care of me, for one thing.

How could I ever have thought of settling down on the ranch and riding herd one day and following the plow among the orchard trees the next, and then building a new shed?

But that is what I am doing. It don't hardly matter what, because loving Feema, just living, is happiness enough, and even poker ain't much worse than an aching tooth, now and then.

There is only one bad spot in the whole layout, and that is that I had to call my son Herbert, which is my idea of a plumb ridiculous name, though what could I do when the sheriff hung around on the christening day?

Besides, Feema insisted. Even to this minute she can't speak of him without adding: "Dear old Herbert Moonie, God bless him!"

By which you may guess that she learned the sheriff put me up to speaking to her on that night in the mountains. You may want to know how it was that she wriggled the truth out of me.

But I would come right back and ask you how it was that she had continued to learn English without ever letting that swine of a Shih Nung suspect it? Or how did she learn to act like a wooden image?

No, there is explanations for a lot of things, but there is no explanation for Feema. She can even make weak Chinese tea taste like a real drink.

But what I mostly wish is that she would get over having stuff burning in the house and making a thick sweet scent of incense trailing around through the place.

"Look here, Feema," says I to her, "what might be the meaning of the fog that we're living in, half of the time? Besides, it makes me sneeze!" And I add: "Ain't it usually mostly only in temples and such like?"

"Hush!" says Feema, and lays a finger on her lips. "But isn't this a holy house? And are not the kind gods around us every day?"

About the Author

Max Brand® is the best-known pen name of Frederick Faust, creator of Dr. Kildare, Destry, and many other fictional characters popular with readers and viewers worldwide. Faust wrote for a variety of audiences in many genres. His enormous output, totaling approximately thirty million words or the equivalent of 530 ordinary books, covered nearly every field: crime, fantasy, historical romance, espionage, Westerns, science fiction, adventure, animal stories, love, war, and fashionable society, big business and big medicine. Eighty motion pictures have been based on his work along with many radio and television programs. For good measure he also published four volumes of poetry. Perhaps no other author has reached more people in more different ways.

Born in Seattle in 1892, orphaned early, Faust grew up in the rural San Joaquin Valley of California. At Berkeley he became a student rebel and one-man literary movement, contributing prodigiously to all campus publications. Denied a degree because of unconventional conduct, he embarked on a series of adventures culminating in New York City where, after a period of near starvation, he received simultaneous recognition as a serious poet and successful author of fiction. Later, he traveled widely, making his home in New York, then in Florence, and finally in Los Angeles.

Once the United States entered the Second World War, Faust abandoned his lucrative writing career and his work as a screenwriter to serve as a war correspondent with the infantry in Italy, despite his fifty-one years and a bad heart. He was killed during a night attack on a hilltop village held by the German army. New books based on magazine serials or unpublished manuscripts or restored versions continue to appear so that, alive or dead, he has averaged a new book every four months for seventy-five years. Beyond this, some work by him is newly reprinted every week of every year in one or another format somewhere in the world.

MAX BRAND®
THE BRIGHT FACE OF DANGER

Through the years, James Geraldi has proven to be one of Max Brand's most exciting and enduring characters, and this volume contains three of his greatest exploits. Geraldi has been dubbed the "Frigate Bird" because of his habit of stealing from thieves, and Edgar Asprey knows just how apt the name is. Geraldi once prevented Asprey from swindling his family out of a fortune, and managed to get rich doing it. That's exactly why Asprey now wants to form an alliance with him. Asprey has his eye on a rare, invaluable treasure, and he knows no one stands a better chance of stealing it than his old enemy, the Frigate Bird.

Dorchester Publishing Co., Inc.
P.O. Box 6640   5384-5
Wayne, PA 19087-8640 $5.99 US/$7.99 CAN

Please add $2.50 for shipping and handling for the first book and $.75 for each additional book. NY and PA residents, add appropriate sales tax. No cash, stamps, or CODs. Canadian orders require an extra $2.00 for shipping and handling and must be paid in U.S. dollars. Prices and availability subject to change. **Payment must accompany all orders.**

Name: _____

Address: _____

City: _____ State: _____ Zip: _____

E-mail: _____

I have enclosed $_____ in payment for the checked book(s).

CHECK OUT OUR WEBSITE! www.dorchesterpub.com
_____ Please send me a free catalog.

MAX BRAND®

DON DIABLO

Throughout his career, Max Brand created some of the West's most exciting and beloved characters. Surely one of these is Jim Tyler, an outlaw who has earned a reputation on both sides of the border for boldness and sheer guts. This volume collects, for the first time in paperback, three of the best Jim Tyler novels. "Mountain Raiders" pits Tyler against a notorious bandit named El Tigre. In "Rawhide Bound" Tyler has to battle the infamous Miguel Cambista . . . and all of his men. And in "The Trail of Death" both El Tigre *and* Cambista return and join forces for what looks like the final showdown with their hated enemy.
